GOLDEN CARGOES

Also by Fiona Buckley

The Ursula Blanchard mysteries

* available from Severn House

GOLDEN CARGOES

Fiona Buckley

**SEVERN
HOUSE**

First world edition published in Great Britain and the USA in 2022
by Severn House, an imprint of Canongate Books Ltd,
14 High Street, Edinburgh EH1 1TE.

Trade paperback edition first published in Great Britain and the USA in 2023
by Severn House, an imprint of Canongate Books Ltd.

severnhouse.com

British Library Cataloguing-in-Publication Data
A CIP catalogue record for this title is available from the British Library.

ISBN-13: 978-1-4483-0922-1 (cased)
ISBN-13: 978-1-4483-0927-6 (trade paper)
ISBN-13: 978-1-4483-0921-4 (e-book)

All Severn House titles are printed on acid-free paper.

Typeset by Palimpsest Book Production Ltd.,
Falkirk, Stirlingshire, Scotland.
Printed and bound in Great Britain by
TJ Books, Padstow, Cornwall.

PART I
WEDDING AT EVERGREENS

ONE

One May Morning

Ursula's Narrative

I remember it so well, that green and gold morning in the May of 1589. As we rode along the track through the woods, the scattered sunshine through the canopy of leaves was strewn before us like a largesse of golden coins. We were happy and as we rode, we sang. We were going to a wedding.

There were six of us. To begin with, there was myself, Mistress Ursula Stannard, in my late fifties by then, but still mercifully hale, my hazel eyes still clear, my hair still dark and my seat still easy on Jaunty, my bay gelding. Beside me rode my seventeen-year-old son Harry, well grown and every day becoming more like his father. He had Matthew's loose-limbed build and Matthew's dark colouring and his strong-boned face, with the same little trace of asymmetry.

I could never look at Harry without remembering Matthew, with whom I had known both ecstasy and heartbreak. I could only hope that Harry would not inherit his father's passionate instinct to adopt causes and give his all to them. As yet, Harry was young and merry and hadn't shown any such tendencies. At the moment he was still rejoicing over the horse I had given him for his birthday, the previous February. The horse was a tall flea-bitten grey with a mane and tail like silver and the head carriage of a prince. Indeed, Harry had taken one look at him and declared that Prince must be his name. My adopted son, sixteen-year-old Benjamin Atbrigge, riding just behind us, was content for the time being to use Splash, one of our all-purpose horses, but in another year, when he too became seventeen, I must in fairness give him a new horse, too.

At home in Hawkswood we were rearing a pretty young

mare, who in another year would probably suit Ben. Her name was Windfall and her history was extraordinary, but she herself was simply a good-looking animal, not a weight-carrier, but very suitable for Ben, who was slight of build. Like Splash, she was what my manservant Roger Brockley called a failed skewbald, for she was mostly chestnut but with white splashes here and there.

Ben had come to me after a tragedy in his own family, and to this day he was a quiet lad, occasionally prone to nightmares. He was more studious than Harry, according to Peter Dickson, their tutor. Dickson wasn't with us, for he was now too old to ride. He had told me that Ben was gifted with figures, which Harry was not, and quite Harry's equal in all other subjects. I had wondered whether he might one day become our steward, when the present one, Adam Wilder, retired. Soon, I would have to talk to Adam and Ben about all that.

For today, however, Ben was a wedding guest like the rest of us, and he too was singing, though his voice was apt to crack, to his embarrassment. Still, he was able to laugh at it. We had taught him the value of laughter, which his father had failed to do.

My other companions were Roger Brockley and my personal maid Fran Dale. Fran was Brockley's wife but somehow I had never got out of the habit of calling her by her original surname of Dale. Brockley was nearing seventy now, but was still as upright as a young pine on his dark chestnut Firefly, who was also old, but was defying time with sharply pricked ears and a gallant tail carriage. Dale was the same age as me and was not a good rider, but I had given her an ambler, a little blue roan mare called Blue Gentle, and in her saddle, provided we didn't travel too fast, Dale felt safe and didn't tire too soon. She and Brockley were only technically servants. With good reason, I regarded them as friends and insisted that when we visited other houses, they should be treated as such and not consigned to servants' quarters.

The final member of the party, and the lustiest singer of us all, was my cheerful groom Eddie Hale, driving a cart drawn by a temperamental mule who was called all sorts of things (she invariably balked when asked to wade across a ford) but was a sturdy animal for transporting baggage.

Today her cart was piled high with boxes and hampers, so that we could all wear fine clothes for the wedding day. Brocade dresses, starched ruffs, best doublets, carefully folded shirts don't fit well into saddlebags, and our saddlebags in any case were full of plainer clothes and accessories. According to the letter of invitation from the bride's mother, Mistress Joan Mercer, the actual date of the wedding could not be set until the sons of the house could be present. They were seamen, apparently, as their father had been, but were expected home at any moment, though their mother could not be sure of the date.

We knew that they each captained their own ship, and sailed together as partners. The *Peregrine* and the *Osprey* were trading vessels. The boys were back from their latest voyage but had goods to dispose of and also to buy and were not at the moment at home though they soon would be. We had been invited to stay in good time, and would remain at Evergreens for as long as it took for the boys to come home and the final marriage arrangements made. We might well be there for a month or two.

Our invitation was a courtesy, a sign of respect. After all, I was the owner of Evergreens. Mistress Mercer was my tenant.

The journey was only twenty-five miles or so, which we could cover in less than a day, even riding at leisure, and it was so very pleasant to be on a joyful errand. Last year, England had been threatened by an invasion from Spain, but the shadow of Spain was lifted now. Without concern, I had left my steward Adam Wilder and my head housemaid, Phoebe, in charge of Hawkswood, and I was free to enjoy this May morning.

My first and best-loved home was Hawkswood, a pleasant house with wide grounds and farmland, within easy reach of the towns of Woking and Guildford. I had inherited it from my late husband Hugh Stannard, and done all I could to maintain it well, but I knew that one day I must resign it to my son. The Sussex house, Withysham, was altogether mine, for it had been a gift from Queen Elizabeth, a reward for certain services that I had performed for her. It was run for me by a competent steward, and I moved my household there now and then, to allow for a good cleansing and sweetening to be carried out at Hawkswood. One day I would live there all the time. Or most of it. I knew I would visit Hawkswood often, as long as Harry made me welcome.

Evergreens too was a gift from the queen. It had a garden and a small home farm, and it stood close to, but did not own, a tiny village called Cutpenny. It was Joan Mercer's daughter, Arabella, whose nuptials we were to attend. She was apparently betrothed to a landowner in the district, a Master Sylvester Waters.

An excellent match, so Mistress Mercer's letter had said, since Master Waters was both well off and personable. She had been able to provide the bride with a respectable dowry but Master Waters had asked for Arabella's hand because he was truly in love with her.

We are all so happy. The moment my sons come home the precise date can be settled, but they are expected within two weeks. The house is full of excitement.

Thinking about that letter as we rode along, I recalled that something about it had given me a curious jog in the mind, but I hadn't worked out why. Nor did I wish to search for an explanation now, because the track ahead had widened a little and taken a gentle upward slope. 'Let's canter,' said Brockley. 'Eddie, you'll just have to tow that devil's spawn of a mule as best you can.'

'She won't canter unless she feels like it but I dare say I'll catch you up in the end,' said Eddie.

Light of heart, we cantered.

Evening was drawing on as we approached Evergreens, but at this time of year the days were long and the sun was still well above the western horizon, throwing its light before us.

The house stood in a little valley, with the slopes of the North Downs rising to our right as we approached. Just before we reached the gatehouse, the track branched to the left, leading downhill to another, deeper valley, in which the village of Cutpenny stood; we could see its roofs and hearth-smoke, and far away beyond those, a glimpse of smoke from the chimneys of Caterham, the nearest town. The land was hilly to our left but the hills were lower than those of the downs except for a single heavily wooded one close by, which rose steeply and all alone.

Harry looked at it with interest and then pointed. 'Somebody lives up there, right at the top. I can see chimney smoke!'

'But what a place to live!' said Ben. 'It must be a struggle either to get down that hill or to climb up it!'

'There's a zigzag path,' I told him. 'A horse can do it easily. Though I've never been up there. We may have time to do that during our stay.'

Two minutes later, we came to the lodge. It was a modern building, thatched and half-timbered, and occupied by a keeper called Joe Jankin. Mr Jankin had a rotund wife and a tribe of youngsters ranging from infants to lads in their teens. I didn't care to speculate on how they all fitted into the lodge; their sleeping arrangements must have been congested, to say the least of it.

Jankin came out to greet us along with his second boy, Robbie, who was sent off at a run to announce our arrival at the house. I asked after Will, the eldest lad.

'Gone to sea along with Mistress Mercer's sons. Allus liked climbing trees, Will did. Now he's climbing rigging. Hope to heaven he don't fall off and land in the sea and drown, but there, he allus did hang on to tree branches like one o' they monkeys. My two elder girls have got wed. 'Mazing how they grow up. But we allus have a few young 'uns coming up to fill their place.'

I wished the family well, nodded to Brockley, who was ready with a tip, and we made our way up the track to the house itself.

Evergreens was much older than its lodge. It was built of grey stone, not that much of the stone was visible, for most of the walls were covered with ivy. 'That needs trimming away from the windows,' Dale remarked, and Brockley, laughing, said: 'We're not here to give orders about cutting the ivy back!'

And so, in good spirits, talking of zigzag paths and ivy, we arrived at the front door of Evergreens, and stepped into as thorny and tangled a tale of passion, cupidity and dreadful

deeds as ever¹ I had met, in a life which had been far from
protected. So tangled, indeed, that I will at times have to ask
someone else to describe their part in it. The beautiful May
morning was so deceptive . . .

We slipped out of our saddles as a couple of young grooms
– I recognized one of them as Mr Jankin's third son, Hal, who
was distinctive because his face was nearly all freckles – came
to help with the horses and the mule.

At the same moment, Mistress Mercer's butler, Charles
Page, a dignified man with a gold chain of office worn over
a black doublet, came out of the main door to welcome us.
We followed him inside and found Mistress Mercer awaiting
us in the entrance hall. I saw to my surprise that her dull
brown gown had no farthingale, that her cap was askew and
her ruff crooked. My surprise was because although I had only
met her twice before, I had formed a definite impression that,
like Page, she valued her dignity.

She had been a good tenant during the two years that she
had occupied Evergreens, but I had never taken to her. I knew
that she had been married young, so that she had a daughter
and two sons, all by now in their twenties, though she herself
was not yet fifty. Her face was unlined but her complexion
never looked cared for and her large grey eyes had whites
with long outer corners, which gave her a curiously fierce
expression. At the moment, though, I felt sympathetic because
she looked quite distracted and I wondered why. She was
smiling, however, and her hands were held out in welcome.

'So here you are. Have you been riding all day? You must
be tired. Please come in. I have ordered a supper, hare pie,
with nutmeg and almond fritters to follow. And I have some
excellent wine that my sons brought home from their last
voyage. They are such good boys.'

At our previous meetings, she had been taciturn. Now, she
was positively rattling. 'They take cheeses and cloth, iron
and leather and tin, and raw materials and made goods to
our colonies in the New World, you know – if you sit down
here, Page will help you to get your boots off – and they
bring home the most wondrous things. Arabella and I have

beautiful matching bracelets of pure gold. Your rooms are all prepared . . .'

'Our hostess seems flustered,' Brockley said into my ear as we handed our cloaks to a maid and seated ourselves on the bench in the vestibule, so that Page could help us off with our riding boots and bring us the soft slippers provided by the house. The vestibule was big and was probably a remnant of a former great hall, which had at some time had a ceiling put in so that rooms could be built above, and had also been cut in half. The other half was now the parlour. Both vestibule and parlour had pairs of antlers as decorations.

'Her letter was excitable,' I whispered back. 'But perhaps, with a wedding to organize . . .'

Page was back with the slippers, having made accurate estimates about sizes. They all fitted, and Mistress Mercer was hovering, wanting to show us into the parlour. 'We are so happy to be here,' I said, as we followed her in. 'And for such a glad occasion. When will we have the pleasure of meeting the bride?' I took a seat on a cushioned settle. 'Arabella, that's her name, is it not? I haven't met her before. Your letter mentioned that she's twenty, just the right age for marriage.'

Mistress Mercer plumped herself down into a chair and then, taking us all aback, burst into unhappy speech. 'Oh, this is dreadful! When I sent out the invitations it was because Master Waters wanted me to, wanted me to put the arrangements in hand at once, and naturally I paid attention to his wishes. Arabella has been brought up to know her duty; when I told her that she was to marry Master Waters, I never thought she would object, let alone persist in objecting, trying to defy me! I had already sent the invitations out. Now, I don't know what to do. I never dreamed she would behave like this, never . . .!'

And with that, to our horror, our hostess put her face in her hands and burst into tears. Dale bit her lip and turned her head away. Brockley's face, with its high, gold-freckled forehead and steady grey blue eyes, became a tactful blank. Harry and Ben looked embarrassed. I went to Mistress Mercer's side and put my arm round her shoulders. 'Where is Arabella now?' I asked her.

'Where?' wailed her mother. 'Where would she be, the obstinate, want-witted, *silly* little girl that she is? She's locked in her room, that's where she is, until she comes to her senses. She's been there for days, on bread and water. I have tried to reason with her, threatened to birch her but still she won't listen. A *perfect* match, and all she will say is that she's fallen in love with Gilbert Gale, the Cutpenny carpenter, and wants to marry *him*! When she could have an upstanding man with a farm and a fine house . . .! And he's not ugly, either. He's a *good* match. What am I to do?'

We looked at her in alarm. She sounded as though she were asking us for advice and none of us had any to give her.

'Master Waters doesn't know about this,' Joan wailed. 'He desires the marriage so much. He's visited us and talked and walked with Arabella, ridden with her, too, she is not being asked to wed a stranger. He did the proper thing and asked me for her hand and I said yes, on her behalf, as I have a right to do and then when I told her, she said no! Till then, I knew Gilbert Gale only as the village carpenter. And when she said . . .'

'How did the two of them come to know each other well enough to fall in love?' I asked. 'I don't suppose you see him often, except when you want to use his services as a carpenter.'

'It started with a dance in the village, on the green. We both went, just for amusement. These rustic dances can be jolly affairs. She danced with him. She talked about him afterwards, but I didn't pay much heed to that. And then – more fool me,' said Joan with feeling, 'I sent her into Cutpenny one day on various errands and told her while she was there to call on him and ask him to come here, to make some extra shelving for the still room. They talked then, it seems. And when he came to see to the shelves, they talked again . . .'

'That's how these things happen,' I said. 'And they can happen fast.'

'I don't know how often they met after that. Arabella admits that they did. Admits! She almost threw it in my face – she's proud of it! They decided they wanted to marry, only they thought they would have to choose their moment as Arabella's mother – me – might be difficult . . .! Hah!' said Joan, and threw up her hands in despair.

After a moment, she added: 'I told her not to be foolish, that what she felt for Gilbert was just girlish foolishness and that her marriage to Sylvester Waters was settled. I never thought she would disobey me. I never thought of disobeying my own parents when they told me I was to marry Captain Mercer. I hardly knew him. He was older than me, a friend of my father, and I had only seen him two or three times. But I did as I was told, of course I did. I paid no heed to Arabella's nonsense. But now . . . oh, what am I to do?'

I had no answer to that and stayed silent.

'I've had her under lock and key now for three whole days, ever since I tried to talk to her about her bridal clothes and she said no, not for Master Waters. Obstinate wretch! It was this damned carpenter for her, or nothing. As it chances, Master Waters had to go to London on business, the very day after I said yes to him. But I have heard from him; he will be back tomorrow or the next day. He thinks it's all settled, he'll come to see her and . . . Oh, dear God! He'll be so angry . . . How will I be able to tell him? I don't know how to face him!'

Again, I had no answer, and kept silent. My first marriage had been an elopement. I had crept out of a window, slipped down a sloping roof and dropped into the arms of Gerald Blanchard, who was supposed to be betrothed to my cousin Mary. Mary's parents, Uncle Herbert and Aunt Tabitha, who had brought me up, never quite forgave me. I think that my theft, as they saw it, of Mary's betrothed, coloured our relationship for ever after.

But Gerald and I were happy. Our daughter Meg was grown up now and married with her own family, and I rejoiced that through her, something of Gerald would live on. He had died of smallpox while Meg was still little. I began a new way of life then, which brought me wealth, and sometimes happiness and sometimes danger. But I didn't forget Gerald and I had a good deal of sympathy for young lovers.

Joan used her sleeve to wipe the tears from her face and said suddenly: 'Would you talk to her? Maybe she'd listen to you, a woman of position, a lady who attends on the queen at times. A lady with your . . . your reputation. She'd have respect for you, maybe.' She looked up at me, her large eyes still swimming with tears. 'Will you, would you, try?'

'Well . . .'

'Just *try*. That's all I ask. I've *got* to make her understand that she is going to marry Master Waters and that's the end of it. I know you can't guarantee anything but for the love of Heaven, couldn't you just *try*? I can't imagine how I could tell Sylvester that Arabella won't marry him. If you can't convince her, then I'll have to beat her until she agrees. But agree she must!'

I considered her thoughtfully. It seemed to me that Mistress Mercer was more than just embarrassed about telling this Sylvester Waters that the wedding was off. I had met frightened people before and I sensed fear now. Mistress Mercer was afraid of this man. I wondered why.

One of the reasons why I had sometimes run into danger was because it's my nature to be curious. I very much wanted to meet this recalcitrant bride and hear her side of the story. I said I would try to help, even though I might not succeed.

By this time, I had realized what had worried me about that letter of invitation. It hadn't said one word about the feelings of the bride.

TWO
Asking Why

However, to begin with, I asked that we should be shown to our quarters, and given a chance to refresh ourselves. 'Of course,' said Joan. 'Page will show you the way.'

I found that I had been given a spacious chamber upstairs, with a view over the kitchen garden which, despite its practical nature, was beautifully laid out parterre fashion, between low hedges of box. The Brockleys were next door to me. Since Evergreens was not large, the two boys and, of course, Eddie, would share the grooms' quarters over the stables.

Washing water and towels were brought. Our luggage had been brought to our rooms and Dale set about unpacking. She helped me out of my plain dark blue riding dress and into a fresh gown and kirtle in my favourite tawny and cream, though with only a small farthingale. I considered that the big high-fashion farthingales were only suitable for formal occasions, or for women who led completely inactive lives. Dale tidied my hair and chose some jewellery for me.

'You had better look impressive, ma'am, if you're to have an effect on this girl, who may well be a proper little termagant.'

'I doubt that, somehow. She sounds like a brave little lass who is in love for the first time and trying to fight for it. I was her age when I ran away with Gerald. But her mother is in a state, there's no doubt about that! Yes, the amber necklace and the matching earrings, the drop ones – they'll do. Thank you, Dale.'

I meant to go downstairs to the parlour, but when I reached the top of the stairs, I saw Joan Mercer hovering about at the foot, evidently waiting for me. 'I am to interview Arabella now?' I asked.

Mistress Mercer started up the stairs towards me. 'If you would! The sooner the better. Please follow me.'

She reached the top of the stairs and then led me off to the
left and round a corner. We mounted a further staircase and
found ourselves on the attic floor. Mistress Mercer led me to
a door that was secured by a padlock. She produced a set of
keys, undid the padlock and opened the door.

'Here is Mistress Ursula Stannard, who has come to reason
with you,' she announced, somewhat tactlessly, I thought.
Come to reason with you. The very words to put up the back
of an angry and determined young woman. I stepped past Joan
Mercer, gestured to tell her that I wished her to leave us, and
waited silently until I heard the door close behind her. Then
I looked at Arabella and also at her surroundings.

It was truly dismal attic room, under the slope of the roof
so that even in the middle there was barely space to stand up
straight. The meagre furniture consisted of a narrow bed
without hangings, a chest with a jug and basin on top of it,
and a single stool. Arabella was sitting on the side of the bed.
I had visualized her as defiant, likely to throw back her head
and refuse to listen to a word I said, but this girl was a picture
of dejection.

She would have been pretty if she hadn't looked so wretched.
More than pretty; strikingly beautiful would be nearer the
mark. I wondered what her father had been like, for she surely
didn't get that pointed, elfin face from Joan. Her hair was
tousled and in need of a wash, but when clean and brushed,
it would have been brown, with a bronze sheen, and her eyes,
though now blurred and red-rimmed with crying, were beautifully set and they were hazel, a lighter, more greenish hazel
than my own. The hands that were clenched on her lap were
small. She was dressed in a dull grey gown, creased as though
she had slept in it. She had no ruff, and her feet were bare.

To start the conversation off, I said: 'Surely this isn't your
usual room?'

'It's for lumber,' said Arabella. Her voice was husky with
crying. 'Mother took the lumber away. She said I was lumber
myself and this room was the right place for me. You are
Mistress Stannard? I've heard of you.'

I crossed the bare boards of the floor and sat down on the
bed beside her. 'You are in dispute with your mother over a

marriage she very much wants for you. Will you tell me your side of things?'

Arabella heaved a sigh and turned her head away. I wondered if she was now going to take refuge in silence. But I waited and at length, she said: 'I don't like Master Waters. He's years older than me. But it isn't just that. I don't like *him*; there's something about him that frightens me. I think he's cruel. It's his eyes. Mother made me go walking and riding with him, and he was friendly, admiring, but I *didn't like him*. He held me too tightly when he helped me in or out of my saddle; if he gave me a hand over an awkward place when we went walking, he would *touch* me . . . you know. Mother keeps saying he's good-looking and so he is, in a way. But it's a cold way. Like an icicle. I wouldn't want to marry him even if I'd never seen Gilbert Gale. Did my mother speak to you of him?'

'Yes. She said he was a carpenter.'

'He lives in the village, Cutpenny, but he's not just a local woodworker. He's a Master Carpenter! He went to London to be an apprentice and learn from a Master of the trade. Now he's a member of the Carpenters' Guild. People come miles to bespeak furniture from him. He makes simple things for the village, but wonderful, inlaid things for people who can pay for them . . . he has money. He owns the smallholding behind his house and he has rented it out; he isn't just no one. He isn't just a villager living hand to mouth as my mother pretends!'

She had been sitting with her head bowed, as though she were addressing the floor. Now she raised her head and glared at me as though I had myself called Master Gale a hand-to-mouth villager. Pacifically, I said: 'Go on.'

Arabella swallowed and looked away from me and said: 'He came back to Cutpenny after his apprenticeship ended because he says it's his home. And he's young and we're in love and . . . it isn't fair, why shouldn't I marry him? There's girls in the village that would love to wed him! But I'm to be pushed off on to Sylvester Waters just because he wants it and I'll have to live in his horrible big house and come into the village and see Gilbert with someone else as his wife, see them with their children . . . and I can't bear it and my mother won't listen!'

'It seems that she knew nothing about Gilbert until after she had said yes to Master Waters.'

'She said yes to Master Waters without asking me!'

'Parents don't always ask their children. But they usually try to arrange good marriages for them. It isn't as if you had never seen Master Waters. He isn't a stranger to you.'

'No, he isn't, he's a neighbour. His house is only a mile away. Yes, I know him. Mother has *made* me get to know him. And I *don't like him*!'

'Arabella, your mother seems very anxious for you to marry him. Perhaps excessively so. Do you know why?'

'No. I think she's afraid of him for some reason.' So Arabella thought that too. 'She behaves as though she owes him something. Me!' said Arabella, and then she was crying again.

I said, trying to sound stern: 'Do remember, Arabella, that it's your duty to obey your mother.'

'And it's her duty to look after me,' retorted Arabella with spirit. Once more, she looked me in the face. 'Mistress Stannard, I know a good deal about you. We once gave a night's lodging to a Queen's Messenger. His name was Christopher something, and he talked about you.'

'Was the name Christopher Spelton?' I asked. Arabella nodded and I silently cursed my good friend Christopher, whom I had known and sometimes worked with for so many years. He was normally so discreet. This time, it seemed, he must have let his tongue off the leash. 'What did Master Spelton say?'

'My mother had mentioned the name of our landlord – your name. And he said he knew you; you lived not far from him. He said you are a half-sister to the queen. Is that true?'

'Yes. My mother was once a lady-in-waiting to Queen Anne Boleyn. She was sent home in disgrace, because she was with child. The child was me. She took shelter with her brother, my Uncle Herbert, and his wife Aunt Tabitha. I was grown up before I found out who my father was.'

'Master Spelton said that it was old King Henry,' Arabella informed me. 'And he said that he not only knew you – he had once wished to marry you, except that he found somebody else and fell in love with her instead. He would have understood about me and Gilbert! And' – there was triumph now in her voice – 'he said you had been married three times, and the first time was when you were the same age that I am now, and that you ran away with your cousin's betrothed. So you know about falling in love. You must do. Were you happy?'

'Yes,' I admitted. I would never regret Gerald and I couldn't deny that, even now when I was trying to persuade another young girl to give up the young man she wanted.

So much for that happy ride through the green and gold May morning. I had been so carefree then, thinking not only that the shadow of Spain was gone, but that with it had gone the last of my curious career as one of Elizabeth's secret agents. I still wore open-fronted gowns with hidden pouches stitched inside, in which I could secretly carry such unlikely objects as picklocks and a small dagger. I continued to carry them, but only out of habit. I hoped never to need them again. I was done with investigating mysteries.

But here, I suspected that there was a mystery. Joan Mercer feared this man Waters. I had sensed it, and so had this unhappy girl.

However, solving the mystery was not what I was here for. 'Arabella,' I said gently, 'I don't know the reason but I think it will distress your mother greatly if you refuse to marry Master Waters. You surely don't want to distress your mother, even if you don't understand her fears. What do you say?'

Arabella's pretty features became suddenly mulish. 'I say no.'

'Won't you at least think it over?'

'I've been shut in here for three days, thinking it over, and the answer is still no. I keep saying, *I don't like him!* I wouldn't like him even if Gilbert didn't exist. You say my mother very much wants me to marry him. But no one's asking *her* to live with him, to swear before God that she will stay with him for life. Only I won't. I won't marry him. I *won't*!'

'Many girls,' I said, knowing that I sounded sententious and privately marvelling at the difference between Mistress Ursula Stannard now, and young Ursula Blanchard who had climbed out of a window and slithered down that roof to defy her guardians and elope with Gerald, 'many girls, and young men too, have obeyed their parents and consented to marriages that weren't to their taste to begin with. They have even done so when they thought themselves in love elsewhere. And then found after a while that their parents had made a good choice after all. Found themselves loving their spouses, being happy. Love *can* grow. I was married three times. I undertook my final marriage for practical reasons, and was amazed at the way love grew. I held his hand as he died and I thought my world had ended.'

'My world will end if I marry Master Waters. I never will. *Never!*'

'Your mother has threatened to use force. Can you withstand that?'

'I'll have to.' The little elfin features were more mulish than ever.

'Do think,' I repeated, rising to my feet. 'Please.'

There was no answer. There was nothing more to say. I left her. I fastened the padlock behind me and went down, to find Mistress Mercer in the parlour, alone. She looked at me with raised eyebrows and I shook my head. Her eyes snapped and she rose to her feet. 'Then I will have to deal with her.'

'I do urge you to wait a little. Now that she's alone, and has heard what I had to say . . . she may change her mind.'

'I'm tired of waiting. Master Waters will be home tomorrow or the day after and he will come to see his bride. Her brothers will be home at any time – could be in two weeks' time, could be late tonight, midday tomorrow. Everything must be as it should be before any of them come. There isn't time to wait. I must make an end of this at once.'

I wanted to plead with her but I knew it would be no use. I was heartsick for the two young lovers who were now to be parted, and full of pity for Arabella, who for all her courage and resolution had little chance of withstanding what was to come. I knew what it would be like. Uncle Herbert and Aunt Tabitha had taken my mother in, had sheltered her and later me, had housed and fed us and even let me share my cousins' tutors. But to my mother they had always been cold; she died when I was sixteen and I think that mostly she died of unhappiness. As for me, they had always resented me and they had beaten me, many times.

Mistress Mercer walked purposefully out of the parlour. I stayed where I was, tensely. A few minutes later, Dale appeared, looking alarmed, and then the boys and Brockley came running in too. 'We were all in the stables, rubbing the horses down and cleaning tack!' Harry gasped. 'But from one of the upstairs windows, there were such sounds . . .'

'I thought someone was being murdered!' Dale stood still, head cocked. 'You can't hear it from here. But what's happening, ma'am? Do you know?'

'I'm afraid I do,' I said, and told them.

'Can't we do anything?' Harry demanded, visibly imagining himself as a noble knight, rushing to the rescue of a belea-guered princess. Just like Matthew! I suddenly thought, with faint alarm. I shook my head at him and sat down. Everyone sat down. We waited. Presently Mistress Mercer came in. She was very pale and seemed to be out of breath.

'All is well. I should have done it before. It was the quickest way out of the problem. I was sorry to have to do it; Arabella was sick before she finally gave in but give in she did. She will marry Master Waters as arranged. Now, it's time for supper.'

THREE
Allheal and Camomile

Evergreens wasn't the kind of house where breakfast consisted of a few snacks eaten standing up. There was a table with benches round it, a white cloth and dishes set out on a sideboard. These included fresh manchet bread, butter, honey and cold lamb chops, with small ale or milk to drink. Eddie ate with the grooms (though I understood that the food was the same) but Harry and Ben joined us, and fell eagerly on the chops.

A pert young maidservant called Cathy was in attendance and I asked her where Mistress Mercer was. I didn't enquire about Arabella. I knew she was lying face down in her bed, too stiff to move and breaking her heart for Gilbert Gale. I rather wished I could meet that young man. Arabella was a girl with character. If she fell in love, I fancied that the man would probably have character as well.

Cathy didn't mention her, either. She said: 'The mistress isn't well, madam. She has a sick headache. It happens to her sometimes. Awful, her heads are. She says they're like hammers banging over one eye and in the end she often brings everything up. She asks if after breakfast, you will visit her in her room.'

'I sympathize with Mistress Mercer,' I said. I recognized Cathy's description of the symptoms all too well. I had migraine headaches myself, on occasion.

While we were eating, Page came in to see if we needed anything more and I asked him why the village was called Cutpenny. 'It's such a strange name,' I said.

Page's usually expressionless face relaxed into a smile. 'The story goes that in the days of King Edward the Fourth, he and a young landowner, who was then the lord of the village, played a game of dice. The young landowner pledged the village and the king pledged half a penny – a penny coin, cut in half. The landowner lost.'

'It sounds like a very uneven wager,' I said.

'I understand,' said Charles Page, 'that there was never any suggestion of sharp practice. It is said that both parties were in their cups.'

We all laughed. I nibbled the last of the meat off a chop bone, brushed away some crumbs and said: 'Cathy, will you show me to your mistress's chamber? Dale, come with me.'

'Show Mistress Stannard the way, Cathy,' said Page.

Cathy took Dale and me up to a bedchamber on the south side of the house. At her knock, a voice bade us to enter and she opened the door. 'Mistress Stannard is here, as you asked, madam,' Cathy said, not herself venturing to enter the room. From the depths of a wide fourposter bed, a wan voice said: 'Please come in.'

A thin, quietly dressed woman came to meet us as we entered, announcing herself as Jane Hayes, Mistress Mercer's personal maid. 'My mistress is far from well, but is most anxious to see you,' she told us, and gestured for us to go to the bedside.

We did so. Joan Mercer peered painfully up at us from the midst of her pillows. Her face was pasty and her brow was puckered. She said: 'My head . . . I am sorry. I think that dealing with Arabella brought this on. I was too long over taking firm steps. I hope she will be quite healed before her wedding day. Mistress Stannard, I keep a potion for my head ready as a rule, but my last phial of it was broken, and now I have none, just when I need it. Once more, can I ask your help?'

Dale said: 'We have a medicine for headaches with us. Would you like to try that?'

Joan Mercer shook her head and then looked as though she wished she hadn't. 'I would rather not. There are things that make me ill; I never eat spices or strong-tasting things. I come out in rashes. I take only potions that I know are safe for me. I don't know what *is* in the one I like to take but I know it won't harm me. It's made for me by Mother Lee.'

'Mother Lee – Margaret Lee, her full name is,' said Jane,

in a disapproving voice, 'lives in a cottage up there on the hilltop, all alone in the woods. She makes medicines for sale. The villagers use her sometimes but they don't like her. They say she's a witch.'

'Yes, so they do,' said Joan. 'Our vicar, Father Dunberry, says we should not buy her potions. Father Eliot, the vicar we had before him, said the same. But her headache potions *work*!'

'Father Eliot used her potions himself, in the end,' Jane said to us. 'He had something amiss with his heart and he'd tried everything else, things from the Cutpenny apothecary, things given him by a physician from Caterham and all no use. Then his housekeeper went and got something from Mother Lee. I know because I know her. He tried it because he'd got desperate. Only it didn't do him much good because he died not long after. Seems he took an overdose of that same medicine. Mother Lee's potions are dangerous, it seems to me.'

'Her headache medicine isn't,' said Joan irritably. 'And don't look at me like that, Jane. I know what you want to say. This new vicar Father Dunberry speaks against Mother Lee every Sunday and if he finds out that someone's used her potions he visits them and puts the fear of hellfire into them. I know. I've heard him! But I need her medicine! And I mean to have it! It works!'

'So what is the difficulty?' I couldn't understand why I was being called to help. Joan Mercer had a house full of servants who were presumably capable of walking up a hill to visit this Mother Lee.

'It's all because of what that vicar's been preaching. None of my servants, not even Jane here, will go up to her cottage now because he says it's a sin to use her magic medicines.' Joan sounded both wan and acid. Jane blushed.

Mildly, I said: 'Back at Hawkswood, there's an aged Welshwoman who is part of the household though she hasn't any special tasks there. Years ago, Brockley and I rescued her from a charge of witchcraft. She attached herself to me after that. She isn't a witch – she's just clever with herbal medicines and capable of being very rude to people who've annoyed her.'

In the folds of my gown, I crossed the fingers of my right

hand. I do not and never have believed in witches, but I sometimes did wonder about Gladys Morgan. She had an uncanny
way of foreseeing the future – at least when it contained
trouble. And there had been one occasion when I had been in
a dangerous situation, but had escaped, and then come home
to find Gladys claiming the credit because she had performed
a spell on my behalf, sacrificing a cockerel at dawn and reciting
incantations. I smiled at Joan and said: 'Surely there's *someone*
who will take your orders?'

'The only one who would do so, I think, is Page, and I
can't ask him. He is not paid to undertake trivial errands. But
these headaches can go on and on and I must be well for when
Master Waters comes home, and my sons might be here at
any moment! Can you, will you, go to Mother Lee for me?
Or send your manservant? Horses can get up the track. You've
just hinted that you don't believe in witches. Jane here'll give
you the money.'

I agreed. I could have sent Brockley, but I did not. Curiosity
is assuredly my besetting sin. This talk of an old woman who
lived in a cottage in a wood at the top of a hill, and made
potions and had upset two vicars in succession, was enough
to make anyone inquisitive. I would go and see this so-called
witch for myself.

It was as I was turning away, having promised to be as
quick as I could, that to my dismay and great surprise, it
seemed to me that Gladys Morgan's croaky old voice was
speaking in my head.

That woman, it said, as plainly as though Gladys, who had
grown lame with age, had hobbled into the room and was
standing in front of me, *is poison.*

Amazed but hoping it didn't show, I shook my head
impatiently and the illusion vanished.

All the same, I nodded sharply to Dale, who was standing
by in silence, and got us both out of the room as quickly
as I could.

I couldn't pay attention to imaginary voices in my head. I had
undertaken to visit an old wit— woman in a cottage up in the
woods, and fetch medicine for my hostess, who certainly

needed it, and I ought to go at once. Jane had followed us out of the room and although her expression was forbidding, she came downstairs with us and from somewhere produced a small cloth purse with coins in it.

I thanked her and after stowing the purse in the hidden pouch inside my skirt, I said to Dale: 'We'll take Brockley. Come, we must have our horses saddled and go at once. Heaven knows what we'll find,' I added thoughtfully. 'Probably a tumbledown hovel with thatch swooping down to the ground as though the house needs to have its hair cut, and an unwashed old hag who'll threaten to put the evil eye on me if I upset her. I shall welcome company! Though – are you sure *you* want to come, Dale?'

'Yes, ma'am. A lady should not be unattended when away from home.'

This actually meant that Dale didn't like me to go anywhere alone with Brockley. Once, long ago, there had been a time when Roger Brockley and I nearly became lovers. It hadn't happened and it never would but there was still a secret bond between us. There had been a time when Dale and Brockley had quarrelled over it. We never spoke of it, but it was there.

Brockley and Eddie saddled the horses quickly. Brockley provided himself with saddlebags. 'Got to carry this medicine somehow, madam.'

Harry and Ben wanted to come too, but Brockley, now taking charge in the absence of their tutor, told them roundly that they were not wanted. Would they please put the mule out to grass and then exercise their own horses, and not up and down that wooded hill.

With that settled, the Brockleys and I mounted and set off.

It wasn't far to the foot of the hill, where to the left a downward path led to the village of Cutpenny. At least, we could see some cottages only a hundred yards or so away. To the right, the track led away across a meadow, and we could see it winding off into the distance, skirting a spinney and a cluster of farm cottages, and leading on uphill towards a distant house, possibly the place where this Master Waters lived. Straight ahead, the path went up into the trees, and then angled to the right, the first leg of the zigzag track up the hill.

It was a cool day. Yesterday's sunshine had gone, and the sky was clouded. The horses managed the path easily, for it wasn't particularly steep, only lengthy because of the long zigzags. The trees, which were mostly oaks, in a stunted form that was probably due to the thin soil and the extraordinary angles at which they had to grow, overshadowed the track, so that we rode through a greenish twilight, as though we were under water.

At the top, we emerged into a clearing, and there we found a dwelling which was nothing at all like the imaginary one I had described to Dale.

This was no tumbledown cottage. It was thatched, but neatly, and it was timber-framed, with a whitewashed filling, probably wattle and cow-dung daub, a material that lasts nearly forever. Its windows were small but they were glazed, and leaded in a diamond pattern. It stood in a garden where I could see onions, carrots and lettuces being grown, and there were frames for peas and runner beans. There was a little flower garden, with hollyhocks and sunflowers and some tall poppies already coming into bloom, and there was a herb patch too, well stocked by the look of it and no doubt the source of Mother Lee's potions. I doubted if she ever gathered wild plants in the light of the full moon.

There was a well, too, and beyond the cottage I glimpsed a stretch of flat ground; the hilltop seemed to be a small plateau. I could see hens pecking about and a couple of tethered goats, and to the right, there was fencing and a gate into a stretch of rough pasture. A donkey had wandered up to look interestedly at us over the gate. The cottage itself had a lean-to, open in front, containing pails and firewood and some milking stools. It had a flat wooden roof where an enormous striped cat was snoozing.

'Do we just knock at the door?' Dale asked, doubtfully.

There was no need. The door was already opening. The woman who came out of it was not attractive but she was not a hag. She was short and thin with a sharp-featured face, and the strands of hair that had escaped her tight-fitting linen cap were grey, but she was upright and moved briskly and wore a well-used apron over a brown stuff gown cut in a bygone fashion, to be worn without a ruff.

She halted in her doorway and we went towards her. 'Ah,' she said as we came within earshot, 'I heard you coming. You will be the people from Evergreens?'

'She'll say next that she saw us in a crystal ball,' muttered Brockley.

'We have come from Mistress Joan Mercer,' I said. 'She has a severe sick headache and needs a potion that we understand you can make for her. We are guests at her house just now. I am Mistress Stannard . . .'

'Aye, I've heard of you. These will be your servants, the Brockleys,' said Mother Lee, interrupting me. Her voice was harsh, her accent that of a countrywoman.

By the sound of it, somebody, recently, had ignored the vicar's strictures and climbed the hill to have a gossip with Mother Lee. She was now grinning and just for a moment, her thin face had something truly unpleasant about it, as though the sharp chin had lengthened and the pale eyes had glittered.

'The villagers and Mistress Joan's servants won't come up here now but children do,' she said, answering my unspoken question. 'For all that their parents tell them no. There's three that are younger brothers and sisters to Joan's maid Cathy. They know all about the wedding and the guests and they've been up and talked about you and the Brockleys. You'd best tie those horses to that gate to make friends with Neddy there, and then come inside.'

We tethered our mounts as instructed and trooped into the cottage, followed by the striped cat, which was probably curious about us. Mother Lee walked in ahead of us.

'I've got some of the headache medicine ready,' she said over her shoulder. 'I keep it by; there's a good many folk use it. It keeps well, stoppered properly, and I put it in proper glass bottles. When I was married, my old man made them; worked as a glassmaker, he did. I've got a whole store of bottles that he made. One of his friends put them glass windows in for me when I come up here after my man was gone. An old hermit's place this was, in the days of Queen Mary, and about as comfortable as a tomb, back then. I've improved it. Sit you down now.'

The front door opened into a room which was living room and kitchen all together. There was a spit over the hearth, a whitewood table with stools set round it, and a pair of basket-work chairs. Along one wall there was a bench with cushions and opposite to this was a window seat, probably a storage chest as well, and beside it, a tall cupboard. The cat at once laid claim to the window seat and arranged itself there, watching us with suspicious green eyes The light was dim, for the small windows kept out light as well as weather and the glass was old-style, thick and flawed and tinged with greenish blue. Underfoot, there was straw.

'I can let Mistress Joan have two phials,' Mother Lee informed us. 'Allheal and camomile, that's what works for her. Well, that and a little extra of my own but that's my secret ingredient. I'll give you some ale afore you start back down. I brew a good ale, I do.'

We sat down on the bench and Mother Lee disappeared through a further door. She didn't shut it after her and by leaning forward, I could see that it looked like a still room, limewashed, with shelving laden with bottles and earthenware jars in various shapes and sizes. Mother Lee, with a basket on her arm, appeared to be climbing, rather stiffly, up a short ladder to get at a high shelf.

The cat was growing restless. It sat up, licked a forepaw and gave a desultory wash to its left ear. Finally, it rose to all four feet and took a leap to the top of the cupboard, which swayed a little. One of its doors swung partly open. I went to close it and caught a startling glimpse of the cupboard's contents.

I had seen such things before but not in the lonely cottages of elderly women who lived – presumably – by making goats' cheese, selling hens' eggs and vegetables and brewing potions. Inside that cupboard, along with earthenware bowls and dishes and several candlesticks, there were two golden goblets. They were small but they were valuable. I didn't even own such precious objects myself. I knew the rich look of gold. I also knew the look of genuine rubies and pearls, and each of these goblets had a pattern of rubies and pearls round its bowl, and another round its foot. I closed the cupboard hastily and resumed my seat.

Mother Lee reappeared, with her basket. Two small rounded bottles with narrow necks were poking out of it.

'Here you are.' She lifted one of the bottles and I saw that a symbol, a circle with a horizontal line across it, was painted on its side. 'This is the one Mistress Mercer wants. I never learned me letters but all I need are marks I can recognize so I made some up to use as labels, so as I can tell which bottle has which mixture in it. This here, with a circle and a stroke across it, this is the brew for sick headaches.'

She gave us a smile which was more like a leer. I didn't take to Mother Lee any more than I could take to Joan Mercer. She said: 'I take care over them signs of mine. Wouldn't do, giving a headache potion to a fellow as has the rheumatics, or offering a nice scented ointment to keep a lady's hands smooth to some poor soul with boils.'

'I should think not!' said Dale.

'Well, it wouldn't,' said Mother Lee. 'And that's all the signs are for, but this last year or two I've had bother on their account. Mistress Mercer, she's got sense and at a guess I'd say so have you, but there's some as think they're magic signs, and I got them from the Devil. This Father Dunberry that's vicar in Cutpenny now, he's made the village folk frightened to come here. It makes me that angry. If I were really a witch, which I ain't, *they'd* all have boils!'

'What's the dosage for the headache potion?' I asked.

'One big spoonful and no more for six hours at the least. Mistress Mercer knows. She sleeps after a dose and when she wakes up, she's better. I've heard there's a fruit called lemon that's good for sick headaches as well, but it's too costly for the likes of me to buy though when I used to ride Neddy down the hill to go to the market at Caterham, I've seen them there. Good market, that is, though Oxted market to the south runs it close.'

She took the bottles out of the basket and handed them to Brockley. 'I saw you had saddlebags. Here, put these in, and take this pretty basket for when you take them in to Mistress Mercer. That'll be two pence.'

My eyebrows rose but the horny palm, with the ingrained dirt in its lines, remained steady. 'There's work in making these medicines, work and knowledge and I got to live. Mistress Mercer, she don't grudge the price of getting rid of her pain.'

I wouldn't grudge it either, I thought. I knew too much about headaches. I brought out the purse and found that there were three penny coins in it and three halfpennies. I paid up. Mother Lee pushed the money into a pocket and then, changing on the instant from a woman of business to a genial hostess, bade us all settle ourselves and she would bring out her ale.

FOUR
Knights and Maidens

The ale was excellent. Mother Lee was skilled at brewing in every way, it seemed. Presently, much refreshed, we bade her farewell and left. At the foot of the hill, Brockley suddenly said: 'I'd like to look at this village, Cutpenny, with its villagers that won't go near Mother Lee except when they have bad headaches, and this vicar that threatens them with hellfire. I think, madam, that I will ride down there while you go back to Evergreens. Mistress Mercer will be waiting for her medicine. Fran, take my saddlebags.'

'Very well,' I said, though I added: 'Brockley, we are not on an assignment.'

'No, madam, I know, but in your service I have formed habits of – shall we say, inquisitiveness.'

I laughed and said that I too would like to know more about Cutpenny. We parted, and Dale and I hurried on to the house. We transferred the phials into the prettily woven basket that Dale had carried on her arm, and went at once to Joan Mercer's chamber. She was lying flat with her eyes shut. Jane Hayes was sitting beside her. She stood up as we came in.

'You have the medicine?'

Dale held out the basket. Jane seized one of the phials, removed its stopper, picked up a spoon that lay ready on a table by the bed, poured out a spoonful and went to her mistress. 'Here's what will help, madam,' she said, speaking very quietly.

Joan moved among her pillows, trying to sit up, though the effort made her forehead pucker. 'They've brought it? Thank you, Mistress Stannard. And Dale.'

Jane spooned the potion into Joan's mouth, holding her mistress's head steady with her spare hand, all her movements gentle and tender. Dale put the basket down on the table and

we started to withdraw. Jane followed us to the door, to
whisper: 'Loud voices hurt her. But she will sleep now, in
spite of the pain, and when she wakes, the pain will be gone.
Thank you for fetching it.'

'I'll stay with you to help, if you like,' Dale whispered. She
glanced at me for approval, and I nodded.

Jane, however, shook her head. 'I know what to do. I will
soon have my lady back to her old self now.'

We left them, therefore, and I suggested to Dale that we
should fetch the embroidery work that we had both brought
with us, and take it downstairs to the parlour. Dale and I always
had embroideries to hand; we regularly made cushion covers
and tablecloths for my houses and garments for ourselves. I
was working on a pair of sleeves and Dale had brought a
cushion cover with a pattern on it that had been designed by
my former companion, Sybil Jester, who now lived with her
married daughter in Edinburgh.

She and I exchanged letters sometimes but they were
growing rarer. As one grew older, I had noticed, things and
even people of the past began to fall behind, as though one
had sailed out from a coast that was now dropping out of sight
beyond the horizon.

We were sewing industriously when we were disturbed by
a scraping noise outside, and what sounded like Harry's voice,
saying something impatiently. I sat up, needle poised in the
air and my ears alert, and made out a few words. *No, not there
. . . round the corner . . . Hurry up . . . Don't make such a
noise . . .*

Dale and I looked at each other, set our work aside and
hurried out of the room. We made for a side door and went
out on to the wide gravel path that encircled the house. A few
swift steps to the left brought us round a corner, where we
found the source of the noises.

'Harry!' I said angrily. 'Come down at once! Ben, haven't
you more sense than to be helping him? And where did you
get that ladder?'

'We found it in a garden shed,' said Harry, backing carefully
down the ladder. He had been halfway up it, with Ben gripping it to keep it from slipping. 'We'd seen a gardener using

it to trim back the ivy and where he put it afterwards. We want to rescue Arabella! We want to take her to Cutpenny village, to the carpenter there, Gilbert Gale. We know all about it; the grooms know everything. And after hearing those sounds we heard yesterday, we can't just leave her . . .'

I looked up and glimpsed a pale face peering down from an attic window. Arabella had seen what was going on, whether or not she was a party to it. I took a deep and angry breath.

'This will not do. You have no business to interfere. We have no authority in this house, and no right to poke our noses into the way Mistress Mercer deals with her daughter.'

'But . . .'

'As a matter of fact, I too am sorry for Arabella, but she will have to do as her mother bids her, and her mother has the right to bid her. She isn't asking Arabella to do anything other than marry a suitable man. Take that ladder back to where you found it at once. Did you manage to tell Arabella what you were planning?'

'No,' said Harry and Ben echoed it. I was thankful to hear it.

I looked at them in exasperation. 'Listen to me. You are not knights on a quest to rescue a maiden who is locked in a tower. You are two ill-informed and very foolish boys acting out some romantic tale of derring-do. It's nothing but a fantasy. This is reality. You are interfering where you have no business and defying your elders, as you very well know. In broad daylight, too! *Very* foolish.'

'No one's about,' said Harry, aggrieved. 'Mistress Mercer is ill in bed. We thought, if we could just get Arabella away . . .'

'Dear God! I have never allowed either of you to be beaten, but believe me, at this moment, I am half inclined to change my mind and get Brockley to do just that. You have much to learn, you two!'

'Brockley did once do that, anyhow,' said Harry, unperturbed. 'Brockley and Wilder. Brockley took a strap to me and Wilder did the same to Ben. Not that Ben worried about it any more than I did.'

'I got used to that, from my father,' said Ben, quite calmly.

I had always thought of Ben as vulnerable, to be treated gently, as though he were made of glass. Now I saw that he was vulnerable no longer. Hawkswood had done that for him. Unfortunately, Hawkswood had also, somehow and by accident, encouraged him to go rescuing imaginary princesses from other people's attics.

'Brockley and Wilder?' I didn't know whether to be outraged or grateful. Harry, confound him, had probably deserved it and Ben had followed his lead, into whatever mischief Harry had planned. But I would have to have words with those two gentlemen, who whatever the provocation had acted without my consent.

'Just get that ladder back to its shed and find yourselves some harmless occupation in the stables. Or I *will* set Brockley on to you.' As though he were a mastiff, I thought, struggling against the memory of my younger self, climbing out of that window, sliding down that stretch of roof as she slithered to Gerald's anxiously waiting arms. That incident was a splendid example of defying one's elders. It was also a valued memory. It was one part of the past that hadn't dropped over the horizon.

'Before you go,' I said, 'tell me, have you warned the carpenter – what's his name? Gilbert Gale – that he was about to elope with somebody else's bride?'

'No.' Ben shook his head.

'It never occurred to either of you that perhaps he might not want to abandon his workshop at five minutes' notice and rush off into the countryside to look for a vicar who'll perform the marriage service without the banns? You young wantwits; you can't even think that far ahead! Oh, take that ladder away before I kill the pair of you!'

'Oh, ma'am!' said Dale faintly as I led her back to the parlour. 'What a thing! Praise be that you stopped them! But I'm sorry if Roger . . .'

'He and Wilder probably had good reasons for chastising them,' I said. I was thinking ruefully that perhaps after all I did need help in educating Harry and Ben.

FIVE
Gems and Jaguars

Brockley returned half an hour later. He looked pleased with himself, but the moment he saw our faces, he asked what was wrong. I told him about Harry and Ben and their attempt to turn themselves into knights errant. And while I was about it, what was all this about Brockley and Wilder having beaten Harry without my knowledge?

Brockley's reaction was unexpected.

He said: 'Well, at least our two lads have good hearts. Their mistake this time was in setting gallantly out to achieve a rescue without working their plans out properly beforehand. Mr Gale should have been consulted! Which I think would have put an end to any such crazy plan. I have now met him and he strikes me as a man of sense. As for the matter, some time ago now, when Wilder and I dealt with them without asking you, madam, forgive me, but they are *boys*. You are a lady and we would not have you otherwise. But boys need someone to play the man's part in their lives. We were not harsh, but what those two young demons were planning was a midnight race on horseback . . .'

'*What?*' I said.

'Their tutor overheard them talking about it but because it involved horses he came to me. I told him not to trouble himself; that Wilder and I would attend to it. Those two wood-wild youngsters could have killed or lamed their horses – or themselves. They meant to have a midnight race, *and* – they apparently hadn't noticed this – in the dark phase of the moon! Starting point, that massive old oak on the east bank of the Hawkswood lake, then across country, round Hawkswood village and back to the oak. They could have broken their necks or the legs of their horses, charging across country in the dark. As I said, we were not harsh, but that kind of thing has to be checked.'

'Dear heaven!' said Dale.

I said: 'God's teeth!' Then I said: 'All right, Brockley. I had no idea that the boys could hatch such a scheme. To risk horses in such a way! That changes everything. You and Wilder did the right thing, though you should have told me, afterwards if not before. At least neither of the boys came crying to me. In future, very well, I will leave these things to you and trust you to keep within reasonable bounds. I am appalled at what you have told me. I'm ashamed of them. You can use your own judgement about today's attempted escapade, Brockley.'

'I will lecture them at length on the virtue of foresight,' said Brockley. 'I won't go further. They acted out of kindness, misguided, but kindness all the same. And now . . .'

I leant back in my chair, wanting to be at ease, thankful, even, to realize that the responsibility of seeing two vigorous lads like Harry and Ben safely out of boyhood into manhood, was not now mine alone. 'What is Cutpenny like, Brockley?'

'It's bigger than I thought it would be,' Brockley said, seating himself. 'I expected that it would be just a tiny place but it's more than that. It doesn't have a market – for marketing, its folk go to Caterham or Oxted. But there's a tavern, called the Crown, and a good-sized church. There's a village green and a sizeable fishpond. I called at the vicarage. Where,' said Brockley wryly, 'the vicar gave me no refreshments but much grave talk.'

'That will be Father Dunberry that we've heard about,' I said. 'He's new, I believe.'

'Yes. He's only been here two months or so. I didn't like him. Long black gown and long solemn face. Puritan leanings and full of superstition. He was shocked to hear that we had been buying Mother Lee's wares. He fears that the Devil has supplied her with the knowledge to create her potions and that we should beware before her brews entrap us to the danger of our souls. I said I would remember what he had said, and got away from him as soon as possible.'

'Poor Mother Lee,' said Dale. 'Not that I cared for her much.'

'There's a well,' said Brockley, 'halfway along the street – there's only one street – and I got talking to some women there, asked them if I could have a drink of water. There was a pewter cup hanging on a chain for anyone to drink from and they fetched me up some water kindly enough. I said who I was and who you were. They all know that the landlord is visiting at Evergreens! They said I'd be welcome in the Crown inn, any time. I told them where we'd been this morning and then there was a sort of disagreement between them, two saying they'd bought medicines from Mother Lee and been pleased with them, and two saying no, she's a witch and the others ought to listen to Father Dunberry. One said that maybe folk ought to be careful because the vicar before him, Father Eliot, had preached against her too, but when he kept getting breathless and his heart kept pounding, his housekeeper had got some of Mother Lee's medicine for him, and after a few doses of that, he died. Then they all nodded, as much as to say: *There you are then.*

'After that,' Brockley said, 'I went on further and saw an apothecary's sign. So I went in and asked for a medicine for my headaches.'

Dale and I gazed at him with astonishment and he grinned.

'Did he supply one?' I asked.

'Yes. I have it here. It smells horrible. I recommend keeping to Gladys' potions, madam. I'll pour this away. The shop was ordinary and looked tidy enough but the apothecary himself is getting on in years and he looks discontented. Lined face, grey hair that straggles. It could do with a wash and needs cutting as well. He hates Mother Lee. He said so. He congratu-lated me on having had the good sense to come to him and not to that old witch up in the woods on the hill. He said they – I think he meant the villagers – would see to her one of these days. I got away from him and went to call on this carpenter that poor Mistress Arabella's in love with.'

He met my eyes. 'He's a fine young man. I don't know what this Master Waters is like but he'll need to be quite impressive to outdo Gilbert Gale. I looked at a bench he was making and murmured something about liking the carving and then he asked me if I was one of the wedding guests at Evergreens and when I said yes, he asked if the marriage was really going ahead. I said yes to that as well and then he asked outright if Arabella's mother had beaten her, as she'd threatened to do. I gathered that Arabella had told him she was afraid of that, during one of their secret meetings. I said I believed so. He looked so stricken. I said I was sorry for them both and came away. What else could I say? Is she still abed, poor lass?'

She wasn't. The parlour door opened at that very moment and in came Arabella herself, pale but dignified. She was still in her drab gown, but she now had a ruff, stockings and a pair of shoes and her hair had been washed. We stood up and she gave us a pallid smile.

'Good morning, everyone. Mother is unwell, as I imagine you all know.' She came forward, moving stiffly but resolutely. *Poor child*, I thought, remembering my own girlhood and the pain that forced me to sleep face down sometimes for three nights after a thrashing. My uncle and aunt both made sure that I would have no visible bruising when I was dressed but the unseen ones made themselves acutely felt.

Arabella said: 'I am acting as hostess in my mother's absence, though she will soon recover now that she has the right medicine. My betrothed, Master Waters, has sent word to say that he is home again and he will visit us soon. I came to say that dinner will be served in an hour. You are the only wedding guests who have come to stay. Most are local folk who will simply join us on the wedding morning. You are most welcome.'

She smiled at us and I saw, startlingly, that my first impression of her had been right. Arabella was beautiful. Very beautiful, even when serious, and when smiling, her whole being was illumined.

She added, in a steady voice: 'Please let us not talk of the last few days. I have accepted that my duty is to obey my mother and make the good marriage she has planned for me. And I am truly grateful for it. Now, how may I entertain you?'

We dined, a stiff meal. Arabella was seated uneasily on a soft cushion and trying to lead the conversation but with difficulty. It centred, I recall, round the good weather we were having and a new breed of cattle that the farm bailiff thought might do well on their land. The meal itself was good, two courses, including fresh trout, pike in a sauce with herbs, fried veal in a seasoned batter, almond fritters and patterned marchpane medallions on a base of buttery pastry.

'We eat more simply as a rule, but you are guests, and wedding guests at that,' said Arabella, gallantly.

I replied by asking her to compliment the cook for me. She brightened a little and said that she liked cooking and had helped to make the marchpane. She took me to the kitchen to express my appreciation in person. I admired the kitchen, which had been improved since I last saw it. It had a stone wall and a stone floor and the two deep hearths that I remembered, but now both of them had spits instead of only one, and there were new shelves on the opposite wall, laden with bowls and platters of earthenware and pewter. The shelves were edged with hooks, from which hung implements, saucepans and tankards.

The principal cook, James Mitchell, was a wizened little man with a hook of a nose and a pair of bright brown eyes. He was below average height but spry and strong, his arms and legs corded with muscle. His voice was strong, too. As we entered, he was throwing out orders to two kitchen maids, a youth who was apparently his assistant, and a spit boy. He seemed to be not only giving orders about supper but also berating them for shortcomings in the dinner, not that I had noticed any. He must be very anxious for perfection, I thought. All of them, except for the youth, who had impudence written all over his face, seemed to be cringing as well as listening. I felt that the internal politics of this kitchen must be interesting.

My compliments were received graciously, however. The servants were introduced to me. The maidservants were sisters, Mary and Phil Drew. The impudent youth was Samuel Hazel and the spit boy was his little brother Silas. After this, Arabella asked us how we wished to pass the afternoon. I looked at her and thought that she probably wished to spend it lying on her bed and having a private cry. I said that I would go for a walk in the fields, and take the Brockleys with me.

It was pleasant outside. The sun had come out and it was

warm. We wandered past fields of wheat and oats, a meadow clearly destined for hay and another where cattle were grazing, mostly small black cows but also a few bigger ones, brown splashed with white, and a bull of the same type. Brockley said he thought the skewbald ones were the new breed that Arabella had mentioned at dinner.

Beyond the fields there was open common land given over to sheep. Their fleeces looked thick. Shearing couldn't be far away.

The common stretched ahead of us, rising gradually, and then, beyond it, on top of a slight hill, was the house we had seen from the foot of the wooded hill. I wondered aloud whether it was the place where Master Waters lived.

It was growing hot, so we turned back. I was thinking that in this warm afternoon a little doze would be pleasant. We went in through the side door that Dale and I had used earlier. It led through a narrow room where cloaks hung on hooks and boots were arranged in pairs along the wall, and then into the entrance vestibule. And there, immediately, we sensed a change in the atmosphere, a feeling of vigorous disturbance which made itself manifest in the very air, even before, from upstairs, we actually heard voices and footsteps and a burst of laughter.

As we stood wondering what was afoot, a young man carrying a heavy roll of something over his shoulder, came clattering down the stairs, shouting to someone behind him that of course he'd said it was to go in the parlour; did those wantwit hired men ever listen?

He came to the foot of the stairs, saw us and stopped. He was a handsome fellow, tall, strong and sunburned. His hair, worn short but curling vigorously, was the same bronze-brown as Arabella's and his eyes were the same greenish hazel. They were full of laughter. 'Ho! We have guests! Mother!'

Joan Mercer, amazingly revived, came out of the parlour. 'So here you are! Have you been walking? Mistress Stannard, let me present my elder son, Hector, to you. Hector, this is our landlord, Mistress Ursula Stannard, and her . . . er . . .'
Like many other people, Joan Mercer stumbled over my precise

relationship with the Brockleys but recovered herself gallantly – 'her friends Master and Mistress Brockley.'

We all exchanged bows and curtseys and then Joan wanted to know what Hector was carrying. 'I thought you were upstairs unpacking, or rather, watching Page unpack for you.'

'Page is hanging up our clothes in a tidy fashion,' said Hector. 'What a great one for tidiness he is! He would go crazy at sea when it's stormy and everything that isn't tied down rolls and slides everywhere. Storms don't even respect the captain's cabin.'

'I dare say not.' Joan sounded tart but she was smiling. 'Where is Will Jankin? I hope you left him at the lodge.'

'Certainly, Mother. He is being joyfully embraced by his father, his mother and a tribe of siblings, all at the same time. We took good care of him.'

'So I should hope. Hector, once again, *what* is that over your shoulder?'

'Let us go into the parlour and I'll show you.'

He led the way and we all followed. Arabella, who had not after all gone to lie down, was in the parlour, sewing. She put down her work and stood up as we came in. Hector tipped the roll, which seemed to be a thick woollen rug, off his shoulder, and opened it out before the hearth, showing us what had been rolled up inside. We all stared at it in wonder.

'Is it a leopard skin?' I asked. Queen Elizabeth had a leopard-skin rug in her study. It went with her, wherever the court happened to be. Elizabeth moved her court from residence to residence, all along the Thames from Richmond to Greenwich. 'Only the spots are different,' I said doubtfully. 'They're . . . well, these are like rosettes.'

'It's a jaguar skin,' said Hector. 'It's a big wild New World cat. About the same size as a leopard but heavier, at least according to one of my crew, who has seen a live leopard, in a menagerie somewhere. Jaguar spots are this different shape. Beautiful, isn't it? And wait when you see what we've brought for our sister's wedding gift, or gifts, rather . . . ah! Here's brother Stephen. You have the gifts, Stevie?'

Stephen was also carrying a roll of something over his shoulder, and holding a small carved box in his hand. He resembled Hector, except for being a little shorter, with lighter hair and lighter eyes, though he too had been browned by wind and sun. He smiled at us all and said to me: 'Good day! Mistress Stannard, isn't it?'

'It is,' said Joan. There were further introductions, in the middle of which, Harry and Ben joined us. Somewhat to my irritation, Hector gazed appraisingly at Harry and said: 'You're a likely lad. You remind me of someone I know. You've got a reckless look like his. And a fine seaman he is. Have you ever thought of going to sea?'

'No, sir,' said Harry, having caught my eye.

'No? Pity,' said Hector. But then Stephen put his burdens down on the table, saying that all this polite bowing wasn't easy when a man was laden like a packhorse.

'But look what we've brought you, Bella. A wedding gift from each of us. Mine is an emerald. Here.' He opened the little box and took out a glittering green stone at which everyone stared in amazement. Brockley said disbelievingly: 'Is that really an emerald? It's the size of a quail's egg!'

'It is truly an emerald, I promise,' said Stephen. He held it out for us all to see closely and we saw that it was fixed in an ornate gold setting and strung on a gold chain.

'We had it made into a pendant for you, sister,' Stephen said. 'In London. We've just been there, disposing of some of the goods we've brought home. We usually make a few trips to London when we're ashore, Mistress Stannard; trade can be quite complicated. But we knew the right jeweller to go to, to get the stone shaped and polished and set and put on its chain. He is a big man in the jewellery world. Theobald Roebuck, that's his name. Let's see how you look in it, sister. The chain is long enough just to drop over your head . . . there!'

It suited her. The deep green stone and the glitter of the gold echoed her eyes and flattered the bronze patina of her hair. She lifted the pendant to look at it closely, and couldn't help but smile.

'That's better!' Hector said. 'We've been waiting to see you smile. What's all this I hear from our mother about you objecting to Master Waters? You're a silly girl. It's a splendid match.'

There was scorn in his voice and Arabella wilted under it, biting her lip. She didn't reply.

Stephen, however, looked at her kindly and said: 'That's not all. Here's what Hector has brought for you, Bella.'

He gave the object that he had been carrying to Hector, who spread it over the table. It was a length of velvet, a fresh light green in colour. I picked up a corner and felt it. Velvet is often a heavy material but this was thin and lightweight. It would be very comfortable for a wearer. It rippled as it caught the light.

'We're taking a score of these velvet rolls – various colours – out to the New World settlements on our next voyage,' Hector said. 'Most of the settlers, poor devils, work with their hands, indoors and out, six days a week, dawn to sunset. But on Sundays they like their bit of finery. This roll of velvet is my wedding gift for you, sister. It should make two gowns. The colour is right for you.'

'I didn't know we had colonies in the New World,' I said. 'The Spaniards do, of course, but surely we English still have to establish one.'

'Not colonies,' Hector said. 'Just settlements, that hope to grow into colonies one day though I doubt it, myself. There are two that we trade with. One's called Roanoke and it's on an island, not the mainland. It's the more southerly of the two. The other is smaller and further north. We don't have settlements in the southernmost part of the New World, of course – that's where the Spaniards are.'

'Why do you doubt that our settlements will last?' I asked.

'They both have harsh climates: the northerly one has hot summers and terrible winters; the other has a sweltering, sticky climate. The settlers have constant bouts of fever and sometimes they're attacked by the natives. The natives are sometimes friendly and sometimes not. The settlers don't have enough women or children, either. Not many women want to go out there, and those that do, don't live long on the whole. We're not sure that either of those little settlements will still be there when we make our next voyage.'

'In that case, we'll have to hunt our own jaguars,' agreed Stephen. 'Still, that can be good fun. We actually went on a jaguar hunt this time. The inhabitants of Roanoke sail to the mainland sometimes to hunt them and the tribes there don't mind. Jaguars are a danger to them. If we want to kill big cats, they don't want to stop us. That rug is the one we killed.'

'Aye, and it was a fine affair,' Hector agreed. 'Though when I got that beast on one end of my spear, and I saw those front claws like steel hooks, I truly thought my time had come. But I held on and thrust harder and it died.'

'You're so boastful, Hector,' said his mother disapprovingly. 'I suppose in a moment you will be telling us tales of your heroic deeds when you were at sea! I am sure you were mighty heroes, but boastfulness isn't a virtue. Anyway, you're here now, not clawed to death after all, and with all these beautiful things!'

There was an awkward pause, until Arabella thanked her brothers, made joyful exclamations over her gifts, and then embraced Hector and Stephen, one after the other. I noticed that they held her gently. Joan must have told them what she had done to their sister. Then the gem went back into its box and Joan called Cathy and another girl, Moll, to take it and the velvet upstairs to Mistress Arabella's chamber.

'We will start work on a new gown tomorrow,' she said to Arabella. 'If we are brisk, you'll be able to have it as part of your bride-clothes.' Arabella smiled, bravely.

Joan said: 'My daughter says that Master Waters is home. He sent word this morning, apparently, while I was abed. He intends to come here to see her tomorrow. I have however sent word inviting him to come on the day after, on Saturday, and to dine with us then. He will admire your gifts, boys.'

To me, quietly, so that her sons didn't hear, she murmured: 'By then, I trust Arabella will not be walking like a puppet doll. I don't wish Master Waters to know how his bride was won.'

SIX
Nothing To Be Done

The next day, taking Dale with me, I went to see Cutpenny and Gilbert Gale for myself. Brockley's report had made me very curious.

He had described the village well. This was no huddled hamlet where villagers barely scratched a living. It was modest in size, certainly, with just one main street. But it had a church and the cottages that lined the street were mostly stone-built with sizeable smallholdings behind them and there was a healthy air of bustle. Half the cottages at least were also workshops of one kind or another. There were craftsmen here.

We didn't seek out the vicar – who sounded unattractive – but we went into the church, which was indeed bigger than one would expect for a village such as this. We were surprised to find Charles Page there, supervising some women who were dusting and polishing.

'I've always liked to serve the church in some way,' he said to us when we greeted him. 'And I can be useful here for I know good cleaning when I see it, and I don't let corners be cut. I helped here in Father Eliot's time and Father Dunberry has let me continue.'

Inside, the church was dim and cool, and splashed with colour from beautiful stained-glass windows, which like the windows of St Mary's at Hawkswood had escaped the Protestant hysteria of the boy king Edward's days. These seemed to depict Christ's various miracles. Dale said she was sure she could identify the wedding at Canaan and the encounter with the lepers.

It was the kind of church that had benches where the congregation could sit during lengthy sermons. An elderly woman in a widow's black gown was seated there, her hands together in the attitude of prayer. She desisted, however, in order to look at us, and when we asked, told us that the church was dedicated to St Mark.

'It did used to be for St Catherine of Alexandria,' she said. 'But when Father Eliot died and this Father Dunberry come, he said St Catherine were Popish and had it changed to St Mark and we mostly don't like it but we've no say.'

'From what Roger said of him,' Dale remarked as we walked away from the church, 'changing the dedication would be just what this Father Dunberry would want to do.'

'I dare say he hates the stained glass,' I agreed. 'He must wonder how it escaped during the days of the boy king. Remember – when ardent Protestants were running about, smashing what they called Popish images? I was thirteen when King Edward came to the throne – I recall it very well. But there were places where the parishioners wouldn't allow their beautiful windows to be damaged. Hawkswood was one of them. Perhaps Cutpenny was the same.'

'Where are we going now, ma'am?' Dale asked.

'I want to see this Gilbert Gale we've heard so much about,' I told her.

'Ma'am . . .' said Dale, uneasily.

'I know,' I said. 'It's none of our business. We're not here on an assignment. But you know me.'

'Ma'am . . .'

'Yes, Dale?'

'There's a joke – well, you know all about it, of course . . .'

We had come to a halt in the main street, though to one side of it. Cutpenny really did have an air of bustle. We could hear hammering from somewhere, and voices calling to each other, a man went past us, driving a donkey cart full of firewood and two women with laden baskets on their arms stepped out of a pie shop opposite and glanced at us with interest.

'Dale,' I said, 'please say what you want to say.'

'It's the joke about the wild geese, ma'am. Some of your friends once said that you, well . . .'

'Now and then hear the call of the wild geese and at once I'm off after a new adventure. I know. And it's nonsense. I don't want any more adventures; I've had more than enough for a lifetime. I just want to look at this young man that Arabella likes so much. That's all.'

'Yes, ma'am,' said Dale obediently. I gave her a really sharp look, but her slightly protuberant blue eyes were limpid and innocent, and the old pockmarks that a childhood attack of smallpox had left on her face were hardly visible. They always showed up more clearly when she was frightened or in any way upset. Just now, she was serene, and perhaps gently laughing at me.

'That's the carpenter's shop,' I said, pointing.

It would have been difficult to miss, for its proprietor had some of his wares on show, out in front of his shop. There was a settle and six armchairs, all decorated with what to me seemed like skilful carving. We edged past it and went inside. The interior was better lit than I expected, because its ceiling was the thatch, into which a skylight had been let. The young carpenter, bent over a task on a workbench, had ample daylight to work by. We darkened some of it as we entered and he looked round.

He straightened up, brushing sawdust from his hands. He had a long blue linen coat over his other clothes, and he had dispensed with a ruff.

'Good day. How may I help you?'

He was likeable on sight. Tall, but not to excess, lean, in the fashion of a man who is healthy and active but well nourished, his face square in shape, his brown eyes deep-set and smiling, his hair dark, with a neatly tended line of beard round his jaw and mouth.

He was a most attractive young man. If I had been twenty – thirty – years younger I could easily have fallen in love with Gilbert Gale myself.

I pulled myself together. Before we set out, I had prepared a way to account for our presence in the shop. although my real purpose was, frankly, curiosity. Arabella's description of him kept echoing in my head.

He's young and we're in love and . . . it isn't fair, why shouldn't I marry him? There's girls in the village that would love to wed him!

I had no right to interfere. Far from it. I had come to be a

guest at Arabella's wedding and I had of course brought a gift
for the bride – a pendant, on a gold chain much slimmer than
the one that held that incredible emerald, but gold, all the
same, and the pendant was a piece of polished amber, warm
to the touch and warm in colour. Amber was said to be lucky.
When I bought it, in London, it was handed over to me in a
plain little wooden box. I now brought it out and showed it
to Master Gale.

'I am Mistress Stannard and I have come to Evergreens
because I was invited to the wedding that is shortly to be
held here. I have brought the bride this pendant' – I opened
the box to reveal the contents – 'and I meant to give it to
her in this box. But it's such a plain box. I would like
to have something prettier.'

'For the bride at Evergreens.' Gilbert said it in a flat tone
and looked away from me. However, he said nothing further,
but beckoned us to follow him to the back of the shop. Here
there was a window and beneath it was a shelf on which
various small wooden objects were set out, including a number
of carved boxes, of various sizes.

'I make these for Oxted market,' he said. 'They sell well.
Would you like to choose one?' He had a country accent, I
noticed, but his apprentice days in London had smoothed the
edges of it away, and his voice was warm, like the amber
pendant I had brought for the girl he was said to love.

I looked at the boxes and handled them. They were well
made, opening and shutting smoothly, polished so that the
wood felt like silk. Various woods had been used. I held
one up to the window light and said: 'What wood is this? I
have never seen it before.'

'It's almost red,' Dale said, peering past my shoulder. 'The
colour of embers.'

'It comes from the New World,' Gale said. 'It's called
mahogany.'

The box been decorated with a spray of flowers in a paler
wood, inlaid on the lid. 'That's pretty,' I said. I asked the price.

'If it's for Mistress Arabella . . .?' said Gilbert.

'Yes, it is.'

'I have met your man Brockley and spoken with him. I

understand from him that you are aware that Arabella and I had hoped . . . oh well, never mind. Only for this box, there is no price. If I may, let me have a part in your gift, so that I can give her something too, but secretly. May I?'

'Yes – as long as it *is* a secret,' I said, on a note of warning as I transferred the amber pendant into the new box.

'Is it really going to happen?' he asked suddenly. 'Is Mistress Arabella being made to marry Master Waters?'

I was careful. 'Mistress Arabella has agreed to the match. Her brothers have brought her some beautiful gifts.'

The brown eyes fastened on me. 'I said: is she being *made* to marry? She said that she would never agree, that if she had to, she would say, *I won't* at the very altar. We are pledged to each other . . . but I haven't managed to see her for a week or more. She was afraid, I know, afraid that her mother would beat her. Is that what happened?'

'Please, Master Gale, there are things that I really don't know. I only know that Mistress Arabella is apparently willing for the marriage.'

This was an honest man and it was hard to tell lies to those steady eyes. It was also pointless. 'She is not willing. She has been forced. There's no need to tell me how,' said Gilbert wretchedly.

'I haven't met Master Waters yet,' I said. 'I understand that he has a fine house and is a man of substance. How old is he? Do you know him?'

'Waters? Yes. He has bought furniture from me. He's about forty and he's quite good-looking. What of it? Arabella and I were meant for each other. Can you understand what I'm talking about?' The brown eyes searched my face.

He was of course, unknowingly, speaking to someone who understood very well. Who had once climbed out of her bedchamber window and . . . I knew, all too well, what Gilbert Gale was talking about. I also realized (and so had Dale, who was looking most uncomfortable) that I had stepped outside my rightful territory and had better retreat. At once.

'I do understand,' I said gently. 'But there's nothing to be done. This kind of thing happens all the time, you know. And mostly it works out well in the end. The girl settles into her

new life and there are children, and the young man she was
first in love with, well, in time he finds another and maybe
with this one there is no impediment and the young man who
once thought his world had ended becomes a husband and a
father and then a grandfather and his first love is just a sweet
memory.'

'In other words, give it time, and I will forget and love
someone else. But this is now and Arabella has been terrified
into obedience. I shan't forget,' said Gilbert. He looked at me
very straightly. 'One day she may need me. I have a reason
for saying so. If ever she does, I am here. She can call on me.
Will you say that to her when you give her the present?'

'Master Gale, I'm her mother's guest and I can hardly
conspire with you behind her back!'

'A promise of help if needed is not a conspiracy. Besides,'
said Gilbert, with a sudden impish grin, 'I know who you are,
Mistress Stannard, apart from being the owner of Evergreens.
Mistress Mercer knows all about you, and has talked of you
to her servants and they have talked to friends in this village.
Our present vicar, who nearly everyone in Cutpenny detests,
has already condemned you from the pulpit as an unwomanly
woman whose shameful behaviour, doing work that is rightly
that of a man, is likely to damn her in the life to come. We
are all agog to meet you. You have broken so many rules of
society, Mistress Stannard. Can you not stretch this one, just
a little, so that Arabella knows she is not friendless? There is
more in this than the fact that Arabella and I are in love.'

'Just what *do* you mean by that?' His gaze was so very
intense, and in his voice I heard an unmistakeable note of
worry. I was already guessing at the likely meaning but I could
hardly ask outright if they had already become lovers. But I
wanted to hear what he would say.

He hesitated for a moment and then said: 'I would like to
get her out of that house. Her mother uses the services of the
old woman up on the hill, for one thing, and I am worried
about that.'

'You mean Mother Lee? But why should that worry you?'

'Because there's trouble brewing. Father Dunberry is brewing
it. He has suspicions about the way his predecessor died. He'd

been ill and using Mother Lee's medicines. Father Dunberry is preaching against witchcraft, saying that Eliot's death was a judgement on him and his housekeeper Mrs Brewer who bought a medicine for him from Mother Lee. He has also named Mistress Mercer, who he says sets a bad example.'

'Do you believe in witchcraft?'

'No, I do not. As I see it, Father Eliot was ill, his house-keeper bought something for him from Mother Lee and he either took too much and killed himself, or died of the illness anyway. But a man with a head full of witchcraft will find it anywhere. Mistress Mercer could herself be in danger.'

'Well,' I said, 'if Arabella is married to Master Waters, she *will* be out of Evergreens.'

'Yes, she will, and if he were a decent man, I might shut my teeth and step aside. But I have seen the way Master Waters treats his horses. He is all spur and whip and he jags their mouths. And his servants say he is a bully. I know from one or two who have left his service.'

'I see. But let us hope that he truly loves Arabella and uses her kindly,' I said. My unspoken question had not been answered. One could only hope for the best. 'Master Gale, there really is nothing to be done. But yes, I will give her your message.'

As we walked back to Evergreens, Dale said: 'It's a sad state of affairs, isn't it?'

'Yes,' I said heavily. 'But it can't be helped and I made a mistake in going to see Gilbert Gale. Though I shall be inter-ested to see Master Waters tomorrow.'

'Oh, *ma'am*!' said Dale, reprovingly.

When we returned, I found a moment to speak to Arabella alone so that I could give her my gift, in Gilbert's box, and also give her Gilbert's message. 'I shouldn't be telling you this,' I said to her. 'Your mother would call it meddling. Don't think too much about it. You have a new life before you and you may be happier than you expect.'

'I doubt that,' said Arabella frankly. 'But I thank Gilbert for having such thought for me. And I thank you for this pendant and oh, how kind it was of you to put it in one of his

pretty boxes. I shall treasure that box always. Master Waters,'
she added, 'will dine here tomorrow. What will you wear?'

'I shall dress for the occasion,' I said.

I did, of course. I had brought more than one gown in my
favourite tawny and cream and I put on the best one. It was
made of tawny silk, with a pattern in the weave, and with it
went a cream silk kirtle with little tawny flowers embroidered
on it. The sleeves of the gown were hugely puffed above the
elbow and tight below, and the puffs were slashed to show
the same embroidered silk.

I often wore amber jewellery with it but I didn't want to
challenge my own wedding gift to Arabella. Instead, I chose
freshwater pearls, with their faint, subtle hints of all colours.
I had a rope of them, with matching drop earrings, and a hood
trimmed with the same pearls. I also put on a good-sized ruff
and farthingale.

To my discomfort, Joan asked me if I would be offended
if the Brockleys were asked to dine in the kitchen. I replied
that of course she was the lady of the house and it was for
her to say who should dine at her table. I suppose my tone
conveyed a message. She changed her mind and agreed that
the Brockleys would be present, and would be described as
friends who had accompanied me.

I told them that this was a special dinner, and asked them
to do justice to it. Brockley donned the soldierly buff that he
preferred for these semi-formal affairs and had fortunately
brought his best suit with him, and not the one that had been
pulled out of shape because he had from time to time worn a
breastplate under the doublet. Dale wore the dark blue gown
and the plain hood she liked for such occasions but with a
well-starched ruff and a respectably sized farthingale, along
with a set of peridot jewellery that I had given her some years
before. The pale green stones were striking against the dark
blue. Dale looked elegant.

Mistress Joan herself was in scintillating pink and green
damask with an open ruff edged with lace and a farthingale
that obliged her, at table, to occupy a special seat like a short
bench so as to make room for it. She too had a rope of pearls,
but hers were deep-sea stones. She had drop earrings of pearls

and gold to match. I wondered at them. Her husband, as far as I knew, had not been more than a fairly prosperous man but these were the trappings of real wealth and strictly speaking were not legal for a woman who wasn't a member of the nobility. Not that I had ever met anyone who took the sumptuary laws seriously or had been fined for transgressing them. Joan Mercer clearly didn't worry about them.

Nor did Hector and Stephen, who were in quilted satin doublets, cream and bronze respectively, with the glint of little diamonds in their ruffs. Their clothing went oddly with their sunburned hands and faces.

Arabella was also expensively dressed, in contravention of the law. Her mother had no doubt chosen her ensemble for her. She had a beautiful and very expensive golden silk gown, with an open ruff too old for her, and an exposed neckline on which her emerald pendant could be displayed. The gown looked new and had probably been bought for her wedding. She was wearing emerald earrings, too. But amid all this richness, she looked like a pale ghost.

There was wealth in this household; no doubt about it. Yet Mistress Joan Mercer had approached me, asking if she could rent Evergreens, as though she were just a yeoman's widow, obliged by widowhood to give up her original home and not rich enough to purchase another outright. Yet she and her daughter were each wearing the value of a respectably sized house, in the form of their jewellery.

Master Waters was late. For a good half hour, we sat in the parlour, watching the windows in vain. I saw a faint glint of hope in Arabella's eyes. She was hoping that he wouldn't come, that he had decided to jilt her, that he had fallen off his horse, that he had woken up with a fever on him, that he hadn't woken up at all but had died in his sleep . . .

But then, at last, came the clatter of hooves outside, and a loud voice shouting at his groom, to take the horses and rub them down and look smart about it, and then Page, in a curiously colourless voice, was announcing: 'Master Sylvester Waters!' As Master Waters came in, Mistress Joan was on her feet, hands extended in welcome, and Arabella had also risen, in order to curtsey, and had sunk down almost to the rushes, her golden silk skirts spreading all around her. I stayed where I was and so did the Brockleys. We looked at him with interest.

I recognized his type at once. I didn't need Gilbert Gale's scathing assessment to tell me what kind of man this was. I had been about the world too much, met too many people of too many different kinds.

Unlike the Mercer boys, Waters was not sunburned. He was tall, with features so clear-cut that the bones might have been sculpted from pale marble. There were some smallpox scars across his forehead but they were faint. One would have called him handsome, except that there was something harsh about his compressed mouth with its turned-down corners. We had already heard him shouting at his groom, who probably knew his work perfectly well and had no need of instruction.

And Mistress Mercer was nervous of him. As she presented him to me, her voice shook a little and I could feel her being anxious to please: it emanated from her like an odour. Again, I wondered why. She was my tenant, not his. He couldn't throw her out of Evergreens. Why should she fear him?

He acknowledged me and the Brockleys courteously enough, his voice now calm and cool. Then he crossed the room, raised Arabella to her feet and kissed her and stood over her, smiling as he said: 'My love, I am sorry I have been so long in London. I had business to deal with and many people to see. But here I am, home at last, and now, look what I have brought you, my dear. I should have given you a betrothal ring before but I wanted to go to London for it and here it is.'

He brought a small box out of his belt pouch, flipped the lid open and held it out to Arabella. She took it from him, still in its box, and gazed at it and her mother, rising to look more closely, exclaimed: 'Arabella, what a lucky girl you are! You are being showered with gifts. What a ring! Look, everyone!'

She took box and ring from Arabella and handed them round. The box was lined with white silk and the ring that lay on it was nearly as spectacular as the emerald. It was a hoop of gold, bearing an immense diamond flanked by two smaller ones, all of them flashing in the sunlight that slanted through the window.

More unexpected wealth. Where did it all come from?

However, we all said the right things and then Master Waters, with a great flourish, put it on the fourth finger of Arabella's left hand. It fitted perfectly. In a small, polite voice, she thanked him. Joan frowned and Arabella thanked him again, more enthusiastically. Then Page came in, followed by Cathy, carrying trays of small refreshments, to encourage our appetites before dinner was served.

The dinner itself passed off well. Hitherto, we had eaten in what Joan Mercer called her small dining chamber. This was her large one. It was the biggest room in the house, panelled in a light-coloured wood, and with a view away to the distant slope leading to the house that Dale and I had surmised was Master Waters' home. We now learned that we had been right, and that its name was simply Waters House.

'Its windows have pleasing views, for miles,' said Master Waters smilingly, to Arabella.

Conversation was harmless, without undertones. Hector and Stephen, spoke of their latest voyage, which they said had been profitable. Their next voyage would carry some luxuries to the New World settlements, but would also carry a cargo of well-made tools for every kind of manual work.

'They need tools above everything,' Hector said. 'They use their tools all the time and sometimes break them, and they have no means of repairing them or making new ones. They have no metals and no smiths. When they see our sails on the horizon, they all come down to the shore to greet us; they are so eager to see what we have for them.'

'Have you never had to fight off pirates?' I asked. 'Your cargo must be quite valuable, surely.'

'We're not treasure ships,' said Stephen. 'We are hardly worth attacking. And there are three of us – we travel in company with a friend who joins us when we sail out of Rye. Also, we're very well armed and our ships are highly manoeuvrable. Father had them built to his own design – based on the Portuguese carrack, three-masted, just under a thousand tons, but faster than the ordinary carrack. He did a good deal of the work himself; didn't want the shipbuilder to know all his secrets. Our friend's ship is the same as ours; based on mine, in fact, and he took the same precautions. Father could have made a fortune as a shipbuilder but he preferred to be a sailor. He loved the sea. Didn't he, Hector?'

'Yes. He was lost at sea,' said Hector, 'but very likely, that is how he would have wanted to go.'

The meal was nearly over and we were eating the Genoa rice and the almond jelly which were the final dishes when the talk turned at last to the forthcoming wedding.

'Today is the thirteenth of May,' Joan Mercer declared. 'The banns can be started tomorrow, the fourteenth. They will be called for the third time on . . . let me see . . . the twenty-eighth and the ceremony can be arranged for the following week. Will that suit you, Master Waters?'

'On any day, at any time,' said Master Waters gallantly. 'As soon as you will. Arabella won't want to delay it, will you, my pet?'

With her mother's eyes on her, Arabella said: 'No, of course not.'

In the evening, the Brockleys and I gathered in my chamber to talk as we often did. Usually, this was just a matter of friends chatting together of trivial matters, but this time Brockley was serious.

'Those two lads didn't get that great big emerald from the settlements they talk about,' Brockley said. 'Emeralds like that come from the Spanish New World. I'd wager they've been robbing Spanish shipping.'

'Well, so has Sir Francis Drake,' I said. 'The queen takes her cut from what he brings home and the rest he divides between himself and his crew. Perhaps these two are doing the same thing. It would explain a lot. It's unusual to see such jewellery in a simple house like Evergreens.'

Part of Dale's character was an odd percipience, which sometimes revealed itself unexpectedly. Now, she said: 'I don't like the smell of all this. Why is Mistress Mercer nervous of that man Waters? She is; she's much too anxious to please him. And she's too anxious to stop her sons from talking about their voyages. If they're robbing the Spaniards she ought to be proud of them. There's something *wrong*.'

'This marriage is wrong,' I said. 'But there's nothing to be done. I shall be glad now when it's over, and we can wish Arabella well, and then go home. We can't change anything. It isn't our business.'

SEVEN
Reversing an Hourglass

I t was Wednesday, the thirty-first of May, and it was Arabella's wedding day.

It was lively weather, with a brisk breeze and intermittent sun and shadow, as large, but harmless, clouds sailed across the sky. The ceremony was to take place at midday, and before ten o'clock most of the guests had arrived. Joan Mercer evidently had quite a big acquaintance in Oxted and Caterham. One notable pair were a Master and Mistress Andrews who were so well dressed and well attended – they had a maid and a manservant with them – that they were surely dignitaries of some kind.

Most people came on horseback and both Eddie and the three Mercer grooms had their hands full, looking after the new arrivals, trying not to get their tack mixed up, and making sure their charges didn't kick each other. One elderly couple, cousins of Joan's late husband, arrived in a wagon, which took up far too much space in the yard, until it was finally pushed into a haybarn.

An unexpected guest – as far as I and the Brockleys were concerned, anyway – was Mother Margaret Lee, perched sideways on her donkey and dressed for the occasion in a scuffed gown of amethyst velvet and a straw hat with a limp brim that flapped in the wind.

We had all dressed for the occasion, of course. Harry and Ben were in their best doublets and hose. Joan Mercer was magnificent in another brocade gown and the same lace-trimmed open ruff. I had chosen my cream and tawny silk and my freshwater pearls but I wore my best ruff, which was edged with gold thread (legal in my case, since I was an acknowledged sister to the queen). Dale still wore her peridots but had abandoned her dark blue in favour of a rust-coloured gown and hood while Brockley was in his best brown doublet and hose with pale green slashings.

'Though after all,' he said as the procession at last set out for the church, all on foot except for Mother Lee on her donkey, 'no one cares what we're wearing. All eyes will be on the bride.'

Arabella was to follow us to the church, escorted by Hector, who was to give her away. They would come on horseback, Joan said.

As far as I knew, no guests from Cutpenny had joined us at the house, but a crowd of onlookers awaited us outside St Mark's. Gilbert Gale was there, I saw, at the back of the crowd, waiting, I supposed, for a last glimpse of the girl he had lost.

We went into the church and Joan led us to seats on a front bench. I had attended the church three times now. Twice, the sermon had included a condemnation of women who did work that was the province of men and all three sermons had seemed interminable. The benches were a blessing.

As I seated myself, I looked round for Sylvester Waters and found him on the front bench just across the nave from us, with another man beside him. We exchanged nods and Joan whispered to me that the other man was Master Waters' manservant, Hammond, who was also his valet and his butler. 'Runs the household. Arabella'll have to get on the right side of him.'

There was a pause, while we all waited, including Father Dunberry, who, dressed in the white and gold vestments expected by the English Church, Puritan leanings notwithstanding, was standing beside the altar, hands folded at his waist. Then, at last, came the sound of hooves outside and a moment later, there was Arabella, on Hector's arm, coming through the door.

The pair of them were something to behold. Hector, upstanding and handsome, was in military buff, with a sword at his side and a dashing cockade in his hat. Arabella was once more in the golden silk gown, with emerald jewellery. Her hair had been plaited and piled into a wondrous confection on top of her head, with emerald-headed pins thrust through to hold it. Her mother had sensibly given her a neat, closed ruff. The neckline below it was still cut low so as to show off the big emerald, but the modest ruff made her look young, innocent, as a bride should be.

Waters and his companion rose to their feet as Hector brought his sister towards the altar. She was pale and grave but had a resolute air. She had accepted her fate, I thought, and wondered if she had seen Gilbert in the crowd near the church.

The ceremony began. We were all asked to stand. Father Dunberry enquired whether anyone knew of any reason why this man and this woman should not be lawfully joined in matrimony. Secretly, I wished that someone would, but no one stirred. He asked who was giving this woman to be married to this man and Hector stepped forward and placed Arabella's hand in that of Sylvester Waters.

Vows were exchanged. Sylvester put a ring onto the third finger of Arabella's left hand. The enormous diamond had been moved to her right hand for the occasion, I saw. It was still much in evidence. Her hand was steady as it received the wedding ring. They were pronounced man and wife and she lifted her face for her husband's kiss in a most natural and willing manner. Everyone cheered. It was done.

After that, we all crowded out of the church, where Sylvester handed his bride up into the saddle of a pretty white mare and mounted his speckled grey gelding. I looked up at Arabella and wished her happy and she smiled and said that the mare was her husband's gift to her. 'She's an ambler,' she said. 'I'm not a good rider so I shall appreciate her easy paces.'

Sylvester took the mare's bridle and led his bride away. The two of them disappeared ahead of the rest of us, as we all set off on foot to Evergreens House, except of course for Mother Lee, who got someone to help her back onto her donkey. We didn't see her again, and presumably, having witnessed the marriage, she just went home.

At Evergreens, everyone gathered in the parlour, a considerable crush, until the feast was served. There was a babble of talk, with women clustering round Arabella to admire her rings and her gown and wish her good luck, and I heard Hector rather tiresomely boasting to someone about the jaguar rug and his exploit with the jaguar on the end of his spear. Joan told him, quite loudly, not to keep giving himself airs but others were laughing and wanting to hear more, and Stephen was positively egging his brother on, so Hector continued to brag and had just launched into a tale of how he had saved his ship from disaster during a storm at sea when he was interrupted by Page, who came in banging a little gong to announce the feast.

We crowded into the panelled dining room. Joan had set the table with her best pewter goblets and her glazed earthenware platters, and there were four fine silver serving dishes, on which some of the food was already set out. Dale and I had helped with the preparations, making the coloured marchpane and rolling out pastry. Joan had been in the kitchen too and we saw how skilled she was, entirely the match of her very skilled staff. The wizened James Mitchell and the impertinent-looking Samuel Hazel had created marvels, including a spun-sugar confection like a three-dimensional spider-web. During the preparations, I had noticed with admiration that Phil and Mary Drew seemed able to do three if not four different things simultaneously; they were the culinary equivalent of jugglers.

Page hadn't come to the church because he was overseeing the final touches. He brought in the main dishes, the platter of roast mutton joints, and the spun-sugar fantasy, with great pomp, including fanfares from the trumpeter in the band of minstrels who had been hired for the occasion. Sylvester and Arabella had the seats of honour, side by side under a canopy. When everyone was full, Hector proposed various toasts – to the bride and groom, to the cooks who had produced so noble a banquet and to the bride's mother who had brought up his beautiful sister . . . at this point Joan began to cry, and any further toasts were foregone while Dale and I tried to comfort her.

After a while, Joan dried her tears and declared that the dancing should begin. Page, Cathy and Moll descended on the room to clear away the remains of the feast and move the tables back. The dancing followed the usual pattern, with

Arabella, who already looked exhausted, dancing with virtually all the male guests, until at last Sylvester made a sign to her, and the two of them quietly withdrew.

I noticed that Joan kept glancing out of the window and when she hurried out of the room, I moved to her place by the window and looked out of it too. On the track between the stable yard and the house, Master and Mistress Waters were about to mount their horses and Joan was kissing her daughter and her new son-in-law farewell.

Dale came to stand beside me. 'I wonder why he didn't marry Mistress Mercer,' she observed. 'They're near in age, after all. She's only forty-two. She was married at fifteen. She could still have another baby. He wants a son.'

'Who have you been talking to?' I asked, watching as the freckle-faced Hal Jankin assisted Arabella, still in her golden gown, up into her saddle.

'Jane Hayes,' said Dale. 'She thinks it would have been more natural, too. He's been married twice, apparently, but he's been unlucky with children. The first one died having their first child, and the baby was stillborn. The second one had a son, but when the child was two, there was an outbreak of smallpox and they all caught it. He lived, his wife and child didn't.'

'I see,' I said. The couple were riding away. Arabella was looking over her shoulder and waving to her mother. 'There's a saying, surely, about third attempts being lucky.'

'Better for Mistress Arabella if it is,' said Dale.

That was it. Arabella was gone, one hoped into a new life that would be better than she expected. Not even her belongings remained at Evergreens for they had gone up the hill to Waters House the day before, in a mule cart.

Joan came back into the house and into what was now a very lively ballroom. 'Well,' she said to me, 'they're away. It's over. I hope she will be happy. I had good reasons for insisting that she should marry Master Waters, but I do wish her to be happy. I want her to realize that I was right.'

I nodded, wondering why Gilbert Gale wasn't a satisfactory choice and why Mistress Mercer and Master Waters hadn't considered each other instead. On Waters' side, I supposed that he had been bemused by Arabella's beauty. Beautiful she certainly was. Without wishing to, she had probably entranced him and blinded him to all else. Like her mother, I could only hope that all would turn out well in the end.

A dance ended. Master Andrews asked me to partner him in the next and I did so. Then with other partners I took part in the two dances after that and I didn't notice Joan again until I left the room to go outside to the necessary house. I had to cross the vestibule to get to the side door and I needed to walk past Joan, who was out there, deep in conversation with Hector. As I went by, I realized that they were quarrelling.

They saw me, of course, but they were arguing in French and didn't trouble to pause or even to lower their angry voices. Probably they assumed that I wasn't familiar with French.

In which they were wrong. I knew French very well. I had lived in France for a time, with Harry's father, my second husband, Matthew de la Roche. I didn't turn my head as I went by; I gave no sign that I had understood, but inside my mind, what Joan was angrily saying quietly translated itself into English.

'*You are a fool, Hector. You always cause trouble in your cups, and if I hadn't stopped you in time you'd have started boasting about other things besides storms and jaguars. I know you! Master Andrews might have heard you and then where would we be? He's a magistrate! My God, why have you no sense?*'

She was speaking fast. She had rattled all that off before I passed out of hearing and was opening the side door.

I thought about Dale's unexpected declaration that something was wrong. Dale's instinctive feelings were often sound. Something was going on here that wasn't within the law and she had sensed it.

Well, I hadn't been sent here to investigate it. I simply wanted to go home, and if my tenant at Evergreens should later be arrested for some misdeed or other, I would be duly shocked and look for a replacement.

*   *   *

Later, when I returned from my call of nature, I found Joan once more watching the dancing. She looked drawn and far from happy and I went to her. 'You seem tired,' I said.

'No. Just anxious. I did make sure that Arabella knows what is to happen tonight. I was taught never to speak of such things but I don't think a girl should go to her wedding quite unprepared. I did, because my mother wouldn't discuss such matters, and it was such a shock, and I wasn't yet sixteen! That first night, I thought my bridegroom had gone mad, and he was bewildered and hurt . . . it's a great mistake. A girl can be just too pure.'

'But you have made sure that Arabella is properly informed,' I said soothingly. 'She will be all right, I'm sure. When next you see her, she will be all smiles!'

'I hope so. I do hope so,' said Joan.

In the morning, I once more took Dale for company and walked down into Cutpenny. The sportive wind had dropped. This was a quiet, sunny day and sunshine brings people out of doors. I found the village full of life, though it seemed somehow disturbed. There were a number of women round the well but they didn't seem to be just filling their pails and carrying them away. The cluster round the wellhead was apparently deep in talk. I didn't stop to find out why, however, but made for Gilbert's shop. I found him at his bench, polishing something, but he looked up as I entered and I said: 'Arabella admired your box and was touched by your thought for her. She thanks you for your concern. I thought you might like to know.'

Gilbert laid his work down. 'I am glad. She has something to remind her of me, for always. I suppose I shall see her occasionally; no doubt she will come into the village to buy things, to attend church . . .'

His voice broke off. I said: 'I caught sight of you yesterday. You were in the crowd that watched us all going into the church.'

'And coming out of it. When the deed was done,' Gilbert said. There was a pause and then he added: 'She looked so beautiful. I knew she was beautiful but I never imagined she could look quite like that, like a princess out of legend, out of song. You cannot know how much I wished she was decked like a princess for me.'

'I think I do know, but it's all over now, Gilbert. She will treasure the box. You will have to be content with that.'

'I know.' He seemed to shake himself and become businesslike. 'Is there anything here that would please you, Mistress Stannard? Something for yourself? Do look round if you wish.'

I had already had it in mind to buy something from him as a friendly gesture and I had given Dale a basket to carry when I had made my choice. I examined his display bench and picked up a pair of swans, mounted on a base and facing each other. The whole thing was about six inches high and it was made from a light brown wood, highly polished and altogether charming. 'What is the wood?' I asked, as I picked it up.

'Sandalwood, madam. It has a faint scent still. I bought a supply of it from Master Hector Mercer. It comes from one of the exotic consignments he and his brother get hold of now and then.'

'From the New World?' I asked. I had heard of sandalwood before but had understood that it came from the East.

'I don't know, madam. But I believe the Mercer brothers trade widely, and sometimes visit markets in the Mediterranean. They talk about it,' said Gilbert, with a glint of amusement, 'in the Crown tavern.'

I could imagine Hector doing that, all too easily. I said: 'This would look well on display in my great hall at home. What is the price?'

We settled a price, while Dale looked along the row of ornaments, found something for herself and declared that she wished to buy a little prancing horse, also made of sandalwood.

'I shall put it in our room at Hawkswood,' she said. 'It will keep my husband in mind of all the prancing colts I wish he wouldn't ride.'

Brockley had the task of breaking in the young horses we sometimes bred. Dale always feared for him. I thought that the statuette was more likely to encourage than dissuade him but I refrained from comment. I wanted Gilbert to have these small successes, and to be paid for them. I did, however, ask what the muttering round the wellhead was all about.

'Oh, it's because that old beldame Mother Lee got on her donkey and came down off her hilltop to watch Bella's wedding. It's started up talk – or started it up again. There's been enough already. Father Dunberry goes on about it. You must have heard him.'

'Yes, I have,' I said, with feeling if not quite with truth. I had been too irritated by Father Dunberry's oblique criticisms of me to pay much heed to his complaints of anyone else.

'And then,' said Gilbert, 'when Mother Lee showed her face yesterday, coming to the church so openly, as if she was an ordinary wedding guest – the village women didn't like it.'

'I see,' I said. 'Well, let us hope it just subsides.'

We paid for our purchases and then left his shop, feeling thoughtful. There was still a huddle round the well and Dale said she didn't care for the look of it. 'I can see that there's trouble coming,' she said.

'You sound like old Gladys at home,' I told her. 'Always forecasting trouble. I wonder she didn't predict it for our journey to a wedding.'

'There's more afoot here than a wedding,' said Dale. 'I'm sure of it, ma'am.'

I remembered the exchange in French that I had overheard the previous evening. Dale was almost certainly right. But I didn't want to know any more about it. 'Let us go back,' I said. 'It's getting hot. Summer is really here now.'

We walked back, silently. The front door of Evergreens was standing open and as we stepped through, we heard raised voices. Then we stopped short, as the shouting suddenly escalated into a wild babble of rage and crying. It came from the parlour. There were words mixed up in the babble. I heard Joan shout the name of Gilbert Gale, and then Arabella's voice raised in a near howl, and saying *no, no, no* before being drowned out by an incomprehensible roar from a man. Waters, surely.

Arabella and Waters? Here, back at Evergreens?

Dale and I stared at each other and then Ben and Harry were upon us, having apparently been lying in wait on the stairs. They were round-eyed with excitement.

I said: 'What is it?' and then stood there, blinking, because what Harry was saying was like the sudden reversal when an hourglass is turned over. One moment, gaiety and hope, and the next . . .

'Mother . . . Mother, listen – it's so awful. We don't understand properly but that Master Waters, he's brought Mistress Arabella back! He says he doesn't want her, that she's damaged goods!'

EIGHT
Fighting for the Wrong

I thought: *Gilbert Gale.* And then, suddenly, remembered something else, something which need not involve Gilbert at all, which had surely been responsible for much injustice throughout the centuries. 'Go to your quarters,' I said to the boys. 'Keep away from this. It's women's business. Dale, come with me.'

I pushed the parlour door open and walked in. Waters was there, with Joan and Arabella. All three of them were red with rage, and tears were streaming down the faces of both Arabella and her mother. Silence fell and they all turned to look at me as I entered. Waters said: 'Mistress Stannard,' and then stopped, and Joan said: 'Mistress Stannard, this is a private matter. I must ask you to leave us.'

'I know it's private. I would not have come in except that I overheard enough . . .'

'You *listened*?' said Arabella. Her face was bruised. She had been hit. She looked at me despairingly.

'Not intentionally,' I said. 'The whole house can hear you! I came in because if I have heard aright, I just might be able to help. I understand that for some reason Master Waters is unhappy about something to do with Arabella. I think I know what that means but may I know for sure?'

I spoke with all the dignity and authority that I could muster. There really are advantages in being known to be a daughter of King Henry, and a half-sister to Queen Elizabeth. Without such advantages, I am fairly sure I would have been turned out of the room for interfering. I almost was; I saw it in Joan's flashing eyes and Sylvester's glower. I stood my ground, determined to be heard.

Arabella, after using both hands to wipe the tears from her face, said stiffly: 'You're supposed to bleed, the first time. He took me and I didn't.' She turned her head away from us, not wanting to meet our eyes.

'Many women don't,' I said. 'I have reason to know it; the best of reasons. It means nothing. Any girl who has led a busy, active life, perhaps ridden astride at times, sometimes doesn't show that sign. I dare say Arabella is such a girl.'

'She is!' said Joan and her face lightened a little. 'She often kilts her skirts and sits astride on a pony, going round our farm.'

'There must have been many virgins who didn't bleed, and so were wrongly accused,' I said. 'As I might have been, except that my first husband didn't even notice. I am sure that Arabella is an honest young woman. That's all.'

I was far from sure, of course, but for Arabella's sake I did my best to sound convincing. I waited.

'Whatever may be true or not true,' said Joan, 'my daughter, Master Waters, is now your wife. You wanted to marry her. You . . . you *demanded* it! You said you were wildly in love with her. Well, you have your wish. I will not let you return her as though she were a horse with a spavin I forgot to mention. You didn't buy Arabella, you married her. Do you hear me?'

Arabella turned back to us and looked miserably at the two of them, first one, then the other. She didn't want to go back to Waters House; of that I felt sure. Between Waters and her mother, she must feel trapped between two ogres.

I bit my lip. If Waters did reject Arabella, might that not be best? Marriages could be annulled. It might be possible to drum up the idea of a pre-contract between Arabella and Gilbert. Not that pre-contracts mattered as much as they had in Popish days, but old ideas don't change as fast as the law does. An annulment might even open the way for her to marry Gilbert. I had probably just fought for the wrong thing. But I didn't like to think of Arabella suffering for something she might not have done.

Might not have done. The phrase repeated itself in my head. Gilbert Gale came insistently to mind. But at least, for the moment, the noise of rage and condemnation had ceased. Sylvester Waters, though grumbling and glowering, was now agreeing to take his wife home.

We watched them depart. He hadn't brought Arabella on her pretty white ambler, but in the mule cart, sharing it with her belongings. He had brought her goods back with her. She sat in it now with bowed head, going away from us for the second time, returning home with the husband she didn't want, who didn't trust her, who from now on would watch her, spy on her, ready to read guilt into the most innocent looks and remarks, probably into the way she breathed.

And all the time, there in the background, was Gilbert Gale. I feared for Arabella.

Arabella herself shall tell the next part of the story. It is as much her story as mine.

NINE
Trade Secret

Arabella's Narrative

I went home with Sylvester in a state of dread.

I say I went home, because I perfectly well understood that from the moment the previous day when Father Dunberry pronounced us man and wife, Waters House was my home, and Evergreens was not. Yesterday, when Master . . . no, Sylvester as I must now think of him . . . took me there as his bride, I had been welcomed warmly. I felt a little encouraged – then.

There were greetings first at the handsome tiled and timbered gatehouse, and then, after we reached the front door, the grooms were smiling as they came for the horses, and we dismounted and there was the housekeeper, Mrs Truebody, at the door with curtseys and smiles.

She was a thin, sandy-haired woman, and I knew her slightly, for I had of course visited Waters House with my mother. I must make friends with her, I thought. She took me upstairs to show me the chamber that had been prepared for us. There was a fourposter bed with new crimson curtains, a clothes press, a chest of drawers for ruffs and stockings and under-linen, and cupboards for any other possessions. I looked at the bed rather nervously.

Mrs Truebody took me downstairs again, and there, Sylvester introduced the rest of the household to me. I made the acquaintance therefore of Gervase Hammond, who acted as his valet, served the meals and kept the other servants in order. He had been beside Sylvester in church at the wedding. He was a tall unsmiling man with black hair and cold blue eyes, and he greeted me with courtesy but not with warmth. I supposed that he was wondering what kind of changes would come into the house with me.

Sylvester presented the other servants to me but my head was spinning, partly with the wine I had drunk at my wedding feast, and I hardly took them in. Within a few minutes of hearing their names, I forgot them.

Some of Sylvester's own guests had followed us from Evergreens, and despite the feast we had had there, a supper had been made ready. It was a jovial affair, with pointed and embarrassing jokes. I ate very little and drank only well water. Then the maids and the women guests took me upstairs and took off my golden silk and all the rest of my clothes and put me into the fourposter bed. Presently, the men escorted Sylvester up to join me. They saw him into bed but after that, Sylvester ordered them out of the room and bolted the door to make sure they stayed out. After that, he said, 'Well, now, my darling,' and got in beside me and began to caress me.

He petted me for some time, and then whispered: 'You are so beautiful. You charmed me the first moment I saw you! I *had* to have you.' Then he clambered on top of me, breathing wine fumes into my face. He was no longer the cool, correct man he had seemed when he was just a neighbour, or even when he had stood beside me at the altar. He was rough. He hurt me. He laughed when I cried out. It seemed to amuse him. He said: 'Now you know you're mine!'

When it was over, he went to sleep though I did not. He woke just after dawn and turned to me and there was a repetition. I felt as though I had been pounded, outside and in. I tried not to show it. Since he could now see my face, I made a great effort to smile and bid him good morning.

But then he told me to get out of bed and he turned back the covers to look at the sheets. To me they just looked like sheets, a little crumpled, but still clean and white but then I learned that this was wrong. The sheets should have been marked with blood but they were not.

It was as though the roof had fallen in.

Whispers about my charm and beauty might never have been. He hit me, knocking me half across the room. He swore at me, accusing me of such things . . .!

'You're going back to your mother this morning, this very day! I'll not have you under my roof, you whore. Does she know what you are? I hope not, but if not, she's in for a most unpleasant surprise. Get up, get dressed! I'll call the girl I meant for your maid. She can see to you. Then it's back to Evergreens you go. They can give you breakfast – if they think you're worth the trouble!'

And so on, on and on. My head was ringing from the blow he had given me. I lay half propped against the clothes press and sobbed. I remember thinking of Gilbert, of how different a wedding night with him would have been. Sylvester hauled me to my feet. I pleaded with him, begged him to tell me what I had done wrong, but he wouldn't listen. He said that if I persisted in lying, he would hit me again. He went out of the room and shouted for someone called Madge, which produced a jolly-looking young maid, who clearly expected to find a smiling pair of newly-weds, and was bewildered by Sylvester's grim face and my scarlet cheek.

Sylvester went into an adjacent room and bellowed for Hammond and meanwhile a puzzled Madge helped me to dress. I whispered to her that I didn't understand what I had done wrong, that Sylvester had just looked at our sheets and then become angry because there was no blood on them. Should there have been? I asked Madge. But why? Madge obligingly enlarged on what Sylvester had told me.

I didn't know how to deal with this. I wanted to lie down on the bed again and cry, but instead I had to choose what to wear, as though this were an ordinary morning. Well, not the golden silk, for sure. I picked out my one black gown instead. I didn't know what was to happen with the silk or any of the other gowns that I had brought. Then Sylvester reappeared, fully dressed, and ordered Madge to pack my belongings.

'All of them. In the hampers they came in – those are in the closet downstairs. Hammond's giving orders to get the mule harnessed and he'll get the baggage taken out there when it's ready,' he informed us.

And so, breakfast-less and in great disgrace, I was returned to my mother's care the morning after I had left it.

And there I would have stayed, I suppose, half married and half not, except that Mistress Ursula Stannard, with her wide experience of life, came to my rescue. Walked in on the uproar and was able to defend me.

By ten o'clock in the morning after my wedding, I had been married, rejected and taken back again and was now, once again, going home to Waters House, not on my gentle white mare, but as I had come, uncomfortably seated on the floor of a mule cart with hampers and boxes joggling against me. My mother had offered the loan of a horse but Sylvester merely said: 'The mule cart got her here; the mule cart can carry her back,' and that was that.

When we reached Waters House, Hammond and Madge came to unload my belongings once again while I stood there in the vestibule, facing Sylvester and pretending not to notice the other servants peeping round the door to the kitchen quarters. Sylvester stared at me, gripped my shoulders painfully in his hard fingers and said: 'If only you weren't so bloody beautiful!'

I said nothing. I was thinking that but for my beauty, I might now be married to Gilbert.

Thinking of Gilbert made me feel bereft. He was four years older than I. I had known him as a boy, learning to work with his father. His father had taught himself to be a carpenter but he had Gilbert apprenticed to a Master Carpenter in London. But when he too was a Master of his trade, Gilbert returned to Cutpenny, because he loved the village.

Shortly after that, his father died. Gilbert found him one morning, lying beside his workbench, overtaken by death when he was working, busy with the legs of a stool. Gilbert took his father's place. A year later, at a dance on Cutpenny's green, we met, trod a measure together and by the end of the evening, we were in love.

We would have married, but Sylvester got in the way. As for whether or not I bled when Gilbert and I first became lovers; I have never known. It was a dull, dark afternoon, and we took the brightly patterned cushions off the settle in Gilbert's back room, to make a couch on the floor. We never inspected the cushions afterwards, or even thought of such a thing.

In the here and now, after staring angrily into my face for some moments, Sylvester let go of me. Then he shouted for Hammond to see that the baggage was taken upstairs again and put away, and told him to order wine to be brought to the parlour. Then he led the way there and I followed, like a spaniel at heel.

The parlour was panelled like the vestibule, but it had mullioned windows giving views to the west, the south and the east. The early sunlight, streaming into the room, imparted an ironic air of cheerfulness. Sylvester pointed me to a settle and planted himself on another. Hammond brought in a tray with a wine jug and two glasses, pushed a table deftly between us, set the tray down and at a nod from Sylvester, poured out two glasses. He bowed and withdrew.

Sylvester sipped his wine and so did I. For a long time, neither of us spoke. Then he set down his glass with something of a bang and said again: 'If only you weren't so bloody beautiful!'

I marvelled silently, for I didn't feel at all beautiful. The black dress was old, my hair hadn't been properly brushed, just coiled hurriedly under a plain cap, and the mule cart had been dusty. I hadn't washed, either.

I couldn't think what to say in answer so I waited. Eventually, he said: 'There are things I must make clear. Whatever the truth may be, I have now accepted you as my wife and we must go on from there. So I will explain your duties to you. They are not onerous. You must see that the house is properly run and that, if I have guests, they are treated with respect. I trust you know how to order a dinner and arrange the seating for dignified company?'

'Yes,' I said.

'Good. Otherwise, your first duty is to give me a son. I had a son once but the smallpox killed him before he was three. I need one to fill the gap, more than one would be better still.'

'I'll do my best,' I said, wondering how on earth I was expected to do such a thing as an act of will. A woman can't choose when to have a child, or decide its sex. Such things are God's will. Timidly, I said: 'What if I have daughters?'

'As long as there are sons, daughters will naturally be welcome. I shall leave their upbringing to you. Except that they will never, under any circumstances, be allowed to ride astride.'

It was a kind of grim pleasantry. I responded with a weak smile. I finished my glass and he poured another for me. 'You will see little of me. I have much to do about the farm, and I have business, too, with your brothers.'

I nodded. I was thankful that neither of my brothers had been present at that dreadful confrontation in my mother's parlour. I had wondered where they were – not in the house, presumably.

'Can you play chess?' Sylvester asked, abruptly.

'Yes, my father taught me.'

'Good. You understand,' my husband explained, 'we must be seen to be on the proper terms for a married pair. I don't want the servants gossiping about us. We must sit together sometimes, play chess, talk.'

I was fairly sure that the servants were gossiping like a sparrows' parliament already, but I supposed that time would erode it, if we acted normally. It would be acting, as if on a stage. I had never seen a play but my brothers had and they had described it to me.

'And it will be better for our sons,' said Sylvester, 'if they are to grow up in a pleasant household.'

'I would want that too,' I said.

'I shall sleep apart from you when you are with child,' Sylvester now informed me. 'It is safer for the pregnancy.'

'How will I know when I'm with child?' I asked him, and he looked astonished.

'Did your mother not explain these things to you?'

'No. When I was ten, she warned me about the monthly thing, and she told me about . . . well, what to expect last night. But that's all. She doesn't like to speak of these things.'

'Good God! I will ask Mrs Truebody to instruct you. She is a widow with three sons. She will know what to say.'

'Thank you.'

'And now,' said Sylvester, 'you had better talk to Mrs Truebody on another matter, which concerns what we are to have for dinner today. The kitchen will want your instructions. I have certain favourite dishes. My chef knows how to prepare them. Finish your wine and then find Mrs Truebody.'

'Yes, I will do that.'

I sipped my second glass of wine. It was at that moment that from the tail of my left eye, I caught movement outside the window. I turned my head and beheld my two brothers, Hector and Stephen, walking away from the house although to my knowledge they hadn't been inside it. And *walking away* wasn't the right way to put it, either. They were *slipping* away, not taking the track down to the lodge but disappearing among the shrubs that grew in some profusion on the right-hand side.

I knew quite well that although the gatehouse had fencing on either side of it, the fencing didn't go right round the house and its grounds. Along most of the sides, there were just tangles of bushes, difficult to push through. Behind the house, there was a topiary garden and then a herb garden, neither fenced at the side, though beyond the herb garden lay meadows where cattle grazed and there was a fence to keep the cattle out. My brothers had seemed to be thrusting their way out through the shrubs, as if they didn't want to be seen.

I thought it strange but I was afraid of asking questions. I must tread carefully in this frightening new world of marriage to Sylvester. I drained my glass. I must seek out Mrs Truebody.

I talked to Mrs Truebody about choosing a dinner and gave my order, but after that, I asked to speak to her in private and she showed me into a room on the ground floor, where she had a writing desk, presumably for household accounts and the like, and a settle where she could read or sew. She invited me to join her on the settle and I explained, somewhat halt-ingly, that although I was now married, there were things I didn't know, and needed to know. Mrs Truebody obligingly informed me, enlarging on what Madge had said. By the time she had finished, I knew all that I needed to know and I had found some of it disconcerting – in fact, alarming.

Innocence is a dangerous thing. At the time when I fell in love with Gilbert, I knew nothing at all except that (in spite of all my mother's efforts to shield me) I had heard hints of a mysterious event that took place after couples were married. Gilbert coaxed me into lovemaking because when we petted, the need – which I experienced but didn't understand – became overwhelming. Gilbert said never mind; it was what lovers do.

Of course, I soon began to realize that the joyful thing we shared in the secrecy of his back room *was* the mysterious thing I had heard whispered about, but even then, I still knew very little. Now, after hearing Mrs Truebody's explanations, I knew much more. A small chill of fear had now rooted itself within me.

I was afraid to ask questions. I thanked Mrs Truebody for helping me to understand things. Presently, the conversation changed and she began to tell me in detail about the ways of the house.

'Master Waters is a good master, as long as he's well served,' she told me. 'He isn't patient with people who don't do their work properly, but why should he, when he's paying them?' She added, quite ruefully: 'I have to be particular myself. Sometimes it causes me to suffer from headaches. I use a potion that Mother Lee makes, her that lives up in the wood on the hill . . .'

'I know her,' I said. 'My mother has headaches sometimes, too.'

'It was Mistress Mercer who recommended her to me,' said Mrs Truebody. 'That apothecary in Cutpenny is useless. Not long ago, I bought a supply of medicine from Mother Lee, and it worked well, but I have nearly used it up by now. I am always so busy. Getting away to fetch fresh supplies is difficult and the maidservants just won't go up that hill to her! All this nonsense about witchcraft! That apothecary is just jealous of Mother Lee; he stirs things up against her. Hammond won't go, either. He takes orders only from Master Waters and Master Waters' – here she lowered her voice a little – 'doesn't believe that headaches exist. If you are not afraid of her, could you perhaps collect some medicine for me? You will want to exercise that dainty white ambler that the master has given you. Perhaps, one day soon, you could take a ride that way and just fetch a couple of phials for me. Just one lasts a long time; a single spoonful is help enough. I can give you the money, and a bag you can tie to your girdle. There's no immediate haste. I have enough for two doses still.'

'Oh, of course,' I said, anxious to make friends. The more friends I had in this house, the better. 'If the master lets me ride out alone, that is. I hope he will. I want the mare to get to know me.'

Sylvester made no objection. 'You are used to riding alone, I know. The mare is gentle. Don't go far. You may visit your mother if you wish, of course.'

So, my life at Waters House began. The nights were hateful: Sylvester took me frequently and always as though he were angry, thrusting fiercely and with no trace of tenderness. But during the day, he was courteous and as he had said, I didn't see much of him for he was usually out on the farm, or riding off to pay business visits which he didn't explain to me.

I decided that I would make a habit of taking a ride each morning, alone. I knew I would be thankful for the solitude. Two days later, I decided to call on Mother Lee and collect Mrs Truebody's medicine.

It was a hot, sticky morning. However, the mare made easy work of the zigzag track and at the top there was a surprise for me, in the shape of another customer, who was just leaving the cottage as I arrived.

'Stephen!' I said.

I slipped out of my saddle and my younger brother gave me a scapegrace grin and helpfully secured the mare's reins to the fence round the pasture. 'How goes it, Bella? Do you like married life?'

'It's what I expected,' I said evasively. The grin became knowing, as though he had heard what I hadn't said.

'You'll tame him,' he told me. 'I heard all about it. *All*.'

'Perhaps I shouldn't ask how you know, or precisely what you know,' I said repressively, and his grin grew still wider.

'That's what I mean,' he said. 'This very minute, you came back at me, quick and sharp. I fancy that you'll deal with him, given time. Don't rush it. But you're not the little mouse you sometimes pretend to be, that Mother makes you be. With Sylvester Waters, you have an advantage that Mother doesn't have. He's in love with you, dear sis. Use your power well.'

'Power? That's one thing I don't possess,' I said with feeling. 'I really am a little mouse, you know. I can't see me taming anything larger than a kitten.'

'You may surprise yourself one day. Tell me, what brings

you here? You surely don't want any of Mother Lee's potions.
You've always been healthy.'

'A headache remedy. Not for me – it's for my housekeeper,
Mrs Truebody. What brings *you* here?'

'The same thing, for Mother. She's had some bad attacks
lately and what with the feeling in the village – well, we're
all wondering how long Mother Lee will still be here. Mistress
Stannard kindly fetched some, but I decided to lay in another
lot, just in case. Look, I'll come with you now and we'll collect
your housekeeper's supplies. If you have enough money with
you, it might be as well to buy extras for her too.'

'What do you mean – about Mother Lee and buying extra
potions in case she goes away?'

'Father Dunberry is fermenting trouble. If you go to church
tomorrow, I think you'll hear a very inflammatory sermon.
There's a rumour in the village that he's going to preach very
strongly about the perils of witchcraft and the likely fate in
the hereafter for anyone who has dealings with the Devil's
folk. Mother Lee may be driven away – or worse. I believe
that Mistress Stannard has a recipe of her own for sick headaches. I shall ask her to leave it with us when she goes home.'

'Is Mother Lee really in danger? Shouldn't we warn her?'

'Oh, she knows. She has ways of hearing the news. She
says she can't run away; she has nowhere to go. This is her
home. Nor,' he added with some irritation, 'will she come
across with the entire recipe for her headache remedy. Allheal,
camomile – and something else, that's what's in it, but the
something else she says is a secret of her trade. Much use that
secret will be to anyone if she isn't here to use it! Well, let's
go inside and get the medicine while it's still to be had.'

I bought several phials of the headache potion and then we
left together. Stephen was on foot and walked beside me until
we parted at the bottom of the hill. I sent my love to Hector
and to my mother, though Heaven knows I had few kindly
feelings for her.

Three weeks after my marriage, having considered matters
in the light of Mrs Truebody's information, I decided that I
must talk to Sylvester. In the evening, across a game of chess,

I said to Sylvester that I had definitely missed a course and that I understood that . . .

He was pleased. He kissed me. And at once gave orders that a guest room should be made ready for him. He also forbade me to ride. I sighed over that, but promised myself that I would give the mare, whom I had now named Snowdrop, a carrot or an apple every day, and I would make the grooms look after her and exercise her with care and plenty of petting. I knew that Mistress Stannard had a habit of saying goodnight to her bay gelding, Jaunty. I liked Mistress Stannard. I would make her my example.

TEN
Taking Sides

Ursula's Narrative

'There's trouble on the way, right enough,' Stephen said, across the dinner table. 'I told Arabella so, when I met her lately, when we'd both been to see Mother Lee and I brought you all those phials, Mother. I think something is going to happen, and soon.'

'I can't believe that. I *told* you,' Joan said crossly, 'that it was absurd to bring me enough potion to cure my headaches for the rest of my life! I know Father Dunberry is preaching against Mother Lee – I've heard him – but so did Father Eliot and nothing happened. It's all just talk and gossip.' She pushed away a half-eaten platter of food. 'It's too hot to eat. I have no appetite.'

It was certainly sultry. We were all perspiring as we sat at dinner, toying with our meal. I wished I had kept to my original plan and had gone home immediately after Arabella's wedding. Joan, very shaken after Master Waters' attempted rejection of his bride, had asked me to stay on for a while. 'In case something more happens. You were such a godsend when he tried to send her back. Just for a month or so? Till I can be sure that things will be straightforward from now on. The boys will be off voyaging, before long. I shall like your company, too, now that my daughter has left home.'

I felt as though my tenant was regarding me as a combination of a companion and a good-luck charm, and I wasn't at all happy with it, but I decided to oblige her. Dale shook her head at me and said I was being inquisitive again. 'Ma'am, you just want to know what happens,' she said.

I said calmly: 'We'll stay for another month and then go home. Where's the harm?' Now, sweltering even though I was in my lightest gown, and thinking how airy the rooms were at Hawkswood, I was regretting my decision.

The heat probably accounted for Joan's bad temper. Brockley used a soothing tone of voice as he said regretfully: 'Madam, I fear the gossip may be true. I was in the village this morning, and the women round the well looked to me as if they were conferring, not just muttering. Also, I saw two men walking round the fishpond, looking down at it. I wondered why. The carpenter's shop looks toward the pond, so I went in there. I bought a workbox for Fran and asked why the men were staring at the pond. Gilbert Gale said that it shrinks in hot weather and that in the Crown yesterday he had heard some of the village men wondering if it was still deep enough to swim a witch. He's worried. He's a decent man and he has far too much sense to believe in witches.'

'*Is* the pond deep enough?' Hector enquired, through a mouthful of meatloaf.

'I think so,' said Stephen. 'Gilbert says that it was deepened many years ago, when he was a child. For the same purpose. There was a suspect witch then.'

'What happened to her?' I asked, with concern.

'She drowned,' said Brockley shortly. 'Gilbert told me.'

'Well, what can we do about it?' said Joan. 'We'd better stay in the house till it dies away or it's all over.'

'I expect we'll miss it, whatever happens,' said Hector. 'We must be off to sea in a few days' time. We mustn't miss the summer season.'

'I wish I could go too,' said Harry, and Ben, who also had a mouth full of meatloaf, nodded vigorously. Harry gave me a wickedly mischievous look. 'We could stow away.'

Stephen and Hector both laughed and I saw Hector studying Harry's face as though wondering whether there really was a possible new recruit there.

'If either of you do any such thing,' I said, 'then the moment you come home again, I will personally kill you.'

'Oh, surely you need not be so harsh, ma'am,' said Stephen, still laughing. 'A few weeks of climbing rigging and scrubbing decks and not doing it properly and getting the rope's end, and they'll wish they had stayed at their books. They would come home as tame as lapdogs.'

We all laughed. I doubted whether anything short of force would detach Harry from Hawkswood, and as for Ben, I was now sure that in a few years' time he would be able to replace my present steward, Adam Wilder.

Someone would have to replace him. Wilder had been grey-haired when I first met him, many years ago. He still performed his duties with perfect competence, but his shoulders were growing stooped. It was time to prepare for the years ahead. Ben had come under my care after being orphaned in a most dreadful manner, but he was not my son and must have wondered what plans I would make for him. One thing I could offer him was a secure future.

Page came in to clear the main course away and bring in a mercifully cold dessert. We were helping ourselves to it and Page was passing a cream jug round when the hammering on the door began.

The hammering was loud and furious. We heard Page go to the door. A moment later, Gilbert Gale, breathless, brushing Page aside, burst in on us.

'It's that poor old woman up on the hill! Father Dunberry is rousing the villagers; he's getting them together to go up and get her and swim her in the pond! He says she killed Father Eliot with her magic potions. He's crazy; they're all crazy; all she's ever done is make remedies that any of the women could make themselves if they'd only be bothered to grow the herbs and do the brewing. Lazy sods and they'll miss her when she's gone and they can't go running to her every time they get a headache or a bad stomach. I can't fight them all alone; I've come for help. Able-bodied men, that's what's needed. Who'll come with me to deal with that mob?'

Brockley and I were both on our feet. 'There are men and lads here in this room!' I said. 'How much time have we got?'

'Maybe an hour if we're quick!' Gilbert said breathlessly. 'There're some who are arguing; they're not all quite out of their minds . . .'

Brockley started to say: 'Not you, madam; you mustn't . . .'

but I was staring in outrage at Stephen and Hector, who hadn't moved. In a casual voice, Hector said: 'She's only an old hag and after all, Mistress Stannard here has headache remedies of her own. Let the villagers have their fun. Swimming a witch might be a laugh.'

Stephen nodded, grinning. Joan seemed unmoved. Brockley looked shocked. Dale said: 'Poor old soul, she'll be so frightened! And if she floats, they'll kill her! How can you?'

I had twice seen a terrified woman being dragged towards a gibbet. I glared at Stephen and Hector. 'I'm really astonished,' I said, 'to find that two fine young fellows like the two of you, sailors who brave storms at sea, are afraid of a bullying vicar and a pack of villagers. Come, Brockley!'

It worked. Hector went crimson and shot to his feet and Stephen made a sudden movement as though he were about to. 'Who says we're afraid of them?' Hector demanded. 'What has that to do with anything? It's a bit of sport! Don't you believe in witches?'

'No,' I said baldly and decided not to add that I had once been accused of witchcraft myself.

'Anyhow, it's no sport for her, poor old soul!' Ben spoke up. 'Horror for her! Harry and me, we're with you, Brockley.'

'What are you all hesitating for?' Gilbert had been standing there, clearly expecting everyone to spring up and follow him to the rescue, and now amazed and angry because we had not. 'Help's needed *now*! Someone's got to stop that mob from going up there! I can't do it alone though if no one will help me, I'll have to try! There's no time to lose. For the love of Heaven, who will come with me? *Now!*'

'We're coming! I have a sword!' Brockley was halfway to the door. '*We're* not afraid of the Cutpenny villagers.' He had picked up my signal. 'Though it could be an ugly business,' he added. 'So, *not* you, madam, for once, not you.'

'We have weapons!' Stephen at least had decided to join us. 'Come on, Hector!'

'And make it quick!' Harry snapped. His rudeness should have made me reprimand him, but I didn't. Something in his voice startled me. All in a moment he seemed to be changing from boy to man.

Hector, now puce with rage, shouted: 'Yes, get the weapons out, Steve. Telling us we're scared! We just wanted to see the sport but if it's a matter of our reputations – all right! We're with you!'

A moment later, all the men had gone, leaving me with Joan and Dale. I was thinking, rapidly.

'Mother Lee should have a woman with her,' I said, addressing Joan. 'If I take Jaunty I can get up there first and get her away. What are the paths like on the other side of the hill?'

'What paths? There aren't any; just a thick wood and a steep slope,' Joan said. She was passive, rubbing sweat from her forehead.

'Then we'll hide in the wood. I'll get her out of sight somehow,' I said.

'No, ma'am, please, what if they catch up and turn on you too!' Dale protested but I ignored her, and moved towards the door just in time to come face to face with Harry and Ben, looking like apprentice pirates, with sword-belts on and short swords at their sides.

'Dale is perfectly right,' said Harry. 'Mother, either you promise not to attempt anything so foolish or . . .'

'Or what?' I tried to brush past them and then to my astonishment, found my wrists being firmly seized by these two lads, respectively my son and my ward. 'Come with us,' said Harry commandingly. 'Dale, you come too.'

It would have been undignified to resist, as well as useless. I had to let them march me out of the dining chamber, across the vestibule, where to my astonishment, I saw Page in the act of buckling a sword on, while Stephen and Hector were handing weapons round to a crowd consisting of Eddie, Hal Jankin, the other two Evergreens grooms and James Mitchell and Samuel Hazel from the kitchen. They took no notice as I was marched rapidly past them and up the stairs. I was escorted to my room, with Dale behind us, protesting uselessly, and thrust into my chamber. Dale was pushed in after me. The door was shut and I heard the key turn and be withdrawn. Harry called: 'No time to waste, we must be off. You'll be safe now, Mother. We only want to protect you!'

Then their feet were running down the stairs and a second later I heard the front door slam. I ran to the window and saw our men running down to the lodge, where Joe Jankin and his sons Will and Robbie had come out to meet them. A goodly force. But the villagers would still outnumber them. The best way and, I feared, the only way to save Mother Lee was to get to her first and get her out of sight.

'It's all right, Dale,' I said. 'Even my very dear son Harry doesn't know *everything* about me.'

The thin kirtle under my light summer gown still had one of my secret pouches inside it and I was in the habit of always shifting their contents into the gown I happened to be wearing. I reached into it and pulled out my picklocks.

'I'll soon have us out,' I said to Dale as I set to work on the lock. 'You mustn't come,' I added. 'I'll go on foot – it sounds as if a horse might be in trouble on the other side of the hill if it's as steep and heavily wooded as Mistress Mercer says. If I make haste, I may yet get there in time. Ah!' The lock gave way. Dale said: 'Oh, ma'am . . .!' but didn't persist. She knew me too well. I left her where she was and sped down the stairs. It would take me maybe ten minutes to get to the foot of the zigzag path but if I got there before the mob did, then I would win.

Arriving in the vestibule, I encountered Joan, who clutched at me and said: 'What are you doing? Where are you going? Surely you're not going to save that old witch yourself?'

'You've been glad enough of her potions!' I snapped.

'When I'm in that pain, I'd seek help from Satan! But I wouldn't challenge all Cutpenny!'

'What a pity!' I shouted at her, and went.

I had the impression that the rescue party meant to make for Cutpenny and confront the mob before it left the village. I hoped so. That would give me my best chance of reaching Mother Lee in time. I used the side door and then, running and walking alternately, my face streaked with sweat in the heavy heat, I made for the place where the track into Cutpenny began. I had to cut through a stretch of wood to avoid the track and knew I must go as fast as possible. Once, I halted to catch my breath and from the direction of the village, I heard it: the sound of human beings baying like animals. I hoped that the rescue party was down there and that the confrontation had begun. If so, I was ahead of it.

I won't soon forget that exhausting climb on foot, the endless zigzagging across the hillside, with the trees arching overhead, and the light beneath them growing livid. The sun had gone in and the sky had suddenly begun to darken but the stifling heat seemed only to grow more intense. The air was thin. At one point, when breathlessness once more forced me to halt, a break in the trees allowed me to look down to a lower stretch of the path. And there was Father Dunberry marching along, holding up a crucifix, and leading a gang of villagers, men and women alike, all crowding after him, some of them with weapons. The pursuit had been harder on my heels than I had thought. And where were the rescuers?

I was still getting my breath but I had to go on. When I came out into the clearing at the top, I was staggering rather than walking.

'Oh, Mother!' said Harry's voice. 'How did you get out?'

The rescuers had not gone into the village to issue their challenge. They had gone up the hill ahead of me and taken their stand in front of the cottage. Harry told me later that it had been Brockley's idea. Brockley had been a soldier and knew something about strategy. He had said that if they were to go towards Cutpenny and block the end of the street, a clever leader could make his mob fall back and appear to disperse – but really to split into two and go across the small-holdings behind the two rows of cottages. That way they might outflank the defenders and start up the hill ahead of them. He reckoned that it might be better to confront them on the hilltop, in front of the cottage.

There they were, anyway: Gilbert Gale, the Mercer boys, Harry and Ben, Brockley, Page, Jankin and his sons, Eddie and the other grooms, James Mitchell, Samuel Hazel and two men I didn't recognize who looked like farmhands. They had the two Evergreens mastiffs with them and they also had an astounding assortment of weapons: a whole range of swords and daggers and some homely choppers and billhooks. Jankin's freckle-faced son Hal was brandishing, of all things, a shovel. And Harry and Ben were staring at me in amazement.

'I have skills that you don't dream of,' I gasped. 'Where's Mother Lee?'

'In the cottage,' Page snapped. I pushed furiously through the line and, still panting and unsteady, I reached the door of the cottage. It was shut and fastened from within. I shouted my name and heard bolts being drawn back. I entered, to see Mother Lee backing away. She sank onto a stool. She was trembling. She looked up at me and said: 'Are they coming?'

'Yes, and you're going!' I seized her arm and pulled her to her feet. 'I've come to get you away. Down among the trees on the other side of the hill. They won't find you there. Come on. Why don't those wantwits outside take you there themselves?'

'It'll be no good. If they don't get me today, they'll get me tomorrow or next week. I knew it'd happen one day. I'll have to pack up, pile all I can on my poor old donkey, along with my stripey cat hissing in a basket, and my goats following and I'll have to leave my hens, and then I'll load what I can on my back and find somewhere else. I'd have lasted longer if Father Eliot had lived; he was no leader of men. And I *didn't* poison him, whatever they may say! Silly old fool took too much of my foxglove medicine if you ask me. I told him what dose to take and I said don't take too much, foxglove is strong, but he was a muddlehead. Nearly killed himself once with his own sister's concoction for a sore throat.'

'Never mind about that. Come *on!*'

I was pulling her towards the door, which I had left open behind me, but she resisted. 'Look out at that there sky. Black as the devil, ain't it? No good out in the open. There's a storm coming.'

'Good thing if it does; it might discourage that mob. Mother Lee, I beg you to . . .'

The lightning flash made us both jump. Through the doorway, we saw it sizzle across the livid sky. It was followed by an almighty crash as though heaven were hurling rocks at the earth. 'Going to run out in that, are we?' said Mother Lee and emitted a cackling laugh that ended in a gulp and then burst into what I recognized as the tears of sheer terror.

I put my arm round her. At the same moment I saw Father Dunberry and his followers burst into the clearing and heard the defenders shout and saw them stand to arms, blades at the ready, ranks closed. I heard the mastiffs snarl. Father Dunberry shouted something and there was a concerted roar of fury from his forces, and battle was joined. Mother Lee and I clung together. The defenders seemed so few, confronting too many.

Nevertheless, they stood. I heard the dogs snarl again and someone screamed, and for a moment, although I couldn't see clearly, it seemed that the villagers fell back, intimidated perhaps by the flashing swords and the canine teeth. Then the lightning crackled again and the thunder roared, and the rain was released, cascading down, pounding the earth. A gust of fierce wind blew it in at the door.

Through her tears, Mother Lee whispered that the goats had a shelter and so had the donkey. It touched me. Even in this extremity, she had thought for them.

Meanwhile, the storm was doing with ease what our line of defenders might have failed to do in the end; it was driving the enemy into retreat. Father Dunberry was shouting that Mother Lee had called up the storm; take courage, all, and follow me! but all his confused forces wanted was to get into shelter, back beneath the trees. And then, the rain turned to hail, a fearful storm of it, bouncing whitely all over the garden.

The enemy, dragging coats and shawls over their heads, drained out of the clearing like water out of a leaking pail. Our own friends turned the other way and came headlong into the cottage. Suddenly it was full of large wet men and also two large wet dogs, shaking themselves all over everyone. The lightning flashed again and once more the thunder sounded as if it were flinging boulders at us. Then came a sudden silence, as the hail died away and the rain steadied to a more common-place downpour. Page slammed the door and threw the bolts across.

He took off a drenched cap and felt his thin head of hair to find out if it was wet. 'Not sure if we'd ever have done it ourselves,' he said, 'but nature's done it for us. Mother Lee, did you call up this storm?'

'Don't talk daft. I wouldn't know how. I don't know any

spells, just how to make potions with herbs any fool can grow if they want to!' Mother Lee was still sobbing. 'And they'll be back once they're dried off. They'll get to boasting to each other about how brave they were until the Devil joined in to help *me* and then Father Dunberry'll add raising storms to poisoning vicars, and he'll lead another mob, all screeching *witchcraft*. I'd best leave, soon as I can.'

'And how're you going to make a home anywhere else?' Hector asked her. He was standing by the fire in his shirtsleeves, squeezing water out of his doublet.

'I got some money and things I can sell though I'd rather not, being as they're pretty. Make me think of when I were young and married and had a home like every other woman!'

'What happened?' Gilbert asked her. He too was in his shirt and wringing out his jacket. 'How did you lose it all?'

'I had childer, seven of 'em. Four died, one girl got wed and went away with her man, Heaven knows where, and the two lads went off as well, said they'd make fortunes in the New World. Last I ever heard of any of them. I got lonely, couldn't make enough of a living selling eggs and goats' cheese. Started making potions. Learned that from my ma. Started selling them. Then there was talk of witchcraft and I left. Left my *home*. Do you know what that means for a woman?'

'Where did you go?' Gilbert asked.

'Didn't know where I was going. Pretty sight I must have been, tramping the tracks with me goats on a string and a mule – it was a mule I had then; my husband left it to me. Had it laden, I did, with all I could bring with me, clothes, a rug or two, pans to cook with, when I had aught to cook. But I had a bit of luck; I come here to Cutpenny and Father Eliot said there's this empty cottage up on the hill; an old man had it, a hermit sort of fellow; grew things and kept a cow, but then he died and left his home empty. I was welcome to the place, so Father Eliot said. I'd never of hurt him, even if he did get nervous about me later. I been happy here. Even got a friend of my husband to put proper windows in for me. Knew it wouldn't last.'

'It will last,' said Gilbert Gale. 'We will approach the Bishop of Winchester if necessary. Father Dunberry will have to listen to what he says for he's a mighty prelate with power over other bishops.'

'What if he likes witch-hunters too?' Ben wanted to know.

'He's got to keep the law,' said Gilbert. 'And mobs aren't lawful. I'll go to him and complain about Father Dunberry.'

Mother Lee looked at him, doubtfully but with a trace of hope. Stephen said idly: 'What were the pretty things you didn't want to sell?'

'Only a pair of pretty gold goblets,' said Mother Lee. 'Present from your mother, lad. A generous lady, is Mistress Mercer.'

'Gold goblets?'

The alertness in Hector's voice should have warned her but it didn't. She reached for the door of the cupboard I had seen on my first visit, and took the little gold goblets out. Hector and Stephen looked at them, first with astonishment and then with horror.

'Our mother *gave* you these?' Hector shouted. He picked one of them up and held it up to the window. The sky was still dark but even so, the jewels flashed. 'When? For what reason?'

Mother Lee looked frightened. 'She said she was grateful. For all the pain I'd saved her. So she made me a present. They're so pretty.'

'*Pretty!*' Hector spluttered. 'They are precious, as I think you well know, for you talked of selling them if you had need. Our mother had no right to give them to you. They were not hers to give.'

He glanced at Stephen and I had a sense that a wordless conversation was taking place between them. 'They're heirlooms,' said Stephen. 'Heirlooms of our family. They've been in our family for generations!'

Hector said: 'We'll take these back.' He put the goblet down, and then, looking round, saw that he was in the midst of a crowd that expected something more of him. He made a disgusted noise, fumbled at his belt, opened a pouch that hung inside his breeches, and drew out a purse. 'Money will be easier to use than goblets if you have to start living somewhere else. Take these in exchange.' He opened the purse and I saw him slip what looked like several sovereigns and angels into Mother Lee's hand.

'The trouble's most likely over for the time being,' he said. He collected up the goblets and wrapped them in his damp doublet. 'The rain's stopped and we can leave. I don't think the villagers are lingering.' He went to the door and peered out. 'No sign of them. They've all gone home to get dry and boast of how brave they were.'

Before we left, I gave Mother Lee a quick kiss and said: 'If you hear them coming back, get out of this cottage and hide in the woods on the other side of the hill.' She nodded, still sitting in a bemused fashion, clutching her money.

As we crowded out of the door, I said to Harry: 'We can do no more and I can endure no more of Evergreens! The moment we return there, we will pack and then leave at once for Hawkswood. We can reach home before nightfall. I have a feeling that a family quarrel is going to break out at Evergreens and I don't want be under the same roof with it.'

'The family quarrel might be quite entertaining,' said Harry wickedly, but Ben said: 'No!' and Brockley said: 'Not my idea of entertainment. What if they want us to take sides? Again! The mistress is right. We leave for home at once.'

ELEVEN

Floods, Mud and Migraine

We did not start for home that afternoon. Before we had reached the foot of the hill, I was already feeling the first ominous twinges over my left eye and before we were in the house, I had a full-blown sick headache of my own. Dale recognized the signs at once.

'Ma'am, you have a migraine. You should lie down. I will bring you the potion that Gladys made. You won't want any of the concoctions made by that witch up on the hill.'

'She's not a witch, Dale, just a grasping old woman with some herblore. She likes to talk about her secret ingredients,' I said. 'I saw poppies in her garden. I would wager that her secret ingredient is poppy juice.'

We were crossing the vestibule. Hector and Stephen had gone on into the parlour where they had evidently found Joan; I could hear raised voices coming from all three of them. The expected family quarrel had begun. The sound of it made my head pound even more. I let Dale take me up to my chamber, where she helped me out of my outer garments, settled me on the bed in my petticoat and drew the coverlet over me.

'I meant us to go home this afternoon,' I said feebly.

'We can't do that now, ma'am. You lie there. I'll get the potion.'

She was back with it in a few minutes. 'There's such a to-do going on in the parlour, ma'am. The boys are going for their mother over something; you never heard such shouting! And she's shouting back like a termagant!'

'The Mercers' family squabbles are nothing to do with us,' I said. 'The sooner we get away from here, the better. Oh, my head!'

My skull felt as though it was being hammered to pieces. Dale held out the cup of medicine and I swallowed it gratefully, though it tasted unpleasant, despite being sweetened with honey. I lay back and closed my eyes. 'Leave me, Dale. I'll sleep this off.'

'I've put a basin beside you, ma'am, but I'll sit in here with my sewing. You'll probably throw up when you wake.'

I didn't sleep it off. I didn't sleep at all. Towards evening I began to feel sick and I called Dale, who held my head while I emptied my guts into the basin. I lay back, expecting the pain to subside. It didn't. Dale fetched another dose of Gladys' potion. This time, I did sleep, and didn't wake until dawn, which should have cured me, because a long sleep usually did. But I awoke to the same awful pain. I couldn't eat any breakfast and before long I was throwing up again, or rather I was trying to. I heaved and heaved on an empty stomach and my stomach muscles began to ache.

'There's nothing for it,' said Joan, who had come anxiously to visit her ailing guest. 'I will fetch you one of Mother Lee's potions. They really do work.'

'Thank you,' I said weakly. I was longing for home, but Hawkswood felt as far away as the moon, and in any case, it was growing stickily hot once more and I could see through the window that the sky was darkening all over again.

I drank Mother Lee's potion. I would have taken anything that might ease the pain. I would have swallowed deadly nightshade if anyone had offered it and I wouldn't have cared if it cured me only of living.

The effect that Mother Lee's potion had was to send me to sleep again. I slept until the evening and then woke, and found, thankfully that at last, the pain was gone. I was weak, as much as anything through lack of food for I had eaten nothing since our interrupted dinner the previous day. Dale brought me some white bean soup. I drank it thankfully and there were no ill effects. Dale must have told Joan, who came to see me again.

She came with a candle because although the long June evening should have still been light, there was another thunderstorm in progress and the only bright light came from the lightning.

'You are better! I am relieved. You have had a dreadful time.' She glanced towards the window and winced as another jagged streak of lightning split the sky. 'My boys left for the coast this morning. Will Jankin has gone with them, of course. I told them they shouldn't travel on the Sabbath, but they were impatient to be away. They were anxious in case the storm had damaged their ships – they'd left them safely laid up, but you never know.'

'They bring home beautiful things,' I said, thinking of the goblets which I somehow felt were more likely to be the spoils of trade and not heirlooms at all. The Mercers were not, somehow, the kind of family that would have such precious heirlooms. 'Are they bound for the New World again?'

'I think so, though they do sometimes visit the Mediterranean.' Joan sighed. 'Seamen live dangerous lives; I often worry. Still, they have a fine crew of strong sailors and there's their third partner – I've only met him a few times; I don't know him well or much about him – but I understand he's a good mariner and skilled with a sword if they run into trouble with pirate shipping. I don't encourage my boys to boast, you see. Hector's always been boastful and I don't approve of that.'

She left me to finish my recovery. The thunder and lightning stopped presently, and I slept again, to the swish of rain and the buffeting of a strong wind. In the morning I was able to rise though Dale begged me not to go downstairs till the next day. She brought me a breakfast of bread and milk with honey and later, a chicken quarter, spit roasted with no garnish except a little ginger, accompanied by a piece of white manchet bread and a small dish of salad.

'That goblin of a cook – Mitchell – he's used to doing special meals for Mistress Mercer after her headaches,' Dale told me. 'I was afraid he'd be difficult about me wanting manchet bread and a chicken joint done special but he said it was no trouble, he was used to it. Mistress Joan sends her good wishes and perhaps you'll join her at supper this evening.'

'I think I will,' I said, attending to the chicken and finding myself hungry. 'When can we set out for home, I wonder?'

'You should have another day's rest, ma'am,' Dale said. 'Besides, the tracks are deep in mud after all that rain. One of Mistress Joan's gardeners has had his cottage clean wrecked, thatched roof torn off in the wind and water halfway up the

downstairs walls. The place is near a stream and it burst its
banks. He and his wife are with his parents in Cutpenny for
the time being. There's been other floods, too. Mistress Joan
went to Cutpenny this morning. She was gone a long time
and came back with her skirts all wet, and said the pond had
overflowed into the church and some of the women were trying
to sweep the water out. There was a spare broom and she
joined in to help them. Some of the cottages are flooded, as
well.'

'Is the carpenter's shop flooded?' I asked, with some
concern.

'Where Gilbert Gale is? No, that side slopes upwards a
little and the cottages and shops there are dry. That's where
the gardener's parents live. The trouble is all on the church
side, so Mistress Joan says. But, ma'am, I've been outside and
looked round and believe me, we oughtn't to travel until the
roads are drier.'

'The sooner we're away, the better,' I said. I felt uneasy in
this house. Joan's dislike of letting Hector and Stephen talk
about their voyages, at least in the hearing of her guests,
seemed a little excessive. Most sailors tell tales of their adventures at sea and most people enjoy listening to them. And why
had she been afraid of a magistrate hearing them?

I found myself wondering if they had been robbing Spanish
vessels and then slipping their haul ashore without paying the
royal treasury its share. Queen Elizabeth didn't at all mind if
her captains attacked Spanish treasure ships and snatched their
cargoes but she expected to receive a fair share of it. Incoming
ships were supposed to sail into certain ports to declare what
they were carrying.

I thought of the valuable goods those two young men had
brought into the house. That emerald pendant. The beautiful
velvet. The jaguar skin. Those goblets!

But it was nothing to do with me. I just wanted to go home.

TWELVE
The Heaviness in the Air

Before we left, I wished to thank Mother Lee for her
potion and see if I could coax the recipe out of her. I
felt that my guess about the juice of the poppy was
probably right but I needed to know the amounts and the
method. The stormy weather had given way to sunshine. It
was a Tuesday morning. I had decided to leave the next day
and trust that the sun would have dried the roads enough by
then. I took the Brockleys with me and we set out on horseback. At the foot of the wooded hill, where the track was
crossed by the one that led between Cutpenny and Waters
House, we met Arabella.

She was on foot, carrying a basket and looking rather weary.
It was nearly a mile to Waters House though it was easy walking.

'You're bound for Mother Lee?' I asked her. 'But not on
your lovely white mare?'

'No. How nice to see you, Mistress Stannard. I thought you
must have gone home by now. I am on foot because I . . . I
had good news for Master Waters, and he says I must not ride.
I may walk; he says that walking is beneficial.'

I took a moment to grasp what she meant by *good news*
and then I said: 'You are with child? Already? Congratulations!'

Arabella didn't look happy. There was no smile in her eyes
and the bronze-brown curls in front of her white cap had none
of the shine that pregnancy usually creates.

'I'm nervous,' she said now.

'You're young and strong. It will be all right,' I said comfortingly. On more than one occasion, it hadn't been all right for
me but this wasn't the moment to say so. 'Are we all going
up to see Mother Lee?' I enquired.

'Yes. She makes an ointment for chapped hands that my
mother uses and provides for the maids at Evergreens. I've

noticed that some of my maidservants have reddened hands. Since none of them will go up to see Mother Lee – they're all saying now that she raised that storm – I said I would go myself and buy a supply of that ointment. I would like to make it myself, and use it for my household, but I believe she never shares her recipes.'

Arabella, I thought, was trying to shoulder her new responsibilities as mistress of Waters House. If in her heart, she still pined for Gilbert Gale, she was nevertheless doing her best. Just as Gilbert, presumably, was trying to do the same thing.

I said: 'I have a good recipe for that kind of ointment myself. I'll give you that before I go home. I use woundwort. You need beeswax as well and some sort of oil . . .' We had started up the zigzag path, with Arabella walking beside me. 'I'll write it down for you and send it to Waters House. We're leaving tomorrow. We were delayed because I had a migraine for two days – like your mother's migraines – and then the roads were so bad after all that rain. Your mother gave me one of Mother Lee's headache potions and it worked. I am going to see Mother Lee and buy some for myself.'

Brockley said: 'If I dismount and set you sideways on my horse, Mistress Waters, would that be more comfortable for you than plodding up this long track? Firefly will only be walking. I am sure that will do you no harm. Madam, do you agree?'

'Yes. I do,' I said. 'You look tired, Arabella. And the sun is getting hot.'

'I do feel tired,' Arabella agreed.

Brockley slipped down and lifted her onto his saddle, seating her sideways as though in a chair. He pulled the reins over Firefly's head, and led the way, walking slowly.

We heard the noises before we actually reached the cottage. The goats were bleating frantically and the hens were cackling as though a fox were on the prowl. As we emerged into the clearing, Arabella exclaimed that there was no smoke from the chimney.

She tried to say something else, but was drowned out because the donkey had galloped to the gate and added a loud braying to the bleats and the cackles. There was no sign of the cat.

'Something's wrong!' Brockley paused to lift Arabella down from the horse, then tossed his reins to me and strode off to the cottage. I dismounted, told Dale and Arabella to wait and went after him. I caught up with him just as he pushed the cottage door open. It hadn't been fastened. We walked in.

We knew at once. The silence had a potent quality and the air was heavy. This house was inhabited by the dead.

The fire had been out for a long time. The trivet was in place, with a pot standing on it, but the fire-pit below held nothing but ash and a few half-burned pieces of wood. It was a few moments before we saw Mother Lee, for she was in a shadowy corner, slumped in one of her basketwork chairs and already, in the mysterious manner of death, sinking back into her surroundings.

'When the villagers came – she was so frightened,' I said. 'She shouldn't have been left alone. Can one die of fear?'

'I don't know.' Brockley went to her and knelt to look at her closely. Then he rose and turned to me. He had gone white.

'Perhaps people can die of fear, but Mother Lee hasn't. She's been strangled.'

She had been gone for at least twenty-four hours, we reckoned. The goats were desperate to be milked, the hens were pecking vainly about in their run and ran towards us when they saw us. The donkey had been lonely and had sensed something amiss. He had galloped to the gate to meet us and his bray was a call for help.

'I know how to milk a cow,' I said. 'I dare say I can milk goats, too.'

'So can I,' said Brockley, 'and there are buckets in that lean-to.'

Dale had also dismounted by now, and she and Arabella had tethered the horses. We found them in the lean-to, where they had found a sack of corn and were filling a couple of pails from it. 'For the hens,' said Arabella. I told them what we had found in the cottage and they listened in horror. 'We half guessed that she'd died,' Dale said, 'but not that way. That's horrible! *Horrible!*'

Arabella said: 'Poor old woman,' and began to tremble.

I found a spare milking stool for her and made her sit down. I sent Dale to feed the hens. Arabella said she would be all right if we went to milk the goats. 'The poor things sound frantic.'

As we worked with the goats, I asked Brockley where he had learned how to milk.

'In France, long ago, when I was with King Henry's army,' said Brockley. 'We lived off the land half the time, stealing other people's vegetables, milking their cows, wringing the necks of other folks' chickens, cutting the throats of calves and goats . . .'

'You must have been very popular with the peasants,' I remarked.

'Not very. But armies have to eat.' Brockley, busily shooting goats' milk into a pail, turned his head to look at me. 'What do we do, madam? Who should we report this to?'

'I don't know,' I said. 'But Mistress Mercer will know. Or Master Waters.'

'Madam,' said Brockley, 'I don't think we should leave Mother Lee as she is. We should cover her with something. Dear God, what a hateful way to die. Who could have done such a thing? One of the villagers? I don't suspect Father Dunberry. We weren't in church this last Sunday but I understand from Page that Dunberry is in a fine state of uncertainty. Apparently, in his sermon, he declared that when the heavens poured torrents of water and hail on the villagers who wanted to swim her, it could have been a sign from God that she was innocent, but on the other hand, perhaps the Devil came to her aid. They are still forbidden to use her potions.'

'It was such a lonely death,' said Arabella tremulously when, having finished with the goats, we went back to her. 'I think she's been a lonely woman, up here with only her animals for company.'

Dale was looking at our pails of milk. 'What are we to do with those?' she asked.

'Put some out for the cat, but otherwise, pour it away,' said Brockley. 'What else?'

I told Arabella and Dale to stay where they were and then Brockley and I went back into the cottage and into Mother

Lee's bedchamber. The narrow bed had a woven blanket on it, a feather pillow and a rabbit-skin coverlet.

'We can't move her,' Brockley said. 'The constable, or whoever comes, will want to see just what has happened. But we can take the coverlet from the bed and throw that over her.'

We did so, tossing it protectively over the pitiful thing that had once been a living woman. Stooping to adjust a fold, I touched Mother Lee's cold hand and my fingers brushed against something that felt like cloth. I peered closer and then lifted the hand. It was cold and still a little stiff, as though the first rigor of death had not quite gone. There was something gripped between her fingers and thumb and further preserved from falling out of them because her hand had been lying on the basketwork arm of the chair. It was a torn strip of black woollen fabric. With some difficulty, I eased it free.

'She fought her assailant,' Brockley said, when I showed it to him. 'She clutched at his clothing and tore at it. Better bring it; it might lead us to whoever did this.'

Dale, however, shook her head when she saw it. 'That kind of cloth turns up everywhere. Roger has a jacket with a lining just like that and Eddie has a pair of breeches of that very material. I doubt if it can tell us much.'

'I'll keep it in case,' I said, and put it away in my hidden pouch. 'Someone will have to take charge of the animals,' I remarked. 'I wonder where the cat is?'

Joan knew what to do, and the law took control. To begin with, two constables came from Caterham but because Mother Lee had died in her home, which was not in a Caterham parish, but within the little parish of St Mark's, which came under Oxted, Oxted was where the inquest was finally held. It took place upstairs in the Bell Inn. It was attended by Oxted's overlord, Master Charles Hoskins, City of London merchant. A local man was appointed as coroner. It was all done correctly but it was nevertheless a highly unsatisfactory affair. The fact that Mother Lee had come so near to being swum as a witch coloured everything.

Anyone who might conceivably have known anything to

the point was called, but nothing emerged except that Mother Lee was a highly suspicious character, though useful in some ways. Some of the Cutpenny villagers were called. None of them seemed anxious to say that they had been among Mother Lee's customers though Joan had to admit to it, because her entire household knew about her headaches. The Brockleys and I and Arabella also admitted it because we had found her and why else would we have climbed the hill? Master Waters confirmed that his wife had gone to buy ointment for chapped hands, for herself and her maidservants. His wife, he said, was a considerate mistress to her servants. There were murmurs of approval.

We all said, which was true, that we had seen no evidence of anything to do with witchcraft; that to us, Mother Lee had seemed to be just an aged woman who lived alone and made a living by growing vegetables and fruit, making goats' cheese and brewing herbal remedies.

Father Dunberry, to be fair to him, behaved well. He admitted to leading a crowd of villagers up the hill because accusations of witchcraft had been laid, and said that it was possible that the storm that drove them all away could have been sent by God to protect her, though there was no certainty and she herself might have called it up. He spoke quite graciously of those who had tried to defend her. Father Dunberry wasn't in my opinion a pleasant individual, but he was honest.

As far as finding the murderer was concerned, there was nothing to get hold of. No one had been seen surreptitiously slinking onto the track up the hill; no one had been mysteriously absent from their home or their duties; since the debacle in the thunderstorm, no one had been heard to utter threats against her. The verdict was that Mother Lee had been murdered by a person or persons unknown. Enquiries would continue. It was obvious, though unspoken, that the said enquiries would be unenthusiastic and would eventually be dropped. After all, the woman *had* been accused of witchcraft.

As the gathering dispersed, Master Waters discovered that Charles Hoskins was staying at the Bell for a few days, to attend to some local business, and invited him to dine the next day. He and Arabella departed with Arabella in a fluster about having to entertain such an illustrious guest at such short notice. I doubted if Hoskins would expect too much. He gave the impression of being slightly amused by these rustic goings-on.

The inquest was held on a Wednesday. On the Friday, most of Mother Lee's goods and all her livestock, which had been looked after meanwhile at Waters House, were auctioned in Oxted. The money raised went to the Crown though I heard that some of it was to be devoted to the relief of the poor in the Oxted district. The cat had emerged from the woods while the constable and some assistants were collecting the other livestock. It looked sleek enough, I heard, and was probably used to hunting voles and such small animals in the woods. However, the Caterham constable said that his cat, a good mouser, had lately died and he would be glad enough of a replacement.

Brockley attended the auction and told me afterwards that he had talked to the constable and apparently, the cat had been put into a lidded hamper that was found in the cottage 'and carried down the hill, spitting every yard of the way' to be settled in its new home.

'Constable says a little butter on its paws and it'll quieten down all right,' Brockley said. He added that the household goods hadn't fetched much. 'They only amounted to some pewter and pottery and a few pots and pans. Not that coverlet – I think it was too old and dirty.'

'Just as well that the boys took back those goblets,' I said. 'They would have caused a stir!'

The weather had continued warm and the roads were long since dry. I wondered, but didn't want to wait long enough to find out, whether Arabella had successfully coped with being hostess to a major landowner. On the Saturday, as soon as we had broken our fast, I and my little entourage said farewell to Joan and her household, and at last, set out for Hawkswood.

Ahead of me now lay decisions about Adam Wilder, and a dozen other things concerned with the management of my home. In August, after the queen had returned from her summer progress, I would be going to court for six weeks. She summoned me to her twice a year, to serve for six weeks as one of her Bedchamber Ladies.

I didn't expect to hear anything more about events at Evergreens, nor did I wish to.

If only wishes were horses. Alas, they are not.

PART II
TREASURE HUNT

THIRTEEN
Lawful Complaint

As usual, in August, after the queen had returned from her summer progress, I joined the court, which was at Whitehall, for my turn of duty, bringing the Brockleys with me. I took up my usual tasks, accompanying the queen as she went about her duties, attending on her when she retired to bed and when she rose in the morning, doing my best to get on well with her other ladies. This was no longer as difficult as it used to be, for they now knew that I wouldn't try to claim precedence because I was her majesty's sister. For the first three days, everything went smoothly.

On the fourth day, to my surprise, I was summoned to attend a private Audience.

I had no idea what it was about. Dale dressed me in my favourite cream and tawny court dress, and my most fashionable farthingale and ruff. She did not accompany me. I was fetched by a page and escorted to one of the smaller Audience chambers. There I found the queen, majestic in cream satin, embroidered in gold, with ropes of pearls and pearl earrings, enthroned upon a dais, with four of the other ladies behind her. Her sweet Robin, the Earl of Leicester, was standing beside her, and on the other side was Sir William Cecil, otherwise Lord Burghley and Lord Treasurer. He had been given a seat. I knew that he suffered badly from the joint evil and sometimes from the gout.

Also present, standing one on each side of the dais, were two men whom I recognized as Sir Charles Howard, Lord High Admiral, and Sir Francis Drake, who had fought so valiantly against the attempted Spanish invasion.

During the Armada crisis I had met them both. Sir Charles was a serious man. His long face, thrown back against his stiff ruff, wasn't much given to smiling. Sir Francis Drake had a fair, wind-reddened countenance, wide in the forehead and narrow in the chin, with a thin blond beard and bright, bold eyes. It was a face that looked out of place above the constricting ruff that propped his chin and bulged up to his ears. Those bold eyes went with loose breeches and an open shirt, a brightly coloured headband to keep the sweat out of his eyes and a belt bristling with weaponry. Many years ago, I had had the misfortune to be a captive on a slave ship. Some of her crew had been dressed like that.

I was bidden to stand to one side of the black and white chequered floor. A moment later, two more gentlemen were brought in and placed in the centre. Then Leicester performed the introductions.

'Your majesty, may I present Captain Geoffrey Tyler, captain of your majesty's ship the *White Hart*, and Capitaine Jacques le Boeuf, captain of a French vessel, *La Princesse*. Capitaine le Boeuf wishes to present a complaint and does so in person because the present confused state of France, after the recent assassination of King Henry the Third, coupled with the ever-present conflict between the French Catholics and the Huguenots, prevents him from being represented by an envoy.

'Gentlemen, let me present to you, Mistress Ursula Stannard, half-sister to her majesty queen Elizabeth; Sir William Cecil, Lord Burghley and Lord Treasurer of the Realm; Sir Charles Howard, Lord High Admiral of England; Sir Francis Drake, master of the *Golden Hind*.'

There were bows and in my case a deep curtsey. I was puzzled and also anxious. The rolling out of all those titles were like a trumpet fanfare.

The purpose of this sudden gathering was made clear soon enough.

Cecil was there because the matter touched upon the Treasury. Charles Howard was there because he was the Lord High Admiral and we were about to hear complaints that concerned a threat to English shipping.

Tyler was there to inform her majesty that her own ships were being preyed upon by unknown men of her own country and he had himself been a victim.

Le Boeuf, who didn't look in least like a bull, but more

nearly resembled a university scholar albeit with a sun-browned skin, spoke good English, and in tones that somehow combined outrage and dignity, was there to complain, on behalf of whoever was now on the French throne, that English pirates were preying on His Gallic Majesty's shipping and to request that this warlike and hostile activity should cease forthwith. He addressed the glittering figure on the dais without either discourtesy or fear. He had a lawful complaint, he said, and beside him, Captain Tyler nodded agreement.

Elizabeth listened to this testimony without interruption. Then she thanked them all for bringing these matters to her attention, and turned to the Earl of Leicester, who began to explain that the complaint was not against pirates in general but against one specific set of pirates, a group of three ships, acting in concert. Sir Francis Drake had been growing restless, however, and at this point Leicester handed the proceedings over to him. Sir Francis, he told us, had a contribution to make.

Sir Francis certainly had.

'One person who is not here present, because he is unwell, is Sir John Norris, with whom I this year went out on a campaign that was not as successful as we had hoped.' Here Sir Francis glanced at her majesty, who tightened her lips.

'We had orders from her majesty,' said Drake, 'to finish off all the Spanish shipping we could find, seize any treasure they were carrying, throw the Spanish out of Portugal and capture the Azores as well. A shopping list, so to speak.'

He paused. Cecil said: 'I thought at the time that a commission as big as that was a little optimistic.' Elizabeth's mouth tightened still more.

'We did what we could,' said Drake. 'We destroyed a good many ships but I am obliged to admit that we made little impression in Portugal and did not succeed in taking the Azores. We also experienced heavy losses of men and vessels.

'However, in the course of our expedition, we at one point sent a detachment of vessels westward to intercept any Spanish shipping they could find, and relieve them of any treasure they might have aboard. Among the detachment was the *White Hart*. This ploy did meet with some success – they stopped two galleons, seized most of what was in their holds and then sank them. But on the way to re-join us, they ran into rough weather and became separated and the *White Hart*' – here Drake bowed towards Captain Tyler – 'was assailed by a trio of pirate vessels, smaller than she was, but very fast.

'Their men boarded her, got hold of Captain Tyler, took him aboard one of their vessels and held him hostage to keep his men quiet, while they seized the treasure she was carrying. Then they wrecked the rigging of the *White Hart* and released Tyler, by which I mean that they dumped him aboard his own ship, all trussed up and in the midst of the wrecked rigging. Bad enough, you might think. But there's more!' At this point, Drake paused in his statement and turned to Captain Tyler, requesting his personal details.

'The pirates were masked,' said Tyler, 'and for the most part silent. But their captain spoke when he warned my crew that I was a hostage. He spoke good English. Those pirates boarded my ship like a plague of locusts, seized the Spanish treasure I had aboard and vanished over the horizon, leaving my ship in no condition to give chase. It was two days before we could resume our journey to re-join Sir Francis' fleet.'

He stopped, and Drake resumed.

'That is not all. Far from it. There have been other reports from English privateers who have been bringing spoils home and been robbed of them – by, apparently, a trio of vessels acting together and manned by English-speaking pirates. There is a lawful privateer – I know him, Reginald Prettyman, runs a ship called the *Sweet Music* – who tackled a Spaniard away over to the west, just as she was picking up the west wind to bring her home. He seized her treasure. He was then attacked himself, by what we think must be the same trio of vessels. Faster than the *Sweet Music* and very manoeuvrable. Two came at him from astern, and one was waiting to block his course ahead. Once more, the captain was seized as a hostage.

'Captain Prettyman fairly ground his teeth when he was reporting what happened. The pirates didn't get away with all the treasure the *Sweet Music* was carrying. Prettyman bawled to his crew to fight back, never mind him, and some of them did, fiercely enough to make the assailants think again. They leapt back to their own ships, leaving some gold and silver ingots and some gemstones behind, threw Prettyman into the sea, and made off over the horizon to the east. His crew rescued Prettyman before the sharks could get him. The attackers' crew were all masked but some of them were heard to speak in English.

'They'd damaged the *Sweet Music*'s rigging badly but Prettyman and his crew made some repairs, and the next day they set off for home, limping because they weren't under full sail. Only to be attacked a *second* time just as they were nearing home waters! Prettyman maintains that the second set of assailants were in fact the same as the first ones – the very same three vessels! And this time they grabbed the rest of the treasure! They must have outdistanced the *Sweet Music*, deposited their first collection of loot somewhere and then sailed out to meet her the second time. He also says that the second time they were better armed. They didn't take him hostage again; they just trained big guns on his ship and threatened to sink her with all hands.'

Drake came to a stop and Cecil said: 'Prettyman is well known to me. He has the queen's commission. When he – or any other official privateer – comes into port with Spanish treasure on board, it is declared on arrival and shared between the captain, the crew and the Royal Treasury. But this trio, though apparently English, definitely do not carry a commission – the queen herself has confirmed this – and they certainly haven't paid as much as a counterfeit farthing into the Treasury. I have the honour to be Lord Treasurer and I resent this state of affairs.'

I had been growing uncomfortable. Inside me, a most unhappy suspicion was uncoiling itself, like a disturbed snake. I half expected to be summoned to the middle of the floor and questioned. This, however, did not happen. Leicester was speaking again, saying grimly that any ship, French or English, that saw the approach of such a trio should open fire at once, and that English ships should be provided with heavier guns.

Sir Charles agreed with this and offered some recommendations concerning the said guns. Still, no one spoke to me or asked anything of me. I just stood there and listened. Presently, Sir Charles finished and the queen spoke.

'We must thank Captain Tyler and Capitaine le Boeuf for bringing this information to us, bitter though it is. We are angry. Angry that our own shipping is being attacked in this way; angry that the ships of our friend the king of France have suffered also. This testimony will be considered now in council.' Her tone was hard. 'This Audience is closed.'

And that was that. Elizabeth rose and in a sweep of immense embroidered skirts, she left the chamber, escorted by her attendant ladies and by Leicester. Cecil, Howard and Drake, however, came down from the dais to join me and the two captains. We were clustered together, marvelling at what we had learned and wondering where to go next. Capitaine le Boeuf said that he would return to his lodgings, but Captain Tyler unexpectedly told us that his home was not far away and that he would be honoured if we would all accompany him there for a little refreshment after this awe-ful audience with her majesty. His wife would be happy to welcome us, he said.

The somewhat rigid Charles Howard hesitated, saying: 'Captain Tyler, surely your wife will be a little overwhelmed if you bring people of our standing to your house!'

'Oh, Tilly won't mind,' said Tyler, unconcerned. 'She loves to have guests. She is now preparing a dinner for any guests I bring home! If I don't bring any, we'll eat it ourselves and finish it for supper. But I should like to please her with company. She would like to meet you, Sir Francis. She loves to hear tales of my seaman's world, which she cannot share. I know that some captains do take their wives to sea with them, but I do not. There are perils on the deep and if anything happens to me, I would like to know that my children still have their mother.'

There was something persuasive about Tyler, a dignified consciousness of being a ship's captain, with all the authority that captaincy implied. Drake said laughingly that he had many a tale to tell and would enjoy a willing hearer. Cecil smiled and said he would have his carriage put to and would be happy to accept the invitation.

Le Boeuf still preferred to go back to his lodgings, but the rest of us, to our own surprise, found ourselves going to dine with Captain Tyler.

He lived in a timbered town house, with dormer windows in its slate roof. As a smiling but very correct manservant showed us inside, the first things we heard were childish exclamations and shrieks of laughter from its upper regions.

'I have four children,' said Captain Tyler, 'aged respectively, seven and a quarter, five, three and a half and one year. They have a nurserymaid who has never yet got them properly under control. Ah, my wife. Matilda, my dear, I have brought you some guests, as you wished.'

I had wondered what Matilda Tyler would be like. I now beheld a darling. She was small, a little rounded, no doubt as the result of producing four children within seven years, dressed well but not too fashionably, with a mere sketch of a farthingale, and with a pair of grey eyes that sparkled with laughter.

I realized very quickly that Mistress Tyler belonged to that fortunate part of humanity which sees people before it sees titles. Indeed, it was soon clear that she simply did not understand the nuances of social position, and was none the worse for it. It had begun to rain while we were walking to her home and her first care was to call someone to take our damp cloaks and hats, and to usher us into her parlour, where there was a fire to warm us. Her manservant helped Cecil out of his carriage and brought him inside after us.

Introductions were made in the parlour, and then the house-keeper appeared with a tray of filled wineglasses. Mistress Tyler herself handed them round, saying: 'I love to have guests, and perhaps hear other versions of my husband's tales of the sea. My life is my home and children but that doesn't mean that the world outside doesn't interest me. Captain Tyler warned me that he would be meeting people who were greatly above us, but I meant no disrespect by asking him to bring you if he could, and after all, here you are and dinner will be ready soon. But first, if it is permitted, may I know what passed at Whitehall?'

Drake, evidently enchanted with her, gave her a bold grin

and said: 'A captain at sea, mistress, is a king as far as everyone else on board is concerned. He may marry folk, and bury them, and even order executions. You must already know that during his latest voyage, your husband met with an outrageous attack upon his vessel. Today's audience at Whitehall was to do with that. Her majesty listened to him with the gravest attention. And there was a French sea captain . . .'

Drake was a lively raconteur. His account of the audience included people's gestures and expressions, which he acted out for us with relish. He had us laughing one moment, shocked the next. Little Mistress Tyler's eyes became round with wonder when he talked in detail of the treasure that had been lost to the trio of English-speaking pirates.

However, he presently reached a natural pause and Mistress Tyler, taking the hint, rose, picked up a little bronze bell from one of the tables, and shook it. 'That will tell my kitchen that we are ready for our first course. Will it please your lordships and your ladyship to follow me into the next room?'

The dining chamber was furnished with tapestries, a big table and an enormous sideboard. The table was set with platters and bowls of pewter and elegantly patterned wine glasses, and all along the centre was an array of dishes: two hot roasted mutton haunches, a marvellous salad of cucumber, herbs and flowers, three vegetable pies, a gooseberry pie and a ginger-bread loaf, sliced in readiness. Mistress Tyler, I thought, had the virtue of hospitality well developed.

We sat down, Tyler at the head of the table and his wife at the foot. Otherwise we were not in any special order; this was an informal occasion. Very informal, considering that it was punctuated by the sound, above us, of running feet, infant laughter and infant howls. Neither of the Tylers took the slightest notice and we followed their example. I was seated on Captain Tyler's right, opposite to Cecil. Drake and Howard were on either side of Mistress Tyler. The manservant who had admitted us then came with wine flagons, one in each hand, and began going round the table, offering everyone a choice of malmsey or canary.

'But where is my wine glass?' said Captain Tyler plaintively. 'My dear, all the guests have glasses but you and I have not.'

'Oh, how could I?' Flustered, Mistress Tyler rose at once, pushing her chair aside. 'I set the table myself and – it was just then that our guests arrived and I ran out to greet them. No, no, Jenson.' The manservant had put his flagons down and was making for the sideboard. 'I will get them. I thought that with the company so distinguished, this might be an occasion for our special goblets, Captain.'

She went to the sideboard, appeared to dive headfirst into it, and then emerged with two gleaming goblets, one in each hand. Jenson, who had been hovering, closed the sideboard doors for her and Mistress Tyler set a goblet before her husband and then carried hers back to her own place at the foot.

Seated as I was, so close to Captain Tyler, I could see his goblet clearly.

It was quite small, but was made of gold, the good, deep gold which has been mingled with only just enough copper to mitigate the softness of the pure metal. And round the bowl and round the foot ran patterned bands of pearls and rubies.

It was identical to the goblets I had seen in Mother Lee's cottage. She had said that they were gifts from Joan Mercer and the Mercer boys had indignantly claimed them back as family heirlooms. They really were most improbable heirlooms for the occupants of Evergreens. It was a house of modest size and Joan Mercer was a tenant, not an owner. The only valuable items in Joan's tableware were a few silver serving platters. Also, being so costly, those goblets were a most unlikely gift for her to hand out to such as Mother Lee, however great her skill with herblore. And here were identical goblets in the possession of a sea captain who had been robbing Spanish shipping. The little cold snake inside me stirred again.

I looked across the table and straight into Cecil's eyes. He must have noticed something in my face, for his eyebrows rose questioningly. I was about to speak, but Captain Tyler forestalled me by starting to describe the history of the goblets.

'I took those off a Spanish captain and a fine fuss he made about it. We had him backed up against the wall of his own cabin with a pike prodding his stomach to keep him quiet, and we took a whole lot of pretty things out of the chest he had there, including a set of twelve of these goblets. It wasn't a particularly gory business that time. My men know their work. If our victims, shall we say, behave themselves, we don't gratuitously slaughter them. We left all but two of them alive but sadly bereft of their treasure.

'Only,' Tyler grimly continued, 'as you know, I was myself boarded and robbed later on, by three nasty wasps of ships whose beastly crew snatched all but two of these goblets. This pair escaped because just before we were attacked, the first mate and I had been drinking from them while we played a game of draughts. When the warning was sounded, we leapt up, and the young sailor who acts as my server ran in and took the goblets and tossed them into a bowl of washing-up water in the galley. Rather dirty washing-up water but it kept them hid throughout the attack. The other ten were taken, as I said, but not these. We still have them, as spoils of war. And now, gentlemen and Mistress Stannard, if I may propose a toast to her majesty . . .'

As we stood up for the toast, Cecil met my eyes again, and I whispered: 'I must speak with you.' Cecil nodded. 'We will return to my house in my carriage.'

FOURTEEN
Assignment

Much later that day, in Cecil's house in the Strand, he and I sat in his study, facing each other across his desk. Because the room wasn't large, much of it was taken up by the big desk in the centre, with its elegant onyx writing set: inkpot, holder for spare quills, a shaped rest for the quill in use, a sander. Beside the writing set stood a couple of upright holders for scrolls, a set of silver paperweights, a small abacus and a little bell that, like Mistress Tyler, Cecil used to call his servants. Round the walls there were shelves full of books and papers. It was a businesslike place.

In one corner there was a secondary desk, also with a writing set on it though this one was merely made of polished wood. Cecil, settling himself behind his own desk, in his elegantly carved oaken chair with the velvet cushions, said: 'This will be a formal business. What you told me in the carriage on the way here has raised a whole series of questions. Walsingham will be very interested. He would have been present this morning except that he, like Sir John Norris, is ill and in his bed. Though he still works as best he can, even so. I shall visit him tomorrow and tell him everything that you have told me.'

He reached into a drawer below his desk and produced a pair of eyeglasses and a crumpled cloth with which he cleaned the glasses before perching them on the bridge of his nose. He said: 'You are wondering why you were summoned to that Audience today. It was because Walsingham and I know that you recently attended the wedding of a young woman whose two brothers are sailors. They sail in company with a third partner, who has not yet been identified. It has been noticed that the bride's family possess much valuable jewellery, and that the elder boy has been heard – in taverns and such places – to boast of robbing Spanish shipping. Yet the Mercer boys don't hold any commission from the queen. We felt that you might think it in bad taste to go to a wedding and spy on the bride's family . . .'

'Yes, my lord, I would!'

'. . . but you are observant. We trusted to that. We have wondered if you noticed anything of interest during your stay. You were summoned to the Audience so that – in case of any persisting scruples – you would understand, before I questioned you, just how serious this business is. In the carriage just now, though, when you told me about those goblets, you took me completely by surprise. That was something I certainly didn't expect. Though I was surprised myself to see the Tylers drinking from golden vessels! I doubt if they often show those off. Still, in this case they did bring out some details concerning Captain Tyler's tale of pirates.'

He picked up the bell and rang it, and a secretary appeared so quickly that I felt sure he had been waiting within earshot.

'Weston, I want you to take notes. Now, Mistress Stannard, repeat again what you said when we were travelling back from the Tylers.'

That he called me Mistress Stannard instead of just Ursula told me that the formalities had begun. I did as he asked, carefully describing the goblets I had seen in Mother Lee's possession, and going on to their indignant retrieval by Hector and Stephen, on the unlikely ground that they were family heirlooms. Weston, at the second desk, wrote rapidly.

Cecil said: 'Hector and Stephen Mercer. Two brothers. Did they ever speak of their third partner? Did they ever mention his name?'

'I heard him mentioned, yes. I think he joins them as they sail from Rye. It was just a reference in passing; they didn't say his name though they said his ship was of the same design as theirs. Their mother says she has met him, but only briefly and knows nothing about him. Oh yes, and I did ask if they ever had any trouble with pirates and they said their ships were well-armed, and were . . . I don't know much about ships . . . but they said theirs were a kind of carrack, based on a Portuguese design but faster, and their third partner had a similar vessel.'

'Very good, Ursula!' Without looking round, I could hear

Weston's quill racing across the paper. 'Can you recall anything else, anything at all, any detail? Did they ever speak of how they dispose of the goods they bring in, for instance? What kind of goods are they?'

'They brought a jaguar skin home as a present for their mother. And they brought their sister a wedding gift of an emerald pendant, and they said they had had it cut and set by a jeweller they knew in London.' I was thinking aloud. 'So they must have brought it home uncut,' I said. 'The jeweller had a curious name – Roebuck, that was it.'

'Theobald Roebuck?'

'Yes. Yes! That is what they said. Or one of them said; I can't remember which.'

'Theobald Roebuck is a jeweller all right. He is known to us. He is also a moneylender with a slightly dubious reputation. That is to say, some dubious people use his services. This becomes very interesting, Ursula. Now – let us return to the goblets. Mistress Stannard, you are truly sure about them, are you?'

'Yes, I am. They are distinctive and I saw them very clearly when Hector and Stephen were taking them back from Mother Lee. Stephen held one up to the light.'

'Good. All the same . . .' Cecil leant back in his chair and contemplated the ceiling beams above his head. 'Before you went to the wedding, we had suspicions about the Mercer boys. This business of the goblets seems to confirm those suspicions but it may not be so certain. There may be other goblets made to the same pattern. For all we know, there's a goldsmith in Spain who makes them as regular stock items. Those that we saw in Captain Tyler's house do suggest that the Mercer boys are self-appointed privateers, but we still can't be sure. The Mercers may have bought theirs or traded for them – costly mementoes, perhaps, of a particularly successful voyage. And if they do have really successful voyages, then perhaps the family jewellery may be the result of honest trading.'

I had something else on my mind. I said: 'How did you know I was going to that wedding? Oh, Laurence Miller, I suppose.'

Cecil ceased his study of the beams and smiled at me. 'You

are a half-sister to the queen and as you well know, for your own protection, we like to know where you are and with whom. Your current guardian angel is indeed Laurence Miller, the senior groom at that little stud of trotters you have at Hawkswood. Yes, he told us that you were going to Evergreens.'

'I suppose I should feel safer because you watch over me but sometimes I feel I am merely being watched. Miller embarrasses me every time I see him. I can *feel* him watching me.'

I saw Cecil's mouth twitch. 'I am aware,' he said, 'because you have admitted it freely to various people, that one of your husbands nicknamed you Saltspoon because of your sharp tongue. How right he was. Mistress Stannard, what you told me in the carriage *may* have made your visit to Evergreens far more important than either Walsingham or I ever expected. Please will you now give me, step by step, an account of everything that happened, everything you heard or saw, during your visit there. Never mind if you repeat anything you have already said. Are you keeping up, Weston?'

'Yes, my lord,' said the secretary. He was a pale young man who didn't look as though he saw much of the open air. But he was clearly competent. His quill had been working so smoothly. Cecil turned back to me.

'Begin from your arrival at Evergreens, and describe every single thing you can recall, of your stay.'

I tried my best. It took some time. *Every single thing*, Cecil had said. That meant including the unhappy story of how Joan had forced Arabella into agreeing to marry Sylvester Waters. I did that with reluctance. Cecil listened without interrupting. Weston's quill softly scratched.

When I finished, Cecil said: 'Tell me, apart from the oddity about Mistress Mercer making such an over-generous gift to the herb woman, and the boys claiming that the goblets were family heirlooms, and your obvious sympathy for the unwilling bride – poor lass, I hope things turn out well for her in the end – did you observe anything that to you seemed strange?'

'Dale did! Dale has a knack sometimes of having feelings about things and she is often right.'

'Go on.'

'She told me that she sensed something wrong and I think

– yes, I think it was because when the Mercer boys came home, they weren't full of tales about their voyage, the way sailors mostly are. Hector Mercer did at one point start to tell us a tale about a jaguar hunt and Mistress Mercer told him not to boast. Oh! I have left something out! I recall now. I *did* overhear something curious.'

'Please tell me.'

'Joan Mercer was angry with the boys about something and it sounded again as though she was warning Hector not to boast. She was speaking French – that's why she didn't lower her voice when I passed close to her. I suppose she didn't think I would understand, but I did. Let me see . . .'

I thought for a moment. 'She called Hector a fool. She said he was drinking too much and causing trouble. She said, *If I hadn't stopped you in time you'd have boasted about other things besides jaguars. Where will we be if Master Andrews hears you? He's a magistrate!* It was at the wedding celebrations, just after the feast. A Master Andrews was one of the guests. I think I have it roughly right.'

'Intriguing!' said Cecil. He leant back in his chair and took his eyeglasses off to give them another rub with the cloth. 'Evidence that the Mercers have been up to something they shouldn't. Though there's still no definite proof of serious wrongdoing. The boys may simply not have declared all their dutiable goods, or maybe broken the law in some other manner likely to interest a magistrate but it needn't necessarily have been wholesale piracy.'

Resuming his eyeglasses, he said: 'Before we can accuse them of bringing in illicit treasure and throwing Captain Prettyman into the Atlantic, we need solid proof. For one thing, ships coming into Rye, as at other ports, are searched for contraband. So far, nothing questionable has ever been found in their ships or we would know of it.'

'Before they came to Rye, couldn't they have landed it abroad?' I asked. 'I know that in Italy and Amsterdam, there are businessmen who act as depositories for other men's wealth. They're called bankers. Turning gold bricks and ornaments and bags full of uncut emeralds into money here might be difficult for the Mercers. Getting it to one of those banks

would be the obvious thing to do. Or would it? They're . . .
they're not . . .'

I stopped, trying to clarify something that I had instinctively
felt. Finally, I said: 'They must be good seamen. They captain
their own ships. I think they know a great deal about ships.
But they're young and . . . and insouciant . . . and not,
somehow, worldly.'

Cecil was frowning. The line that was always there between
his brows had deepened. 'Walsingham and I know about those
bankers, and about their English clients. We have many agents,
abroad as well as in England. We also hear news now and
then from men who have their own callings but are in a
position to hear things – I think you understand me – and who
sometimes pass useful information to us. We pay them, of
course.'

'Yes, I know.' I did know. Walsingham in particular was
an information-hungry spider who lived at the centre of a
vast web of agents. He had inherited a network dating from
the days of my father King Henry, when there wasn't a well-
to-do house in the land that didn't have among its servants
at least one spy in the pay of the Crown. The spy would
listen to the talk at table, reporting anything that sounded
seditious. King Henry lived in fear of traitors. Walsingham
had taken over that network, and improved on it. I waited
for Cecil to go on.

'Through these informants,' he said, 'we know who
approaches these establishments and who does not. One thing
I can tell you, straightaway, is that the Mercers have never
even landed in Italy or the Netherlands, as far as we can tell.
They have certainly not had dealings with the bankers in those
countries. But you say that they have dealings with Roebuck.
He has contacts with these foreign bankers.'

He pushed his chair back, got up and began, limpingly, to
pace the room. I could see that his gout was troubling him
and I wished he would sit down again. Weston rested his quill,
but his eyes were on Cecil, as were mine.

After a moment, however, he threw himself back into his
chair and said: 'Ursula, the treasure is the key. We need to prove
that the Mercer boys really do bring home treasure that they

can't account for legally. If they are going to use Roebuck, then they have to get it to London. Tell me, if you were the Mercer boys, how would you go about it? Your brains are younger than mine and they are brains descended from the Tudors who have always been . . . highly intelligent.' He meant *more devious even than I am* but was too wary to say so.

There was a silence, while I tried, inside my head, to become Hector or Stephen, young ship's captains, with treasure in my hold, that I had snatched from both Spanish and English vessels. What in the world, I asked myself silently, had made me behave like this? Why wouldn't I seek a proper commission? I found an answer. The trio just didn't want to share their gains with the Treasury as well as with their crews. And perhaps didn't want to limit their operations to Spanish shipping, either!

Slowly, I said: 'If when they tie up at Rye, their ships are innocent and they're not known to have called at any foreign ports, then they must still have landed their treasure somewhere else first. Presumably somewhere else in England.'

I thought a little more. 'Perhaps the third member of their little fleet goes to the bankers for them. No, that's not right. In that case, why would they need Roebuck? Assume that they do land their – shall I call it loot? – in England. They would most likely bring it secretly ashore somewhere along that south-east coast. Is that a suitable coast for secret landings?'

'Yes, it is,' Cecil said.

'The third member of the group sees to that, perhaps, while the others are tying up at Rye! He lands it, hides it, and then brings his ship into Rye later, as though it has nothing to do with the Mercers. Then, once they are all ashore, they can retrieve the loot at leisure and take it wherever they like. In a cart, perhaps, with vegetables or hay on top. I suppose it would be heavy but it need not be bulky. You could put a fortune in gemstones into quite a small bag.'

Cecil raised his eyebrows. 'Have you ever thought of going in for piracy, Ursula?'

'Dale gets seasick.'

Cecil and Weston both burst out laughing. Cecil pulled a napkin out of his sleeve, wiped his eyes on it and then said:

'You do me good, Saltspoon! No wonder the queen likes your company. You have just presented me with an entire theory of how they could bring it into England and get it all the way to London, concealed! Now, let me see if we can build on this!'

He got up again and went to his shelves. He pulled out a scroll, brought it to his desk and unrolled it, weighing it down at the corners with his silver paperweights. It was a map.

'This shows the coastline round the south-east corner of England. It's a lonely coast. It is patrolled but believe me, it takes a *lot* of patrolling. They could approach a lonely stretch after dark, as near as possible, and bring the contraband ashore at night, in a small boat or boats. They'd need good weather! Then it could be hidden until they're ready to take it inland and hide it, perhaps to take it to London bit by bit. There are caves near Hastings, but we know about those. No one is hiding illicit treasure in them, I assure you.'

'You could simply arrest the brothers and make them talk,' remarked Weston from behind his desk.

'That's what Walsingham would say,' said Cecil. 'But I don't agree. What if the Mercers are innocent and there is no loot to find? Mistress Stannard's suspicions may be unfounded, and Walsingham's ways of asking questions sometimes produce the wrong answers. Men may make false confessions just to stop the pain. I prefer that honest men should sleep easy in their beds and not be afraid of being taken to the Tower because of mere appearances. Let us consider this map.'

I pulled it nearer to me. There were words written here and there but they were too small for me to read. Cecil took off his eyeglasses and handed them to me. I put them on and almost jumped, because the magnified writing leapt out at me as though it was coming straight off the page. I had never looked through magnifying lenses before. The words were place names. *Hastings. Rye. Romney Marsh. River Rother.* I had heard of most of them but they didn't tell me much now.

Cecil, however, was thinking aloud. 'If they land their treasure somewhere along that coast . . .' His eyes gleamed suddenly. 'Romney Marsh! Great heavens, yes! From there, they could use waterways to bring things a good way from the coast by water. Again, at night. We've already guessed that they have small boats available. What then, though? The water-ways would only lead them a little way inland.'

'They have legal goods to move,' said Weston. 'After clearing the customs at Rye, the Mercers presumably load things on to a wagon or a cart, much as Mistress Stannard has surmised. They could meet the illicit cargo somewhere – at the coast or if the waterways are used, then inland, just where the waterways go no further. Somewhere away from prying eyes, anyway.'

'They could transfer the loot to the carts and pile the respect-able goods on top!' I said, inspired. 'And hide everything, as I suggested, under piles of vegetables or whatever. It would be a sensible precaution anyway. Even the legitimate goods are valuable and even on land, robbers exist. They could hide the loot somewhere near home and take it piecemeal to London and to this man Roebuck. Piecemeal would be best. Not so noticeable and easier for Roebuck himself to handle.'

'I *do* think you would have made a splendid pirate, Ursula.' Cecil was wrinkling his brow. 'Of course, this unknown third partner might bring it the whole way to wherever they keep it pending disposal. In that case, setting men to follow the Mercers after they come ashore at Rye wouldn't help us much. Though since the Mercer brothers are the ones using Roebuck's services, they do presumably take charge of the loot once it's inland.'

He stopped to think further and then said: 'It becomes a fair assumption that whoever brings it in it is hidden some-where in the vicinity of Evergreens. They would want to be able to get at it without too much difficulty. Could the hiding place be in Evergreens itself?'

I shook my head. 'Not actually in the house. It isn't that sort of house. No priests' holes and when there were extra guests at the wedding, the attics were used as bedchambers. There are cellars, but the servants go in and out all the time, fetching up barrels and kegs. But I agree that the hiding place is probably nearby. You mentioned the caves near Hastings. Perhaps there are inland caves somewhere near Evergreens.'

'Thank you, Ursula!' Cecil sounded pleased. 'Yes. Though we still have to find out who is the other partner in the trio.'

He hesitated, and I said: 'Yes?'

'The queen feels it personally,' said Cecil. 'You heard her say that she was angry, and so she is. She is very angry that English ships are being preyed upon by English pirates. She is so angry that during that Audience she said little, because to express her outrage fully would have been to lose her dignity. And now we have this complaint from a French seaman! France is much concerned with her own muddled affairs just now, in the aftermath of King Henry's murder. But she will sort her business out before long and return to the world of foreign policies and we want her to be friendly. Capitaine le Boeuf is a Huguenot. In other words, one of a sect regarded with suspicion by French royalty. He has called on us for support. When France settles down, her new monarch may not like that. Ursula, as you surely know, together, England and France are a bulwark against the Spanish and King Philip may not have finished with us. A confused and outraged France, victimized outside her realm by English pirates, and then finding that though the English are trying to put this right, they are also giving assistance to Huguenots – well, it isn't at all a desirable prospect.'

'I can see that,' I said.

Cecil said: 'It would be useful to have somebody at or near Evergreens, looking for evidence at that end. It would be a much smaller area to scour than Romney Marsh, or a long length of the south coast.'

There was silence for several moments.

Then Cecil said: 'It would mean actual searching, looking for the place where the loot is kept while it is being gradually exchanged for money. Caution would be needed. These young men might turn ruthless if they felt threatened.'

My tongue acted by itself, without my permission. 'I have an excuse to be in that district. I am the landlord of Evergreens. I also have experience in secret work. With the help of Brockley, who is always my right hand, I could search.'

Many, many years before, I had been travelling to Cambridge, in the company of Rob and Mattie Henderson, now long dead, good friends, who had once cared for my daughter Meg when she was a child. As we rode into East Anglia, the land grew flatter; the skies were wider and the wind brought us the scent of water, of marshland and sea. A flock of geese flew overhead, filling the sky with their wild, cold calls.

I was already an agent for the queen with a reputation for getting into dangerous situations. Rob Henderson, riding beside me, had asked me if I would ever settle for an ordinary everyday life and then he answered his own question. He said that I wouldn't, that I would always be ready to answer the call of the wild geese. And I had known that he spoke the truth, that within me there was a wildness. And also, I was a huntress who would never be quite content unless I had a quarry to pursue.

After a few moments, Cecil said: 'I agree that you are as well suited as anyone to undertake this. If you choose to go, I can obtain permission for you to leave the court before your official time. The queen would consent, I think.'

'Yes.' *What am I doing? What am I saying?* I heard myself stating that I would wish to start soon. 'Next week, perhaps – Monday the fourth of September. That will give us, I mean me and the Brockleys, time to pack up and send to Hawkswood for a carriage to come and collect our baggage.'

'I can arrange transport for you, tomorrow if you like.'

'Thank you. I would want to pause at home for a few days. There will be things to attend to there. But I would not waste needless time. I can reach Evergreens in half a day.'

'So you are volunteering.' Cecil was all sobriety now. 'You can stop taking notes, Weston. Ursula, I agree that you are the person best suited for this. But the decision must be yours, not mine.'

Then I did hesitate. Difficulties had suddenly reared up in front of me like awakened dragons. 'Where in the world would I start? I would still have to cover a formidable amount of ground.'

'Well, as you have said, that wouldn't include Evergreens house itself. It could include its grounds and its land. Caves, if there are any. The houses or the land of possible accomplices. Under the floors of deserted outhouses or barns. Things dangled down disused wells. You can only try – and take care.'

'I can't intrude on my tenants for too long. Being their

landlord doesn't entitle me to that. Or . . . let me think . . .'
I was warming to the scheme. 'The Brockleys and I could
stay in Oxted. Perhaps the Old Bell can find room for us. I
know. I can pretend that I am considering buying some land,
or a house, in the district.'

'Why would you want to? People might ask you.'

I ruminated. 'I can say I have distant relatives who wish to
lease a house in the district. I am seeking one on their behalf.
They live in the north of England.' I was inventing, sentence
by sentence. 'One of them has a wife who was born and reared
in this area and wishes to return here. They are elderly,' I said
thoughtfully. 'Hunting for such a house themselves would be
too difficult for them.'

I tried to visualize my imaginary relatives and then remembered Uncle Herbert and Aunt Tabitha, who had brought me up.
Uncle Herbert was now crippled with the joint evil. He certainly
couldn't go hunting for houses.

'As their deputy,' I said, 'I can reasonably ride round the
locality, going here and there. And I can call on my tenants
at Evergreens to ask their advice.'

I could call at Waters House, too, and ask after Arabella.
And I could go into Cutpenny and see Gilbert Gale. I hoped
for his own sake that by now he had found a new love.

'You are sure?' Cecil said. 'We shall pursue the matter at
our end, as it were. Perhaps it's time to take Roebuck in for
questioning. Even if he isn't handling loot for the Mercer
brothers, he may be for somebody else. Ursula, I have heard
the jest that a friend of yours once made about the cry of the
wild geese. You may be about to set off on a wild-goose chase
in good earnest. There may be nothing to find and even if
there is, you may never find it. Or you may happen on it the
day you arrive. And you may run into danger. Take care.'

FIFTEEN
The Goldsmith's Tale

The Old Bell in Oxted was busy when we arrived. The public room was crowded but there was a lively fire. It was raining and we were glad to come indoors and stand by the fire, letting our cloaks steam. It turned out that the available accommodation was limited, but there was one reasonably sized bedchamber for me. The Brockleys would have to share a kennel-sized room over the stables. Eddie, who had once more accompanied us as groom and mule-driver, would have a pallet in the grooms' dormitory. However, the inconvenient sleeping arrangements didn't prevent the Brockleys and me from gathering in my room to talk before supper.

'Once again,' I said, 'I will go over our plans, and Brockley, please don't tell me again that this task is absurd. I know it is. But we still have to do it.'

'The right way to do it,' said Brockley, 'is for you to arrange to be told when the Mercer boys have arrived in Rye, and then be on hand to meet them as they return to Evergreens and try to see where they store whatever goods they bring with them.'

'They may not be the ones who bring it inland. There is this unknown third partner. He may be the one who does that – and hides it, presumably, not far from Evergreens.'

'There's too much presuming,' Brockley complained. 'As I keep saying, madam. Are we *really* going to ride haphazardly round the district, looking for places where a treasure just might be hidden?'

I had only told the Brockleys the full details of my plans when we were well on the road to Oxted. This was because I knew quite well what Brockley would say about them, and I was right. His grumbling had started when we were refreshing ourselves in a Reigate tavern, and he had repeated himself at intervals ever since.

'Not quite,' I said, patiently and not for the first time. 'The excuse of looking for a suitable house for my imaginary cousins will allow us to ride in all directions unquestioned. Wherever we go, we will have our eyes wide open. Just in case we come across something that gives us ideas. We might even enjoy it. Yes, it's serious business but the two things aren't incompatible!

'We must find ways to search obvious places such as Evergreens itself, its land, its outhouses and so on. I think we should also search the grounds – garden and farmland – of Waters House. He's a member of the family now and there's no doubt that Arabella was forced into that marriage. It's supposed to be because Waters was crazy in love with her but there could be a . . . a . . . practical aspect as well. That could be difficult but we must try.'

Part of me agreed with Brockley, that our plans were absurd. The chances of finding what we sought were very poor. Yet somehow the prospect of this whole ridiculous adventure made my spirits rise, and I knew quite well that once the search was under way, Brockley would warm to it as he had warmed to other assignments in the past. Dale, dear loyal Dale, would join in because she loved us both. She would trust us to keep her from harm. And there were reasons, good reasons, why we must undertake this apparently ridiculous quest.

'We have to try,' I said, 'because we owe it to the queen, to England. English ships have been attacked. That has made the queen angry and it makes me angry too. Anything that could help to put a stop to it is worth the effort.'

Autumn was near. Leaves were still green, but it was a tired, heavy green, and windy weather had begun to tear some of the leaves down before they had had time to turn. The wet day had led to an equally wet evening. A servant had been sent to light a fire in the hearth and Brockley was squatting on a low stool beside it, tending it with a poker.

Looking up, he said: 'I doubt if the Mercer boys will go to sea in winter. Winter's a time for repairing ships and cleaning the barnacles off their hulls. The Mercers should soon be coming home from their last voyage of the season, that is, if they aren't home already. But if they're not . . . madam, you may be right that the third partner is the one who will bring the loot to its hiding place. I think we should be on the watch for any wagons or laden pack horses arriving in the district and try to see what happens to their contents. What do you say?'

'I agree. We must keep our eyes open all the time, for anything at all that might bear on this. I intend to call on Joan Mercer tomorrow,' I said. 'We'll find out then when the boys are expected. Now, just to be sure that we all know the story we're telling, let's go through it again. John Thornton is a distant cousin of my mother. He and his wife Catherine live in the north of England – in Yorkshire – because John is a Yorkshireman. He owns three farms and lives on their rents. Catherine, however, was born in this district.'

'We had best be vague about exactly where,' said Brockley. 'Or for sure we'll meet someone who knows that there never was a girl called Catherine born in Oxted or Cutpenny or Caterham – none of them are all that far away – who married a man from the north. Old inhabitants have memories like Norman castles – nearly indestructible.'

'We needn't be too knowledgeable about distant cousins,' I said. 'We only know that Catherine was born somewhere in this part of the world. In old age, she has become homesick. So on their behalf, we're looking for a house near here. Have we all committed that to memory?'

They had. 'So,' I continued, 'we enquire of the landlord here whether he knows of any likely houses for sale or lease. And naturally, as I am the owner of Evergreens, we make a courtesy call there, and also we ask Joan's advice. If we hear of any houses, we will visit them and that will be an excuse for travelling about the locality. And somehow or other, we must search Evergreens and Waters House, and their land. And look for caves, of course.'

'Inland?' Dale queried.

'Oh yes. There are inland caves,' Brockley assured her. 'There are some near Dorking, I believe, so why not here?'

I said: 'I only suggest that we search Evergreens, as a matter of thoroughness. I really don't expect to find anything in the house. When I was given the deeds of Evergreens, I was also given a detailed description of it. I believe Cecil drew it up. There are no secret places there.'

'I would agree with you, madam,' Brockley said.

Thoughtfully, I added: 'If I were a pirate hiding stolen gold, I'd prefer not to carry it into my own home. The servants might find it! But it might be on Evergreens land. As far as I know, all the outbuildings are in constant use, but there may be chinks, as it were. And the Waters land certainly has some wild areas. Anyway, I must visit Waters House and see how Arabella is.'

'There's nothing to be done for Mistress Arabella, madam,' Brockley demurred. 'She's wed, she's Mistress Waters and that's that.'

'I know, Brockley. But if she's well and content, that would be something to tell Gilbert Gale.'

'Would he want to know that, ma'am?' Dale asked, shocked.

'It might be a relief in a way,' Brockley told her. 'It might make him freer in his mind. I don't think he would like to think of her unhappy and pining. He struck me as a decent young fellow.'

'But what if she's not happy?' Dale asked.

'We hold our tongues,' I said. 'What else can we do? Now, shall we go to supper?'

The landlord of the Old Bell was heavily built with thick lips and large pointed ears. He was a constantly busy man and though civil to his guests, he didn't hobnob much with them. To talk to him, you had to catch him in flight, as it were, between doing something in the kitchen and attending to the brewer who was delivering beer casks at the back door, while simultaneously shouting up the stairs to someone to make up the bed in number two or check all the mousetraps.

When we did finally pin him down, he had just come out of the kitchen, where, to judge from the bloodstained hands that he was wiping on an equally bloodstained apron, he had been chopping meat. He was courteous enough but unhelpful. He didn't know of any houses nearby that were either for sale or rent. Did these people want land with their new homes, or only gardens or not even gardens?

The Brockleys looked nonplussed but I said firmly: 'They have farmland in Yorkshire, which is rented out and is their source of income. They will keep all that. They will want a garden, and they'll employ a gardener.'

He shook his head slowly, but just then, the brisk young serving man who had brought us our breakfast came by and stopped, having overheard us.

'Caterham's the place to go,' he said. 'There's a fellow there who does it for a living – finds places for folk to live, I mean. Can't see how he makes a living at it, myself; folk don't move about that much. There's newlyweds wanting homes, of course, and folk dying and leaving places empty. His name's Rivers, Henry Rivers. Lives opposite the church of St Lawrence. My sister lives close by; she knows him.'

I thanked him and since the landlord was almost hopping from one foot to another in his eagerness to attend to beer barrels and mousetraps, we took our leave.

'We must see this man Rivers,' I said, as we were getting onto our horses. 'He might give us some useful excuses to poke about in various places. But first, Evergreens.'

At this point, I was interrupted by Eddie, who had just given me a leg-up into my saddle. 'Madam, you have told me the purpose of this journey and I have remembered something. On the way here, when we were passing Mother Lee's hill, I heard you remark that though her cottage may still be empty, no one would want to cart treasure all the way up there. But my dad once worked as groom to a goldsmith. He never saw anything of the work, of course – never saw a gold brick in his life. But he sometimes heard the goldsmith talking to his son that he was training up. He used coal for his fires, and it seems that one time he had a dispute with the merchant – thought he'd been given short weight so he went to where the merchant stored his coal and insisted on having his sacks weighed on the great big scales the merchant had.

'My dad couldn't recall what the outcome was, but he did hear his master say that he'd sat himself on the scales, just for fun, and now knew he weighed twelve stone. And since a gold brick weighed two stone, he said, *Son, your father is worth six gold bricks.* He was making a joke of it. Well, quite a few gold bricks would only weigh as much as three or four people, and if you can get a cart up that hill, with a sturdy horse in the shafts, getting a load of valuables up there wouldn't be so difficult.'

'Yes! A small cart could get along that track,' I said. 'Thank you, Eddie!'

'All the same,' I said as we set off, 'that hill would still be quite an obstacle, despite that goldsmith's tale. I never knew anything before about Eddie's forebears. I must ask him if he has any more good stories for winter evenings. Brockley, if you had some bags of emeralds and a whole lot of gold and silver ingots to hide, where would you put them?'

'What would they be in?' asked Dale. 'I mean, boxes, sacks . . .?'

'Gemstones in bags, and if there are several bags, then I expect they'd be stowed in chests,' I said. 'The ingots . . . I don't know . . .'

'Boxes,' said Brockley. 'Nailed shut.'

'And given that these things can't be hidden in your house, where would you put them for safety until you could dispose of them – bit by bit?'

Brockley reined in Firefly, who had taken exception to a wood pigeon when it rose up in front of him with a clatter of wings, and said: 'Burying it would be ideal but difficult. At the back of a cave, with broken rock on top, to look like a rockfall, maybe. Or down a well, though it would need to be one's own well, madam.'

'There's a well at Evergreens,' said Dale.

'In use all day,' I said, thinking of the servants I had seen, forever dipping buckets of water to drink or cook with or wash floors with, or boil linen in. 'For now, we are going to call on Mistress Mercer and I shall ask her about houses for sale or rent. I'll ask after her sons, too. You never know what may emerge.'

'Yes, I know about Henry Rivers,' Joan told me, as we sat in her parlour, nibbling nuts and raisins and drinking cider. 'My sons consulted him when I was looking for somewhere to rent. He was the one who told me that Evergreens was available. I'm sure he can help you. He doesn't actually make a living at it, of course. He's a pieman – makes hot pies for the local workmen to buy as noon pieces.'

'Indeed? Madam, we must sample his wares,' said Brockley. Our eyes met, with a glint of amusement. Years ago, when I was engaged on one of the unusual duties I undertook for the queen, I had worked for a while in a pie shop.

'And your sons?' I said conversationally to Joan, as I scooped up a handful of raisins. 'Are they still at sea? The autumn gales will start soon.'

'Oh, they're already home, though they're not here now. What a pity you missed them. They spent two nights with me and then went off to London – they always come home with business to see to; disposing of the goods they bring back from the New World. They'll have timed their visit to London to fit in with a market.'

I wondered precisely what the goods consisted of but this was a question I could hardly ask. Joan's mind was elsewhere, anyway. 'I am always relieved to see them safely ashore,' she said. 'Every time there's a high wind, I worry. I imagine what it must be like at sea.'

As if making a casual enquiry, Brockley said: 'Do your sons always sail together, Mistress Mercer?'

'Oh yes, always. The *Peregrine* – that's Hector's – and the *Osprey*, that's Stephen's, are sister vessels. They sail in company with another ship, the *Silver Mermaid*, to make a little fleet. It's safer if ships travel in groups.'

Captain Tyler and Capitaine le Boeuf had both been attacked by a group of three smaller vessels. The *Peregrine*, the *Osprey*, the *Silver Mermaid*? Every small piece of new information that came my way drew suspicion closer to certainty.

I had better be careful. I thanked Heaven that this time I had not brought Harry and Ben. If we were approaching the kernel of a business involving piracy then I didn't want my two boys anywhere near it. Danger was built into it.

Mercifully, Harry, full of the vitality of a young man nearing eighteen, had been happy to stay at Hawkswood and practise the art of being the master of my house and lands. He had done so before and now had a taste for it. Meanwhile, Ben would go on learning about the management of Hawkswood estate. The tutor Peter Dickson would help them both and as long as nothing happened to Adam during the next four or five years, so that Peter and Adam were both there to guide and instruct, the future of the boys and of Hawkswood would be provided for.

I emerged from these cogitations, to realize that it was time for us to leave. I dared not question Joan any further about the activities of her sons. *Joan, dear, can you tell us where your sons hide the jewels and ingots they steal from other ships and bring home in wagons disguised as haywains or vegetable harvests?*

I could scarcely imagine what the reaction would be but it certainly wouldn't include a helpful answer.

There was just one question left that I could ask. 'And how is your daughter Arabella?' I asked. 'I hope she is happily settled now as Mistress Waters?'

'I see little of Arabella,' said Joan, evasively. 'I think she is entirely taken up with being the mistress of her new home, and after all our . . . our conflict, I think that perhaps she herself doesn't want to see too much of me. She might have to eat humble pie and admit that I was right! They entertain, I believe, but they don't entertain me. Nor do I intrude on them with invitations. I dare say the boys will call on their sister, when they come home.'

Conversation lapsed and I took the hint. I thanked Joan for her hospitality, declined her polite (but not enthusiastic) invitation to dine, and led the Brockleys out of the house.

'Cutpenny,' I said as we rode through the arch of the gatehouse, nodding to Joe Jankin on the way. 'Today we are paying calls, and hoping to pick up something useful, though it isn't likely. I want to see Gale and not just in case he has news of Arabella. There may be useful gossip in the village. After that, we call at Waters House. Tomorrow we start serious house-hunting.'

'You make it sound real, ma'am,' said Dale.

'I'm almost beginning to believe in it myself,' I said. 'But that will make us seem all the more convincing.'

SIXTEEN
An Inhospitable House

Cutpenny hadn't changed. We rode slowly along the street, nodding now and then to people who recognized us, and dismounted at Gilbert's door. Within it, we could hear the sound of a plane in use. A pair of village boys appeared as if by conjury, and offered to hold our horses. A couple of farthings changed hands and we left the horses with them and went inside. Gilbert looked up as we came in, realized who we were, and stopped work.

'Mistress Stannard! And Master Brockley and your wife! Are you making another stay at Evergreens?'

'Not this time,' I said, and came out with my tale of seeking a house for imaginary relatives. 'We just thought we would call on you while we were here. To see how you . . . how things are.'

Gilbert stood back from the workbench, brushing his hands together. 'My work prospers.' Then, abruptly, he said: 'Have you called on Mistress Arabella?'

He hadn't found a new love. His eyes were hungry. 'We haven't visited Waters House yet,' I said. 'I understand, though, that she is with child. I hope all goes well. It seems that she sees little of her mother. I wondered if you had news of her.'

'I don't know of anyone who has,' Gilbert said. 'The Waters House servants come here sometimes, buying this or that, but Mistress Waters never comes. It's as if she has vanished into that house. A couple of weeks ago, Mistress Pole – the apothecary's wife – told me that she had to deliver something to Waters House and saw Arabella walking in the garden, but that's all. It's as though she's hidden behind a stone wall. So, she is with child. I hope . . .'

He stopped. His brown eyes looked straight into mine. 'If you call there and manage to see her, or even just find out anything about her, would you tell me whatever news of her there is? And once more, if you can, tell her that I am at her service, if ever she has need of me.'

I looked at him with pity. Love, the genuine thing, is the most glorious of emotions. It is also the most painful. Denied, it can gnaw you from within, making the whole world meaningless. I had only experienced it once, and that was with my first husband, Gerald Blanchard. The pain of his loss had been so intense that I had never spoken of it, to anyone. On the outside, I had kept a calm face. I had had much to do, to find a new way of life for myself; to care for my little daughter Meg; to pay her nurse. Inside, yes, I was gnawed.

You recover in the end as you might from a wound. Blood ceases to flow; the scar ceases to ache; it becomes possible to begin again. My new beginning had been Matthew, but I knew before long that what I felt for him was mainly physical, born from the demands of a hungry young body. My marriage to Hugh had been for practical reasons and the deep contentment I had found with him had been unexpected. Perhaps that was better than passion. Passion was like a climate in which there were occasional thunderstorms. The very strength of the feeling can sometimes cause explosive moments. Even Gerald and I had had those.

If Gilbert's feelings were passionate in the same way, and I thought they might be, I pitied him.

'We certainly intend to call at Waters House,' I said. 'If you wish, we will tell you any news we hear. After that, we intend going to Caterham and the quickest way is back through Cutpenny anyway so we may see you again then.'

Gilbert gave me a sudden wry smile. 'She's someone else's wife. I've no right even to think about her. I know that. If she is happy, I will be glad of it and in time I shall stop thinking about her. I worry about her, that's all.'

Very gently, Dale said: 'We understand.'

As we rode away from the village, Brockley, quite abrasively, enquired: 'Madam, are we here to look for a treasure hoard or to find out how Mistress Arabella is faring?'

I decided to ignore the abrasiveness. 'Both,' I said calmly.

'Double duty. We're going to Waters House now, keeping our eyes open. Then we'll go to Caterham, returning through Cutpenny, and see this man Rivers. Perhaps we should have gone to Waters House first, but I really did want to see Gale.'

The tracks were muddy after yesterday's rain. We were well on our way to Waters House, with Brockley grumbling that the mud would mean washing fetlocks when we got back to the inn, when he suddenly stiffened and reined in. 'Madam! Stop a moment. Look what's been along this track ahead of us.'

'Someone's ridden along here before us,' said Dale, peering down over Blue Gentle's shoulder. 'But why shouldn't they? There are hoofprints going the other way as well. Just people going to and fro from Waters House.'

'Not those prints,' said Brockley. 'Over here to the left – partly on the bank – there are wheel marks too. A wagon, I'd say, and a big horse in the shafts. Maybe the driver had to move over to let someone past. That's why the marks have gone onto the verge. Big horse, heavy wagon. The hoofprints point forward.'

I leant down but I couldn't see what Brockley was seeing. I was willing to take his word for it, but . . .'

'But what does it prove?' I asked. 'Anyone might use a wagon to bring in something heavy. Maybe Master Waters has just bought himself a new sideboard.'

'Or the Mercer boys have been taking chests of gems and boxes of ingots to a place of safety.'

'We had better track these marks and see where they lead,' I said.

But we couldn't. The ground rose a little and the path, having been drained, grew drier. The marks faded out. There was a fork just before we reached the steeper track up to Waters House, and a well-used track led off to the left. We couldn't see any wheel marks on it. Brockley did think that he could see a trace of a wheel mark on the path up to Waters House, but admitted that it didn't mean much. Master Waters might of course be hiding illicit treasure in his cellars to oblige his brothers-in-law but it was far more likely that he really had been buying a sideboard or a dining table or a wagonload of logs for winter firewood, or a cartload of fat, snorting pigs for his farm, or . . . the possibilities were endless.

'Well, let's get there,' I said impatiently.

It was my first visit to Waters House. I had to explain us to the lodge-keeper, before he opened the gate for us and sent his boy running ahead to announce us. When we reached the front door, a couple of grooms were there to take our horses, and a sandy-haired woman, dressed in black and with a bunch of keys jangling at her girdle, had stepped out of the front door to greet us and tell us that she was the housekeeper, Mrs Truebody.

'I understand that you are Mistress Ursula Stannard and her companions the Brockleys, who attended the master's wedding. Welcome to Waters House. Please come in. I will tell the master that you're here.'

'How does Mistress Arabella fare?' I enquired. 'We understand that she is with child. She and Master Waters must be so happy.'

'Indeed they are.' It was a brief and expressionless reply. 'Come this way.'

She showed us into a parlour and asked us to wait. She then left us and after that, no one came near us for some time. There was no sign of the usual offering of things to eat and drink.

'This is a peculiar house,' said Dale, in a half whisper.

'More than peculiar,' I said. 'Inhospitable.' We continued to wait until at last, Brockley said: 'I can hear footsteps.'

So could I. They were heavy; not Arabella's.

The door opened and there was Master Waters, tall and cold-featured as ever, but behind him came the expected refreshment tray, in the hands of a big dark man, dressed in black, like Mrs Truebody. I had rarely seen a chillier pair of eyes. Waters, addressing him as Hammond, told him to set it out on one of the small tables with which the room was furnished, and the dark man did so, drawing the table in question closer to us and arranging things on it with skilful neatness. I realized that I had seen him before; he had of course been beside Master Waters at the wedding.

He withdrew, and Master Waters said: 'I trust you are all well. What brings you back to this part of the world? Are you staying with Mistress Mercer at Evergreens?'

'No, at the Old Bell in Oxted,' I said, and launched into my tale of elderly cousins who had commissioned me to find a house for them. Master Waters nodded sagely and regretted that he didn't know of any suitable property in the neighbourhood.

'And how is Mistress Arabella?' I asked, for the second time.

The words *Where is she?* hung in the air.

Waters seemed surprised. 'Did Mrs Truebody not tell you? Arabella has gone on a visit to some of my relations. She is quite properly anxious to form friendships with her new family. My aunt Susannah – she lives in Kent – has been eager to see my new wife and Aunt Susannah can't travel nowadays. She's too old. So I have sent Arabella on a visit. I expect her to make a stay of some weeks. I am so sorry.'

There was no invitation to stay and dine and I would have declined it, anyway. We took our leave. Hammond showed us out. Our horses had been well cared for, we saw. Their hooves and legs were clean and their coats had been brushed. Brockley's dark chestnut Firefly was clearly in a bouncy mood. He whinnied shrilly as he was led out and when Brockley mounted, he tried to prance. We bade goodbye to the grooms and to Mrs Truebody, who was standing in the front doorway to see us off, and rode away, with Brockley firmly controlling Firefly's antics and telling him to remember he was an old gentleman now, not a silly colt.

But when we were through the gate and out on the track that led back towards Evergreens and Cutpenny, Brockley said: 'Master Waters was lying. Mistress Waters hasn't gone to visit his relatives. She's upstairs in Waters House. When Firefly whinnied, I saw her face appear at an upper window. It vanished almost at once; I think she was jerked back. But I'm sure I'm right. It was Mistress Arabella all right.'

'So what do we tell Gilbert Gale?' Dale asked. 'He is expecting us to tell him something, is he not, ma'am?'

I was thinking. Finally, I said: 'We don't want to start trouble. Arabella is married and in the care of her husband. She's pregnant, we know that. We had better say that we weren't able to talk to her but we did catch a glimpse of her and we think she's all right.'

'But do we believe that?' Dale said.

'I don't,' Brockley said roundly. 'But I don't think we can do anything about it. Mistress Stannard is right. We can't interfere.'

'I wonder if her mother knows more,' said Dale.

'I asked her,' I said. 'You were there. I met with a stone wall. She said she doesn't see much of Arabella and thinks that Arabella may not want to see much of her, as she might have to admit her mother was right. I doubt if we'll get anything further from Joan.'

We bypassed Evergreens and went straight on, back to the village. Gilbert Gale heard our approaching hoofbeats and stepped out of his workshop to meet us. He looked at us without speaking but his face was one expressive question.

We drew up and I said the words I had planned. 'We weren't able to see Mistress Arabella, but we did catch a glimpse of her at a window. She is safe enough. Her husband seems anxious to protect her.'

Gilbert was a long way from being gullible. He looked up at me, very straitly. 'I hope that's true. But should you have the chance, mistress,' he said, 'tell her that if she needs me, I am here.'

'He saw through me,' I said ruefully, as we set out on the road to Caterham. 'I hope he behaves sensibly.'

'There isn't much we can do about that, madam,' Brockley said. 'We'd better see this man Rivers.'

He wasn't difficult to find for his pie shop was doing brisk business. We ourselves were feeling the need to eat by that time. We found a small green, tethered the horses nearby, and the Brockleys went to buy pies for us all, and ask a few questions.

'What is he like?' I asked when they came back.

'Younger than I expected,' sad Brockley. 'Sleeves rolled up, long wrists, long fingers, spotty face, long hair tied back. Businesslike. And knowledgeable. I asked a casual question about caves – said someone had told me there were caves nearby and I'd been surprised because you never find caves inland, do you? He said that yes, he knows of one cave, a couple of miles north-east of Evergreens. He also gave me the names of three possible houses, two in Caterham and a lonely one that you come to if you ride past the cave for another half a mile or so.'

'I wonder if that's a likely hiding place,' I said. 'If the occupants are paid, they might be willing to co-operate.'

Brockley said: 'Apparently, the place is a farmhouse called Three Springs but there isn't a farm there now. The couple who lived there grew old and sold the land. Then the man died and his wife went to live with a married daughter. The house is empty, except that there's a pair of servants, a man and wife, looking after it and feeding a few hens, until someone else takes over. Rivers knows because they sometimes come into Caterham to buy things and they told him about the house being up for rent – there's a landlord – because he's known for advising people who are looking for houses. We can look for the cave with the excuse that we're going to Three Springs.'

'Tomorrow,' I said. 'We've done enough here and there riding for one day.'

SEVENTEEN
Mad Jack Johnson

'It's strange, ma'am,' Dale said the next morning, as we once again skirted Evergreens, and rode on past its fields, 'but this feels almost jolly. A lady with her maid and a gentleman in attendance; what could be more commonplace? No one would guess what we're about. I suppose that what we are doing is dangerous but it feels more like an outing.'

'The fate of England doesn't hang on it,' I said. 'English pirates preying on English ships is treachery, and if they aren't paying their share into the Treasury, that's theft. But it isn't conspiring with Philip of Spain to help him launch an invasion. We know what that means.'

There was a sober moment, as we remembered the previous year, when Philip had sent his Armada against England and I had found myself caught up in an attempt to discover his battle plan. The fate of England had been in the balance all that year. Then we came to ourselves, and laughed, because the dull weather had given place to sunshine, and even Dale, who had never been much of a rider, was happy in Blue Gentle's saddle because the pace of the little ambling mare was so smooth that Dale had only, as I had heard her say, to sit there and be carried.

It was at that point that I noticed that Brockley's doublet was bulging oddly, that he had saddlebags slung in front of his saddle and that he was wearing a sword. I was so used to him that although I must have seen his saddlebags and sword from the moment we set out, I hadn't paid attention. Now, I said: 'Brockley, you're wearing your breastplate! And what is in those saddlebags?'

'If we're at all likely to find ourselves exploring a cave, madam, we might need light. I've brought a couple of lanterns and a tinderbox and I obtained some food and a flask of water from the inn, in case we miss dinner, as we did yesterday. And yes, I have my sword and breastplate. We are challenging pirates, madam, and such men are as dangerous as the Spaniards they rob. I notice that you have as usual an open skirt over your charmingly embroidered kirtle and I would be very surprised if you haven't got a set of picklocks and a concealed dagger about you.'

'Yes, I have. I decided to carry them today,' I said. 'This isn't such a jolly outing after all, Dale.'

'If we find a cave, ma'am, please, I won't want to enter it.'

'I wouldn't let you enter it,' said Brockley. 'Or you, madam, unless I knew it was safe.'

And for a few fleeting seconds, it was there again: a moment in which Brockley and I were linked, as we had sometimes been in the past, caught up in adventures, dangers, which Dale did not share. Bonded as we had been when we hovered on the brink of becoming lovers. We had drawn back from that brink, but ever since, there had been occasional times when we remembered and though our bodies were not united and never had been, never would be, still our minds were connected. To cover the moment, to prevent Dale from noticing it, because she sometimes did and it hurt her, I said briskly: 'I suppose we'll be taking the left-hand fork at the foot of the slope up to Waters House. It's the only one going in the right direction. I imagine it will lead to this place Three Springs that Rivers told us about.'

'Didn't he say there were caretakers there?' Dale remarked. 'They'd use the track, I suppose. Isn't that the turn?'

As we guided our horses to the left, however, all of us glanced up towards Waters House. Brockley said: 'Mistress Arabella is there, right enough. I know I saw her.'

'*We* can't do anything about that,' I said. 'But I would like to know much more about Waters. He may well be hand in glove with the Mercer boys. With Joan's connivance, he has just become their brother-in-law. Well, for Waters, having Hector and Stephen as brothers-in-law might be a blade with a double edge. I think we should call on Joan Mercer again, once her sons are back home. They're Arabella's brothers, after all. *They* may be interested in her welfare.'

Then Dale made us laugh. 'We want to know what they are up to,' she said, 'and we want to enlist their help for Arabella. It's like a fork with two prongs.'

The track wound round the foot of the hill where Waters House stood, and met a broader road, which I knew would take us to Oxted if we turned on to it and rode southwards. The path that we were on resumed on the far side. 'I think we go that way,' said Brockley, pointing.

We crossed and continued eastward. The country grew rougher and a steep hillside arose on our left. There was a place where, at one time, there had surely been a landslide, for the ground at the foot of the hill was a mass of lumps and bumps, as if, during the years, grass had grown over rubble. The hillside above was steep enough in places to present perpendicular patches of rockface.

Brockley saw it first. Despite the steepness of the hill on our left, there was a zigzag path just like the path up to Mother Lee's cottage and Brockley, rising in his stirrups, suddenly pointed. 'There's the cave!'

'But is it?' Dale asked. 'I can only see a dark crack in the rock, slanting sideways.'

'It would look bigger at close quarters,' Brockley said and began to dismount.

'Are we going up there?' Dale asked doubtfully.

'I am. You and the mistress stay here and hold my horse,' said Brockley, delving into his nearside saddlebag and removing a leather bag which presumably held the lantern and the tinderbox. 'I'll go up and see what there is to see.'

'Dale can hold the horses,' I said, slipping out of my saddle. 'I'm coming up to the cave as well.'

'But, madam . . .!'

'Yes, I am, Brockley. Don't argue.'

The path was steep and before we were halfway there, I was out of breath. Even though I had no farthingale and only my smallest ruff, I was hardly dressed for tackling such a climb. By the time we reached the cave mouth, I was damp with sweat as well. Even Brockley was panting a little.

Once we were there, the crack in the rock still looked like a crack. It didn't in the least resemble my idea of a cave mouth. However, it was big enough for a man to pass through. Brockley put the leather bag down and took out the lantern and tinderbox. While he was lighting the lantern candle, I stepped up to the crack and peered in, expecting to see darkness. What I saw instead was something like a room, dimly lit, which puzzled me, for not much light could get in through the crack, even if I were not blocking it. Then I realized that it was lantern light, though I couldn't see where the lantern was. There was something that looked like a table and something else that seemed to be trailing blankets as if from a disturbed bed, and then I jerked back, quickly. '*Brockley!*'

I said it fiercely, but in a whisper. 'What is it?' Brockley asked, also in a whisper.

'There's a light inside and somebody is there. I saw a movement.'

From somewhere within the cave, there was a rustling sound. We both tensed, listening. The rustling was followed by a couple of bumps and then a voice growling what were surely curses. There was an echo in the cave, confusing the sound. Alarmed, I drew further back and Brockley, drawing his sword, put himself in front of me, just in time, before an astounding apparition burst out of the crack.

It was roughly human-shaped, but its bones jutted as though they were ready to break through its dirty skin. It was long-legged and long-armed, with grey-brown hair streaming over its – his? – shoulders, a beard stretching halfway down the naked chest and the prominent ribs, and no garment but a loincloth. It – I couldn't then and can't now think of the creature as *he* – had gaps in its teeth and its voice was distorted. It waved its bony arms in wild shooing gestures and shouted incomprehensibly. I shrieked and Brockley raised his sword. At that moment, it finally achieved something intelligible.

'Who're you, interfering wi' me, wakin' me up, not harmin' 'ee am I, sleepin' in my own home? Get away from me! Get away! An' put that bloody sword away; what you think I be, summat in some old tale of knights and ladies? Get *away*, you . . .'

At this point, its gestures became not only wild but rude, and though whatever it was saying was now dissolving back into incoherence, I did make out a few more syllables. It was calling us extremely offensive names. Then it discovered that its loincloth was slipping and it stopped waving its arms, clutched at the cloth with grimy and overgrown fingernails, turned its back on us and disappeared into the cave. Its curses mingled with the echo as it retreated into the depths.

Brockley sheathed his sword and with shaking hands, extinguished the lantern and returned it and the tinderbox back to the bag. We didn't speak. We just fled from the cave and back down the path to our horses, and Dale, and the normal world.

We found Dale staring and trembling. She had seen the apparition rush out of its cave and had thought it would attack us. 'What *was* it?' she said, tearfully, as Brockley took Firefly's reins from her and thrust his bag back into its saddlebag.

'I think it, no, he, was some kind of hermit. Mad and half-starved,' he said. 'If we had taken the food up there with us, I'd have suggested that we leave it at the cave mouth. I expect he lives there, the poor devil.'

Shakily, I said: 'I don't think the Mercer boys will be storing any treasure there. Unless that thing is guarding it, but it wouldn't make a very safe guardian. No, we can forget the cave.'

'Let's go away, ma'am,' pleaded Dale.

Brockley helped me to mount and then swung into his own saddle and we set off, briskly. We had gone some way before I at last found humour in the situation. 'We start out to look for treasure, and find a mad hermit instead. When we get home, how Harry and Ben will enjoy the story!'

'He smelt,' said Brockley. 'Probably hasn't washed for years. I wonder how he lives at all. I'd wager there's a longbow hidden in that cave and that our apparition knows how to set snares and I wouldn't bother myself planting a vegetable patch anywhere near that cave. I dare say he sneaks out at night to steal onions and cabbage for his supper.'

'We had best get on our way to this farmhouse,' I said.

Thankfully, we left the madman and his cave behind. A canter brought us over the top of a gentle rise, and there below us, were fields and a farmhouse, presumably Three Springs. We saw one spring as we rode down the slope, for it started out of a patch of rock to our left, and ran on in the form of a rivulet, bypassing the house below and meandering off into the fields. Smoke was rising from one of the farmhouse chimneys. 'Someone's home,' I said.

The gate to the yard was open. We trotted through, to be greeted by indignant honking from a flock of geese and loud baying from a pair of big dogs, which rushed out to bound round our horses' legs. Firefly tried to kick them. A woman came out and shouted to the dogs. They left us and returned to her but the geese continued to honk around us until the woman fetched a broom, with which she shooed them away.

'I be sorry,' she shouted. 'Never can keep them pestilential geese in order. Be you new tenants, then? I'm Mrs Munn, caretaker and housekeeper. My husband's out, went early, took a cartload of vegetables to Woldingham market!'

Mrs Munn had a worn air, I thought. Like the cave apparition, she had only a few teeth left, and she was thin. Her cap was pushed back and the hair it revealed was scanty and dry, grey with yellow traces. She didn't look like a well woman, though she seemed brisk enough.

'We're sorry to intrude,' I said, dismounting, and letting Brockley help Dale. 'I am not a new tenant, but I have come to look at Three Springs as I am looking for a property to rent on behalf of someone else. My name is Mistress Ursula Stannard and these are my friend Frances Brockley and her husband Roger Brockley.'

I launched into some brief explaining about my imaginary cousins. Mrs Munn curtsied and said we were very welcome. Would we come in and have some refreshment and did we want to water the horses? We said yes so she led us to a trough.

We let the horses drink and then Mrs Munn showed us into a stable. It was clearly in use for there were two stalls with filled hayracks. We stalled our mounts and Brockley, on the helpful excuse of fetching more hay from an adjacent barn, managed to glance into the only two other outbuildings. Returning, he shook his head at me and seized a moment to whisper: 'Nothing anywhere, just empty. No disturbed floors.'

After that, Mrs Munn took us indoors, into a big kitchen

with benches and a couple of chairs, a table in the middle and a fire with a bubbling stockpot on a trivet. We all sat down and she offered us cider.

'We had a shock on the way here,' Brockley said, as Mrs Munn filled his tankard. 'Do you know anything about a cave up on the hillside where it's very steep and there's old rubble at the foot? The cave looks like a big slit in a rock-face. We were curious enough to stop, and we went up to look at the cave. We got a fright.'

'A mad-looking man jumped out at us,' I said. 'Skinny, long wild hair and beard and nothing but a loincloth on, and he cursed us for waking him up. At least, I think that's what he said.'

'Oh, him,' said Mrs Munn, not at all surprised. 'Everyone for miles knows about Mad Jack Johnson. That's his name. Hermit, he is. But he don't harm no one. There's some say that he had money and land once but lost it somehow and it sent him crazed. He lives in that cave, and folk take food to him. Vicar at Woldingham, over to the east, that's our parish, he approves, says that's charity. Keeps Mad Jack from stealing anyhow. Poaching, that's another matter. We all reckon he does a bit of that. He's given other poachers the scare of a lifetime now and then.'

Mrs Munn giggled, and we laughed, too. I could well imagine the feelings of a country poacher, encountering Mad Jack by moonlight, all gaunt and hairy, mouthing oaths and waving long arms and looking like a cross between a crazy man and a monstrous spider.

We finished our cider. 'You'll want to see everything,' Mrs Munn said. 'So as to tell your cousins about the house. Not that there's much. There's a garden, at least, it's mostly a kitchen garden. Not flowers and such. We grow herbs and beans, onions, cabbages, peas, marrows, all what you'd expect. We got fruit trees: apples – lots of apples; I brew me own cider – and we got plums as well. This is a nice quiet place. That's what your cousins will be after, I take it, madam. We got a pig, mind you, and them geese and a few chickens in a run. Up to them if they keep 'un. Well, you've seen the kitchen. Now, there's the parlour . . .'

'How long have you worked here, Mrs Munn?' I asked her, as we surveyed the parlour. It was dusted but had the drab look of disuse.

'All my life, so has my husband. We both had parents working here – that's when there was the farm as well.'

We went on from the dull parlour to the rest of the ground floor. There was a study but this too was dusty; the farm was gone and no one was keeping accounts for the vegetables and the orchard. The rest of the ground floor consisted of a dairy, a cold room where some meat joints hung, and a cider press. Upstairs, three bedchambers led in and out of each other and there were cupboards, one containing sheets and towels. The rest were empty. Dale asked about the necessary house and Mrs Munn showed it to us. It was a square stone building, just outside the back door. 'It's well-built, no draughts and the floor's cobbled,' said Mrs Munn.

Brockley asked about the attics and we were shown them. There were two. One was clean and empty and the other was given over to the storing of apples, which were set out on trays, no apples touching another, so that no rotten apple could infect its neighbours.

This was not at all a likely place for the Mercer boys to use for hiding treasure. There were no safe hiding places – or any hiding places at all come to that – and I couldn't see Mrs Munn being a party to such a thing, nor could it possibly be done without her knowledge.

We took our leave, murmuring platitudes about thinking things over. We had now discovered some places where the Mercer boys were *not* hiding their illicit treasure. In retrospect, Mad Jack Johnson provided us with both laughter and pity, and I know I pitied Mrs Munn. But as far as treasure-hunting went, it was an empty haul.

'Perhaps,' said Brockley, 'they'd be more likely to store anything nearer Evergreens.'

'Yes. This has been an interesting waste of time!' I let us ride on for a few more paces and then said: 'I keep thinking about Waters. Joan Mercer is afraid of him; I'm sure of it. I believe he frightened her into giving Arabella to him though I don't know how. I doubt if the goods can be hidden at

Evergreens, either in the house or on its land. But maybe they are hidden on Waters land. That's our next objective.'

'But, ma'am,' said Dale, 'how can he frighten Mistress Mercer when he is part of it all? If you meant that he might have threatened to tell on her, he can't do that without telling on himself.'

'I said, I didn't know how he could frighten her; I just think he did. Not necessarily by reporting that she is a party to piracy! By now, of course, Arabella may know something. I don't want to put her in danger but if we could speak to her in private . . . if she is kept from being private with us, well, that's a clue.'

'Going back to the idea of searching the Waters land, I think we could only search after dark,' said Brockley.

'We'd have to use lanterns,' I said, 'and be very careful to shield them from the house.'

I then met Brockley's eyes.

'Not you, madam!' said Brockley. 'I know who I can ask to come with me. Gilbert Gale!'

And now, once more, I must leave the telling of this tale to Arabella. She was the one who lived it.

EIGHTEEN

Two Cats: One Mouse

Arabella's Narrative

I didn't know it at the time, but even before I was married to Sylvester Waters, I had begun to change.

My mother, I know, was always subject to my father, when he was alive. Towards me, however, she was stern. She had clear ideas of how young women should think and behave. They should obey their parents. They should never challenge their parents or husbands by becoming angry with the decisions that were made for them. No young lady should ever show anger or even feel it.

My true rebellion began when my mother thrashed me to make me agree to marry Master Waters.

It was the first time she had beaten me, because up to then, I had always been dutiful, said, done, what was expected of me. If I hadn't always *thought* what was expected of me, well, that was another matter. What happens in the privacy of one's own skull is beyond anyone's reach.

I won't describe the details of what my mother did to me. The pain was beyond endurance. In memory, I can still hear my screams. She left me lying on the floor, my body a mass of throbbing, burning misery, my face wet with my tears, my soul in despair. I knew I couldn't endure this again. I hadn't the courage. I couldn't appeal to Master Waters himself; my mother would half-kill me if I tried and I knew by instinct that Waters would merely assure me that he would make me happy and that I had a duty to obey my mother.

I longed for Gilbert, dear Gilbert, who had no power to help me but would be so angry if he knew what was happening to me. That was when the strange new feeling began to grow within me, a vigorous little seedling breaking through the soil. Anger was forbidden to me, but before God, I was angry now.

I wasn't going to forgive my mother, or Master Waters either, for what they were doing to me. I would wait. One day, my time would come.

During the preparations for my wedding, I pretended to be complaisant and because I was young and pliant enough, I did to some extent begin to hope for the best. Perhaps it would be all right. Perhaps I would get used to Sylvester. Even though . . .

How I wanted Gilbert. How I wanted his kind eyes, his warm voice, his caresses . . . those caresses, that had awakened such extraordinary feelings inside me. Had apparently stirred equivalent feelings inside him. So that two or three times . . .

I was so ignorant. That first time, when Gilbert and I were in his back parlour, petting each other, and feelings that I at least didn't understand suddenly took hold of both of us, I didn't know that what we were doing could engender a child. Gilbert said he had been careful, and I just thought he meant careful not to hurt me. I also know that once – in fact it was the second time, late in March – when he said, *Sorry, I didn't get out in time*, I hadn't the slightest idea what he meant. At later meetings, he sometimes seemed to be worried for me in some way and twice he asked me if I was well. I always said yes. I think he was too polite to ask outright if I had come on when I expected, and I was too ignorant to fill in the rest.

Just before the wedding, when my mother solemnly explained to me what would happen on the wedding night, that just confirmed what I already suspected, that Gilbert and I had done it three times already. But even then, I didn't realize that our lovemaking could have had results, not until Mrs Truebody explained things to me and told me a good deal more.

After that, as well as being angry, I began to be afraid. For now I knew that I was with child when I married, and the best I could hope for was that everyone would think the baby was premature.

I still hadn't reckoned, however, with all that Mrs Truebody knew.

While informing me of the realities of life for women, she had told me of her own life. She had been married at sixteen, had had five children within eight years, reared three and lost two in a smallpox outbreak. By the time she was widowed, she was still only twenty-eight and by then, she was weary of childbearing.

She had been left with enough money for the time being and had chosen not to remarry. Instead, she had attended to the care of her three surviving children. By the time she was forty, her eldest child, a son, had a position as manservant in a house some distance away and the other two, both girls, had been safely married off. Her responsibilities were over and her money was running out. And so, she had become a house-keeper to Master Waters.

'Shortly after that,' she said to me, 'he fell in love with you. It was a relief to me. He had his eye on me before that, and I didn't like it. I have *no* desire to marry again, ever. Oh, my husband was kind enough, though he was many years older than I was, but the constant childbearing! I can only hope, my dear, that you have an easy childbed and that you don't conceive again too soon. Suckle the baby as long as you can; that will help to delay things. By my reckoning, you'll give birth at the end of February.'

I soon began to feel heavy and I felt my stomach swelling, though I tried to conceal this. Bulky skirts can be useful in that way. Three weeks after the wedding, I told Sylvester that I had already missed a course, so that I could date the moment of conception as far back as I could. I hoped I could carry the pretence through. A spell of hot weather in August made me feel tired and by the end of the month I felt very heavy indeed and hardly knew how to hide it. I once or twice caught Mrs Truebody glancing at my middle, as though she were suspicious. As though she had noticed that the swelling had begun too soon.

I was trying to make something of my marriage because there was nothing else I could do. But all the time, I was afraid, and I was angry. I was even angry with Gilbert. He'd tried to be careful, but he hadn't been careful enough! And yet I still ached for him, and dreamed of him at night.

No disaster had yet struck on that morning – it was the last day of August – when I was upstairs in my still room, labelling the jars in which I had put my newly made gooseberry preserve. The sound of a horse's hooves drew me to the window and I saw a stranger dismounting at the front door. Then I returned to my labelling but was interrupted by Madge, who came hurrying to tell me that I was wanted in the parlour. 'And there's to be one more at dinner, ma'am.'

I tidied myself and made haste. Sylvester was in the parlour along with the stranger. *What a contrast!* I thought.

Sylvester was a tall man and he was always, somehow, cool-looking and pale, clean-shaven and dressed in cool colours. Today he was in light grey, slashed in sleeves and hose with pale blue.

The stranger was also tall, but he was dark, a handsome man with wide shoulders and strong facial bones. He wore warm colours, a tawny doublet and hose with slashings of crimson. *One cold and pale*, I thought; *one warm and dark*. He rose courteously as I entered, and bowed, and Sylvester, who hadn't risen, said: 'Arabella, my dear, this is an old friend of mine, Captain Julien, as he prefers to be known. Though I always think I should say Capitaine, since he is a Frenchman.'

'I am content to be Captain Julien when with English friends,' said the stranger, smiling. 'Mistress Waters, you may have heard of me from your brothers, for we usually sail in company. The seas are so perilous these days, and not just because of wind and water. My ship is the *Silver Mermaid*.'

I curtsied and said that yes, I had heard of him and heard the name of his ship. I was happy to meet him. Were my brothers now at home?

'Yes,' Captain Julien assured me. 'We went to London when we first landed from our latest voyage, but your brothers are now at Evergreens. We are all safe, though we had rough weather at times, out in the Atlantic.'

'You are brave to venture, time and again,' I said politely. 'Was the voyage profitable?'

'We think so,' said Captain Julien, and with that, a slightly awkward silence fell. I made to seat myself but Sylvester said: 'My dear, would you inform the kitchen? There will be one more for dinner, which Captain Julien and I will take in the dining chamber, alone together, as he has confidential matters to discuss. Yours will be served here in the parlour. Make sure it is a good dinner; with an extra course. We must respect our guest.'

'Of course,' I said. I dropped another curtsey and left the room. I had no intention of lingering outside the door to eavesdrop. Accident took a hand. As I closed the door, I realized that my bulky skirts had caught in it. I turned back to loosen them, which meant opening the door a fraction. Neither my husband nor Captain Julien noticed, for they were deep in conversation, and I heard my husband say: 'Now what is this grave news that will mean so much talk over dinner? You alarm me, Julien.'

Grave news for the husband usually means grave news for the wife. I froze. The captain said: 'Theobald Roebuck has been taken to the Tower. We must act. We have already thought about moving our base to Italy; well, the time is now. This last voyage was profitable and this time we have got everything into the hands of the bankers. What is left over from the previous voyage had better stay here and be retrieved later, when it's safe. The boys should keep away for the moment.'

At that point, I stopped trying to free my skirt and found myself listening intently. What were they talking about? What was left over from the previous voyage that had to be retrieved when it was safe? What was secret about the profits of my brothers' voyages? Suddenly, a memory had flashed into my mind, of the time when I had been standing in the parlour and caught sight of Hector and Stephen creeping off the premises by pushing through the bushes, as if they didn't want anyone to realize that they had been here. Had they been hiding something?

In the parlour now, Captain Julien was saying: 'It certainly can't stay where it is – it must be put somewhere that doesn't link us to it, where it really *can* remain safely for a while. If we need to get away at speed, then we don't want burdensome baggage.'

Sylvester said something about having to wait until his wife had given birth and by then I came to myself and eased my skirts free in a hurry, afraid of being caught. I closed the door very gently. Much of what the captain had said was bewildering, but whatever it was, it reeked of danger.

I wanted to think about it but couldn't, or not just then, for I had a dinner to create. I felt almost too heavy and tired for the task but I must make the effort and make haste, too. There could be gooseberry pie, yes, and we had a couple of tiny piglets hanging in the cold room; we could serve sucking pig . . . I was hurrying along so fast that I collided with Mrs Truebody and she caught hold of me. 'Mistress Stannard! Whatever is the matter? You are all put about!'

'We have a guest and there's to be an extra course at dinner. I must instruct the kitchen!'

'I'll come with you. Don't worry; we're all used to this kind of thing.'

She duly came with me and I was glad of her help. I still hadn't grasped the name of our cook. He was a powerfully built dark man with one gold earring. He made me quite nervous. I only ever addressed him as Master Cook, which he seemed to like. However, like Mrs Truebody, he was helpful, regarding the prospect of an unexpected extra course at such short notice as quite normal. When I began to talk about sucking pig and started to describe the syrup that was to go inside it, he waved a careless hand and said: 'I know. Leave it to me.'

'I'm eating separately, in the parlour. The gentlemen have private business and will eat in the dining room.'

'You want both courses for yourself, madam?'

'Yes,' I said. 'Small amounts.' I'd enjoy a helping of roasted piglet, I thought.

Sylvester told me afterwards that the dinner had been most satisfactory, and gave me an approving nod and a ghost of a smile. Things between us were improving, I thought. Something might build, given time, some sort of affection, partnership . . .

Disaster arrived the very next day.

Sylvester had gone to attend to something on the home farm while Mrs Truebody had joined me in the still room because, she said, winter lay ahead, and all the stores must be listed.

'I am glad that you can write,' she said. 'You can prepare labels for the jars of preserves.'

'There's much that I don't know,' I said. 'This house is very different from Evergreens. There, I knew how many candles had to be ordered for the darker evenings. How many do we need here? And what about salt for salting the meat in November? I shall become familiar with all this in the end, but I do need advice now.'

'The salt is a regular amount,' said Mrs Truebody. 'Here are the accounts for last year.' She put a ledger in front of me, opening it to the right page. 'Candles – that could be different, now that you are here, and soon there'll be a child. Let me see – here's what we ordered last year. We did it in three stages and . . .'

I was suddenly finding it hard to concentrate. Mrs Truebody's voice had become remote, as though it were a long distance away. Black dots had begun to dance before my eyes, getting between me and last year's ledger. There was a strange sensation within me, as though something inside was alive, moving.

Then I was lying on the floor with Mrs Truebody bending over me and saying: 'Come along now. Up you get. You fainted, but only for a moment or two. You'd best have something to eat. I'll order a boiled egg for you and a new roll and some butter. Remember you're eating for yourself and the little one now. Come along.'

She helped me to rise. 'I caught you before you hit the floor,' she said 'You've come to no harm.' She put a hand on my stomach. 'Your baby is still quite safe. He or she is . . .'

Her face went stiff. She jerked away from me as though I had stung her. 'Your baby moved!'

'Did it? I thought I felt something, just before I fainted. I don't know much about these things.'

'But you've barely been wed three months! If you took on the very first night, you'd still only be three months gone!'

I looked at her in bewilderment. 'I don't understand.' Here, by the sound of it was something that Mrs Truebody had *not* explained to me. She did so now, however.

'I never felt the quickening before four months and with most, it wasn't till the fifth. And you're bigger than you ought

to be and from the first, you had a sort of look . . .' Her voice
trailed off. She stood there, staring at me, looking as though
some sort of light was breaking in her mind. In a wondering
voice, she said: 'I think you'll give birth long before the end
of February. Well before Christmas, most likely! Dear God
Almighty – *you were with child before you married, you
whore!*'

She had hold of me by the shoulders and shook me. '*Who's
the father? That carpenter Gilbert Gale, isn't it? And you
thinking you could pass his brat off as the master's heir?*'

'No!' Denial was my only defence. 'Of course not! How
could you think . . . are all women the same, about these
things?'

'The master knew you weren't pure, didn't he? He *knew*!
He tried to send you back where you came from! But that
Mistress Stannard spoke for you, telling some tale about – yes,
as you've just said – *women aren't all the same!* And the
master, being fool enough to be in love with you, believed
her. Wanted to believe her. Well, now he'll know the truth. He
was right after all. Meanwhile, madam, your bedchamber is
where you'd better be.' She was gripping me fiercely. 'We
can't have you trying to escape his retribution, can we?
Hammond!'

Plump little Madge put her head round the storeroom door.
'Did you call, Mrs Truebody?'

'*Get Hammond! Now!*'

Madge fled. I stood unresisting, knowing that resistance would
fail. If I broke away from Mrs Truebody, someone would stop
me before I got out of the front door and where could I go,
anyway? Would even my mother take me in? In the distance,
I could hear Madge shouting for Hammond and then there were
rapid masculine feet approaching, and Hammond strode in.
'What is it? What's amiss? Mrs Truebody? What is this?'

In a few short sentences, Mrs Truebody told him. '. . . so
you see, the master was right all the time, what he said the
morning after the wedding. She's spoiled goods.'

'I'll send for him.' Hammond spoke across me, as though
I wasn't there. 'Best lock her in her chamber, meanwhile.'

Again, I didn't resist. I was a helpless mouse and two great big cats had their claws in me. I was marched upstairs to the bedchamber and pushed in. The door was shut and I heard the key turn in the lock. I sat down on the bed. I put my hands protectively over my belly. I must try to protect the child at all costs. The child had done no wrong.

I had a surge of anger against Gilbert but then it subsided. It wasn't Gilbert's fault. It was an accident. Gilbert would never harm me of his own choice. If Sylvester now rejected me, said a tiny voice of hope inside me, then perhaps our marriage could be annulled somehow. Gilbert now was my hope for the future.

I don't know how long it was before Sylvester came back. I think it was about an hour. I know that as I sat awaiting him I was full of dread. But when I heard his feet on the stairs, I sat up straight, my hands clenched in my lap and my head up. I didn't want to cringe. I hadn't asked to marry him. I had been forced into it. I said to myself that I was growing tired of being batted about like a tennis ball between my mother and this man. I would try to keep some trace of dignity. If I had been allowed to marry Gilbert, none of this would have happened.

The lock turned and Sylvester came in. He shut the door behind him and came over to me. He stood in front of me, looking down at me. In scathing tones, he asked: 'Have you any idea when the bastard you carry is due?'

'Mrs Truebody thinks before Christmas.'

He went on looking at me, hands on hips. 'I loved you. I really loved you. Part of me still does – *you*, not the thing you now carry, that is none of mine. You haunt my dreams with your graceful movements, your lovely hair like autumn beech leaves, and your eyes, the eyes of a wood elf, brown and green, and the green soft and subtle as moss, or leaves in spring.'

I stared at him, marvelling at these imaginative flights and wondering what they presaged. Nothing good. His eyes were so cold.

'But now . . .' he said, and his voice turned savage, '. . . *now*, you have tried to palm me off with another man's brat.'

'I didn't know. I didn't know I was with child; I didn't understand these things until Mrs Truebody explained them . . .!' But he wasn't listening. He made a sound like a snarl and pulled me off the bed.

My mother had used a birch. Sylvester used his riding whip. It seemed to take for ever. The whole household must have heard my screams but no one came to help me or even protest. When I was on the floor in a state of collapse, he tried to kick me in the stomach but I drew my knees up, pressing my face against them, wrapping my arms protectively round them, lying on the floor like a curled hedgehog. Except that I had no spines.

He stood over me, looming. I whimpered, terrified. 'Bad blood,' he said. 'You and your mother both. Did you know that your mother poisoned Father Eliot? He had found out too much about things your brothers were doing, and she did it to protect them but it wasn't a nice thing to do, all the same. Don't you agree? Your mother a killer and you a whore. How did I ever become entangled with such filth?'

I didn't answer. I could only cower and sob. And be full of fear, and hate. And anger.

NINETEEN
A World Has Ended

Ursula's Narrative

At the time, I of course knew nothing of this. But I began to worry seriously about Arabella after Brockley went into Cutpenny to talk to Gilbert Gale about searching the Waters grounds, and then brought him back to the Old Bell.

'You've shut your shop?' I asked him. 'We didn't mean you to do that – you'll lose business.'

'Master Brockley has explained about the help he needs, madam. If Waters has been hiding loot on his property, I can believe it and I'm only too glad to help search for it,' said Gilbert, standing very upright in the middle of my chamber, his cap in his right hand, and his brown eyes serious. 'Only, madam, there is something I have been worried about now for a long time. I am afraid for Mistress Arabella, only, trying to explain . . .'

He started to twist the cap round and round in his hands. 'I will help you in any way I can,' he said. 'You have only to ask. But . . . Madam, there is something I want to tell you but I'd find it easier, talking to another man.'

'Dale and I will wait downstairs,' I said.

It was dinner time and we had intended to dine at the Old Bell, anyway. Dale and I ordered our meal. The landlord's son had recently been out on the bank of the nearby River Eden, equipped with a longbow. 'Do you like mallard?' enquired the landlord, grinning.

We were therefore able to have roast mallard with a sauce of mustard and honey. With it went green peas, fried beans, apple tart and small ale. We had barely begun, however, before the men came downstairs. Brockley and Gilbert exchanged a few quiet words, and then Gilbert left. Brockley came over to us. 'Well?' I asked, with my mouth full.

'Is that duck? I'll have the same. It was a simple story, madam. Gilbert is very young in some ways. He has heard the tale of how Waters tried to reject Mistress Arabella the day after the wedding and why. He has also heard that she became with child very quickly. He said that he and Mistress Arabella were lovers on three occasions – when they somehow succeeded in being alone together for long enough. He says . . . he is afraid that perhaps her baby may be his.'

A maidservant came to take Brockley's order. After that, I said to Brockley: 'I suppose Gilbert didn't want to mention those things in front of ladies. It's as well he's told us, though. I can see myself,' I said with feeling, 'taking on another ward. If Waters throws Arabella out and Joan won't take her back, I mean. We'll have to wait and see, though. It may well be all right, and the child really is Sylvester's. They won't be the first couple to start a child during their honeymoon.'

'Let us hope so,' said Brockley, earnestly.

His order arrived and we ate in silence for a while.

And then, in the space of half a minute, all our plans were overturned.

Eddie Hale came hurrying in search of us, accompanied by Abel Parsons, another of my grooms, who must have come from Hawkswood. I stood up at once, realizing that Abel must be here with a message, and that it was almost certainly urgent.

'Madam, so sorry to disturb you but . . .'

'What is it, Abel? Just tell me.'

'It's Master Wilder, madam.' Abel sounded as breathless as though he had run all the way from Hawkswood. 'He fell ill this morning. He was in the storeroom, seeing what had to be bought for next month and then – well, I wasn't there, but Phoebe was – he suddenly said he couldn't breathe, and he choked and fainted and fell down and when he awoke, he was frozen all down one side . . .'

'Stroke,' I said. I rose quickly to my feet. 'That's called stroke. I must get home.' I remembered that Abel had just arrived after a long and hurried ride. He must be hungry. I sat down again. 'Abel, take some dinner while we finish ours.

Then we'll pack and start for Hawkswood immediately. Who is in charge there meanwhile? And where is your horse?'

'Master Harry is ordering things at home, madam. He was the one who sent me. My horse is in the stable here. I took Splash.'

'Harry did the right thing. Come, order yourself a meal; ask for what you want. I'll tell the landlord it is on my bill.'

Abel was in too much of a fluster to eat much. While we hurriedly finished our own dinner, he took a slice of cold chicken pie and a glass of small ale and nothing more. Then the Brockleys made haste over the packing and I paid the landlord. In little over half an hour, we were on the road. Illicit treasure would have to wait. Searching the Waters property must wait too. I had come to Oxted on an assignment for Cecil, but even Cecil, even my sister the queen, all the pirates of the Spanish Main at once were nothing in comparison with Wilder.

We went through Cutpenny on the way home and let Gilbert know what had happened. Then we set out in earnest and in haste. Brockley and I went ahead, galloping wherever we could. Eddie followed with the heavy baggage in the mule cart. Dale, who couldn't cope with fast riding, was in the mule cart too, and Abel, whose horse, Splash, was getting on in years, rode at an easy pace beside the cart, leading Dale's mare.

Wilder had been the main supporting pillar of Hawkswood since long before Hugh brought me there. He had been born in the service of Hawkswood. He had married within it; he and his wife had reared their children there and seen them leave to make their own way in the world. There, he had lost and mourned his wife and seen her buried in the graveyard of St Mary's, the village church, in the Hawkswood plot. If Adam Wilder had been stricken, I must be with him.

By early evening Brockley and I were dismounting in the Hawkswood courtyard, which at Hawkswood was also the stable yard, and the household was all round us.

They were all of a babble. Phoebe, who like Adam, was past middle age, looked shocked, as if her greying hair had become suddenly greyer. Aged Gladys was much to the fore, declaring that she had a herbal posset ready for when Wilder became conscious again. The younger maids, Jennet, Bess and Margery, were excited and scared both at once, wondering what would come of all this. Tessie, who was married to Joseph Henty, another of my grooms but often came to help in the house, was with them, trying to reassure them. Tessie was older than they were and she was a good soul, who had once been Harry's nurse.

But furthest to the fore, with Ben at his shoulder, was Harry. I was out of my saddle first, before Brockley was down. For one insane moment, I looked round for Wilder and then pulled myself together and said to Harry: 'Where is he?'

'Welcome home, Mother! Come with me – we'll go to him. Ben, get everyone back to their duties.' I looked at him wonderingly. On the day when we were at dinner at Evergreens and Gilbert burst in to demand help for Mother Lee, Harry had taken charge, like a man, not a boy. Now I heard the same note of command. He said: 'I had him carried to his chamber and laid on his bed.'

Adam Wilder had two rooms to himself in the servants' wing. They were of reasonable size and when his family visited him, they were always squeezed in with him. That was Wilder's own choice. I would happily have let them use our spare bedchambers but he wouldn't have it. Servants were servants, he said, and shouldn't use their master's rooms. He didn't say it with humility. There was nothing subservient about Wilder. He knew his work and knew his place, but considered it to be a place of dignity which he was well content to occupy.

Now, he occupied it still, but differently. Someone had got him into his night-rail and he had been covered with the squirrel-fur coverlet that I had given him last Christmas and positively bullied him to accept. There was a cup of water by his bed. He lay half on his side, his left eye was closed and all that side of his face was drawn down and distorted. His right eye rolled a greeting at me and he tried to speak but the left side of his mouth seemed to be frozen and he could only manage the bare imitations of words out of the other side.

'Sor . . . ry . . . mad'm. So s . . . orry. Trou . . . ble . . .'

'You have no need to be sorry for anything, Wilder. We'll

soon have you right.' I was lying and we both knew it. 'Rest easy.' Phoebe had accompanied me and I turned to her. 'He should have some soup, hot but not too hot. Is anything ready?'

'I told Hawthorn to make chicken soup. I'll heat it myself. I can do it in minutes,' said Phoebe, and made for the door.

From the bed came of a murmur of, 'Thir . . . sty.'

I picked up the cup and helped him to drink, dribbling the water into one corner of his mouth. It was unbearable to see him like this. He was a tall man and all the time that I had known him, his hair had been gradually greying and I always thought of him like that. I suddenly realized that for a long time I hadn't really looked at him. Now I did, and saw that his hair was white rather than grey and that it was scanty on top. I could see the pink scalp below. He wasn't just growing older; he was old. Old and now ill. I tried to hide my tears. He needed care, not weeping that might alarm him.

In a short space of time, Phoebe was back, with a gently steaming bowl and a spoon. 'It's a good clear soup, easy to swallow, madam. Though I put camomile in it to please Gladys, madam; she was in the kitchen, going on and on . . .'

'I will attend to Gladys,' I said. 'Feed that soup into him. I'll fetch a glass of canary wine and help him to drink it. And I'll give him Gladys' posset too. I doubt if it can cure him, but I don't suppose it will harm him, either.'

'You'd best take a camomile posset yourself, mistress,' said Gladys, meeting me as I left the room. 'Nasty shock you've had, an' all. Don't want you getting stricken like him.'

'You and your camomile possets! What good do you think a dose of camomile will do Wilder now?'

'Won't mend him. Might make him a bit more comfortable. What else can we do?'

One thing we could do was to see that someone was with him all the time. Harry and Ben said that they would take turns, and their tutor Peter Dickson said that during the day he could do an hour or two here and there, though he couldn't offer to sit up at night. He was too old for that, he said, and wouldn't be able to keep awake.

With the help of Harry and Ben, I thought we could keep a continuous watch over Wilder without too much difficulty.

I had heard of people, stricken like this, who made recoveries of a sort, had learned to speak coherently again and to walk with the aid of a stick. It was something to hope for.

But during the night, Harry came to me and called my name. I woke instantly. He was standing beside me, candle in hand.

'Mother, I think he's gone.'

Half asleep still, I got out of bed, pulled on a dressing robe and went with him. There were two big branched candlesticks in Wilder's room and by their light I could see how still he now lay. His right arm was outside the covers and I lifted it, feeling his wrist for a pulse. I found nothing.

'I tried that, as well, Mother,' Harry said. 'He was restless for a while and seemed to gulp for air. He stretched up that right arm as if he were reaching, groping for something. I kept talking to him, saying, *It's all right, just go to sleep*, things like that, and then his breathing slowed. His arm sank down. I wanted to call someone but what could anyone have done? His breathing stopped and then started again and then stopped . . . and there's been nothing since.'

'No. I think you're right. But, Harry, I think we should both watch beside him until dawn. He shouldn't be left alone. If by any chance . . .'

'We'll sit together, Mother.'

There was no chance that Wilder would revive. We both knew that his stillness was not that of quiet sleep, but of death. But the dead should have company, at least for a while. I opened a window, instinctively following the ancient custom. The soul must be free to take wing. After that, we just sat, one on either side of the bed. We didn't talk much, if at all. I think I may have dozed in my chair once or twice but never deeply or for long. Wilder was changing already, sinking deeper into the peace of eternity. His face in the candlelight was austere and calm.

It felt as though a world had ended.

TWENTY

Precedence, Pigsties and Byres

At daybreak, the house began to stir. Harry, being young, was able to keep awake and see to things but I was forced to retire to bed and sleep for a few hours. When I awoke, I found that in the meantime Harry had been making sensible plans. Two of our grooms, Joseph Henty and Simon Alder, had been despatched to the town of Epsom, where I knew Wilder's two married sons both lived. There were two daughters as well and where they were, I didn't know, but Harry said he hoped their brothers would.

Dr Joynings, the vicar of St Mary's church in the village, had been summoned and had brought with him two village women, Mrs Dodd and Mrs Henty – who was Joseph's mother – to see to the laying out. They had been dealing with such tasks for many years.

'I hope I have done everything right, Mother,' Harry said when I joined him in the great hall, just in time for dinner. 'John Hawthorn's seen to the meal without asking for any orders; he knows what's best to do; leave it to him, he says. Gladys has been getting under his feet, wanting to make camomile and lavender possets for us all, to calm our minds.'

I began to laugh but stopped short. Laughter was out of place. 'How long will it take to get Wilder's family here, I wonder?'

'We should hear from the sons soon,' said Harry briskly. 'My message will have reached them by now.' I looked at my son, marvelling. He seemed to have grown, not physically, but mentally. He said, 'Mother, there is much to consider. Who, for instance, will replace Wilder?'

It was over. Adam Wilder had been laid to rest in the graveyard beside the church where he had worshipped all his life. In the church and at the graveside, Dr Joynings had spoken movingly of Adam's long service to the Stannard house, of his honesty and good nature and competence. His two sons and his two daughters and their spouses, standing around the grave, had said amen. The grandchildren had said it too. There were fourteen of them, all ages from two to twenty. I was ashamed that I had known so little of Adam's family. He had rarely talked about them, and they rarely visited him. Now, I thought them a family to be proud of.

Many of the villagers had attended, for they had known Adam and liked him, and some of my friends and neighbours were there too. My old friend Christopher Spelton and his wife Mildred, a former ward of mine, came from West Leys, their farm to the north-east of Hawkswood, and my friends Thomas and Christina Ferris, from White Towers, the house nearest to mine, came as well. No one came, however, from Christina's girlhood home, Cobbold Hall, which was also quite near. Christina's parents were long dead and she had inherited the place, which had had a succession of tenants thereafter. I had never come to know any of them well. Now, the place was empty, awaiting new occupants, and had been so for months. I would have liked to ask if any new tenants were in prospect, but this was not the moment.

The weather was kind, dry and not cold. Everyone was invited back to the house and we all trooped there on foot. John Hawthorn and Ben Flood, his short, bald and, in culinary matters, highly gifted assistant, hadn't come to the church but had stayed behind to prepare the meal that everyone needed by then, especially those who must travel some distance to their homes.

Over the hot vegetable soup, the cold chicken quarters, the rolls and honey and the ale, there were speeches. Then the guests began to depart. I bade loving farewells to Christina and Mildred, particularly to Mildred, who was now expecting a child. 'A death and then a new life to balance it!' she said, crying a little, for like everyone who had known him, she had valued Wilder.

The stables had been crowded and two of Adam's grandsons had turned their ponies into a field. Our grooms went to help their young owners catch them and there was some unseemly merriment when the ponies almost let themselves be caught and then shied away at the last moment, kicking up their heels.

'If anyone tells me that horses have no sense of humour, they should try this!' said Eddie, breathless after failing for the third time to get a halter on to the wicked little bay gelding belonging to Thomas Wilder, Adam's eldest grandson.

At last it was done. The guests had gone. The house was quiet once more. Too quiet, without Adam's guiding presence. I went to sit in the small parlour, my favourite place, to catch my breath and think about all that I must do the next day, and there, Harry came to me.

'Mother?'

He was hesitating in the doorway. I called him in, waving him to a settle. 'Be seated, Harry. You bore yourself well today; I am pleased with you.'

'Well, I did manage to catch young Thomas Wilder's pony when Eddie and Thomas couldn't,' said Harry, letting himself be amused for a moment. But then his face became sober. 'Mother, there is so much that Adam was going to teach me, and now he can't. But there are things I ought to know, things to do with one day being the master here, that even Master Dickson doesn't.'

'What things, Harry?'

'Well, things like exactly what to wear and what to order in the way of food for certain occasions, and . . . orders of precedence, who to seat where if you're holding a big feast, with important guests there. There are rules but I don't yet know them. Who will instruct me?'

'I will, Harry, as soon as I return from this task that Cecil has set me. I know the rules you mean; I learned them at court. You're right, they are important. There are other complications, too.'

I had found out about those soon after I learned that I was a half-sister to the queen.

Once Elizabeth knew that I was aware of my parentage, she had let me become known – though unofficially – as her half-sister. She didn't wish me to retire from public sight, but to attend on her at court from time to time. As a result, my status in society rose. Hugh never objected, fortunately. He was himself a man of some status and calmly accepted my visits to the court, sometimes accompanying me. He also accepted the fact that people of rank would seek my friendship, as a way, usually, of getting closer to Elizabeth. Now and then, we had to entertain them.

We never held enormous banquets such as the queen and her great lords did. We lived in a plain manor house, and our standards were those of well-to-do yeomen, with perhaps just a few little extras. Hawkswood carried the right to take deer within its own boundaries, so roast venison sometimes appeared, and I occasionally amused guests in a fashionable manner with a cold pie full of live songbirds which would fly up, singing – or more likely twittering in alarm – as soon as the crust was lifted. Though I didn't do it often. Before the pie was opened, I had to see that all the dishes were covered and provide napkins so that the guests could drape themselves protectively. I considered it a troublesome dish.

But however exalted the company, the number of courses at a Hawkswood dinner was restrained, and few dishes were exotic. No one, however illustrious, was ever confronted at Hawkswood with roast peacock adorned with its own plumage and tail, nor did we ever serve swan, baked inside a coffin of pastry and dressed with pepper, salt, butter and ginger.

Theoretically, I knew how to prepare these dishes; at court, the queen approved of her ladies witnessing their preparation, though none of her cooks would have let us far enough into their territory to beat an egg, let alone dress a swan. I had also been taught a good deal by Aunt Tabitha, who knew in theory how to prepare a peacock though I don't think she ever actually tried it. But such things were not for Hawkswood.

However, since we did occasionally have people of rank to dine on our venison haunches and enjoy (or be targeted by) our singing birds, precedence was important. Place a man of dignity too near the salt, with others above him, and you could make an enemy for life. Allow too many top table dishes to be served to those at the lower tables, and you could damage your own status.

Yet the status itself carried problems. I did not – must not

– boast of my royal descent. I had to uphold the standards of hospitality and dignity that were expected of me, but on the other hand, I knew how unwise it would be to trade on my royal connections.

I must never forget the unwanted bastard brat I had been, or treat my loyal servants as though they were a separate and inferior species. At court, I had once seen a man – I think he was an Egyptian – walk along a rope that had been strung tautly between two trees. He walked that rope as though it were a broad path while the queen and her court watched with open mouths. Sometimes I felt as though, socially, I too walked a tightrope. Harry would have to remember that his family had beginnings both humble and royal, and learn to walk that tightrope, too.

I had been careful not to seem ambitious and Harry must learn that as well. Ambition could send you to the headsman, especially when allied to royal blood. Youth was no protection. Lady Jane Grey was younger than Harry when she went to the block.

Harry, my dear dear son, you have the reckless good looks of your father, but don't have his reckless ideas, his passionate beliefs, please don't!

'There is much you need to learn, and Ben too,' I said. 'I haven't forgotten. It has occurred to me that Ben could be trained to replace Adam Wilder, but this sudden death has taken us all by surprise. As yet, Ben is too young. I think I shall ask Master Dickson if he feels equal to stepping in. He knows the ways of this house. If I give him the authority, I think he can fill the place until Ben is ready. By then, he'll be wanting to retire himself.'

Harry looked relieved. 'I would want Ben to have a place here. He still at times feels . . . orphaned.'

'He shall have a place here, I promise. And I *won't* be long about this treasure hunt. Heavens, Harry, I feel as if I'm being torn in two, between Cecil's – and the queen's – requirements, and your needs. I hope you never have to deal with a divided heart.'

'Ben is having to do that, Mother. I know he is. He has said so to me – just once. He loved his father and yet, look what happened! He doesn't like to talk about it. But if I were in his position – well, I can't imagine what I would feel, or do.'

'I hope you will never have to find out,' I said comfortingly. 'Harry, when I go back to Oxted, I shall be less than thirty miles away. If any emergency arises, you can just send for me, as you so wisely did this time, when Wilder fell ill. I can be here within hours.'

'I shall be glad to think of that. I wish,' said Harry unexpectedly, 'that I had known my own father. I think you once told me that I look like him.'

'Yes, you do.'

'And didn't you once tell me that he had another son, older than me? So that I can never inherit any of the French property. I asked you about that, I recall.'

'So you did. And yes, Matthew did have another son, who has no doubt come into his inheritance by now.'

'So I have a half-brother that I've never met!'

'You have quite enough relations without unknown French half-brothers,' I said, with some asperity. 'Ben is more of a brother to you than any foreign ones can ever be. You also have a married half-sister, and a whole brood of nephews and nieces. Don't be greedy.'

Harry laughed. 'I only wondered . . . Mother . . .'

There were more questions. Harry seemed worried about orders of precedence and wanted instruction at once. I told him some main principles and hoped he would remember them. We would have to go over it again when I came back from Oxted.

And even as I was talking to Harry, I was wondering about outhouses in the grounds of Waters House, and wondering too how Arabella was faring. I had an odd sense of responsibility where she was concerned. I had, after all, thrown her back into her husband's unwelcoming arms, the morning after the wedding. Had I done right or wrong?

As it turned out, I couldn't go back to Oxted at once. It quickly emerged that there was a good deal of business concerned with Wilder. He had apparently saved his wages over the years and built up enough money to buy a smallholding near

Guildford. He had rented it out and it had been profitable. He had left a will, though it didn't turn up until Dale and I were clearing his room out. His family had taken some of his belongings, but quite a few things remained. We came upon the will at the bottom of the chest in which he had kept the account books and some books of his own, including a vernacular Bible, two manuals on the duties of a steward and a volume of poetry.

The smallholding was to be sold and the proceeds divided between his sons, and there were various other bequests. Wilder had kept his wife's jewellery, which was more valuable than I would have expected, and this had to be divided between his daughters and daughters-in-law. Some money was to go to St Mary's church in the village. I had to recall his eldest son from Epsom to help with it all.

Between attending to all that and at least beginning to give Harry some of the instruction that I knew I should have given him before, it was the sixth day of November before I could return to either Oxted or Evergreens.

I had in the interval corresponded with Cecil and been encouraged to go on seeking the Mercer boys' treasure. Nothing had come to light along the south-east coast, it seemed. By this time, the excuse of looking for a house seemed stale. After some thought, I decided just to deposit myself on Joan Mercer and announce that I had come to carry out an inspection of Evergreens, its land, stock and account books. I would say blandly that from time to time, I carried out the same inspection of my other house, Withysham in Sussex.

There was some truth in that except that Withysham had never been let and I sometimes removed there while Hawkswood had a thorough cleansing. While I was there, I naturally enquired into its affairs. That was different, but there was no need to tell Joan so.

It was highly unlikely that any treasure had been hidden at Evergreens, either in the house or on the land. The house was unsuitable and every part of the land was being busily used. I now decided that nevertheless, the possibility shouldn't be ignored. We should try to look, to peer in attics and barns and garden sheds, without alerting Joan. We would even try to look at the walkway round the roof though I was fairly sure that nesting seagulls had laid their claim earlier.

Joan welcomed us with what I can only call a difficult smile. I had the right to inspect my own property and therefore she tried not to seem displeased. She didn't succeed very well. On the other hand, Page took us in his stride, and with slightly twitching lips, told us that he understood that we had come to create our own small imitation of the Conqueror's Domesday Book. He promised us full co-operation.

The Mercer boys were in England for the winter, but were not at home. They were at the coast, overseeing repairs to their ships, Joan told us, as Cathy welcomed us with wine and rosewater biscuits.

'I am so sorry I missed them,' I said. 'Will they be returning here soon?'

'They will be here for Christmas, certainly,' said Joan. *Christmas is over six weeks away. These nuisances surely will be gone by then.* She might as well have said it aloud.

Later, the Brockleys and I foregathered in the chamber I had been given, and we once more went over the plans we had made before we left Hawkswood.

'We are assuming,' I said, 'that there is something to find. I saw those matching goblets in Mother Lee's house and I saw them again in London, in Captain Tyler's house. They are part of a set of twelve – well, we hope there's only one set. Cecil thinks others may exist. But if there's only one set in the world, then the other ten goblets were stolen from Tyler by these English pirates.'

'In which case, those goblets can only have got to Mother Lee's cottage through the Mercers,' Brockley agreed.

I said: 'I have told Mistress Mercer that I have come to inspect Evergreens – all of it. Lofts, cellar, outhouses. The hen house, the pigsty, the cattle byre, the stable, the sheep barn. Fran and I will stay in the house. We will peer at the account books and try to find opportunities to search the rooms. You can take the outside. Take notes, as though you really were looking at the state of the outhouses, and counting the stock.'

'Roger thought it would be awkward, carrying quills and an inkpot about,' Dale said, 'but he has had such a brilliant idea.'

'I've brought a slate,' said Brockley. 'It's a fair size. And after all, we're not *really* intent on listing the number of laying hens or how many piglets there were in the sow's last litter, are we?'

The plan wasn't easy to carry out. Joan seemed to have her eye on Dale and me. We had little opportunity to prowl about inside the house though we tried, seizing every chance to go into the various rooms to study floors and walls. With great solemnity, I examined the accounts and checked various things against the information that Brockley brought me from outside, but I found nothing amiss, and I hadn't expected to.

Meanwhile, Brockley also had difficulties. Wherever he went, one or other of the farm workers always wanted to go with him. Not, he thought, for sinister purposes but because the small farm attached to Evergreens really was well run and the bailiff and his team were properly proud of it. They wanted to show it off. They talked to me as well as to Brockley.

'Makes a good bit of money, our farm does,' said Mr Jonas Hardy, who combined the positions of bailiff and cowman, beaming happily through his permanent pepper and salt stubble and his few remaining front teeth. 'Missis, she do take an interest as much as any man. We've improved that there cattle herd. And as for the sheep . . .'

There was a shepherd, a jolly soul called Ed Robbins. He had a fat and jolly wife and, like the lodge-keeper Jankin, a large family of youngsters. He was only too glad to describe to Brockley how he had improved the wool yield by bringing in 'that big woolly ram from abroad.'

We never did find out what he meant by *abroad*. He told Brockley that he had been born at Evergreens, where his father had been a shepherd before him, and had never been further than Caterham in his life. I suspected that to him, *abroad* could mean anything from the adjacent county to Cathay.

Since I really was the landlord of Evergreens, much of this was of interest to me but it wasn't what we were there for and it was maddeningly difficult for Brockley to look for signs of disturbed flooring or hidden compartments in barns and byres, while Hardy and Robbins were at his shoulder, describing their successes.

At one point, he did discover that the outside wall of a hay barn was longer than the inside one, which suggested a walled-off compartment at one end, but when he showed interest in the matter, Hardy laughed and showed him a door, partly obscured by hay bales, in a corner of the barn. It led into a narrow room with casks inside it. 'Here's where Missis keeps the wines she makes, from cowslips and dandelions and parsnips and the like. So did others afore her. We've allus had tenants who did a bit o' brewing.'

Brockley said that after that he hardly dared to look suspicious about anything. Nor had he noticed anything else that seemed mysterious.

'So that leaves the Waters property,' I said. 'We shall have to do it, as I expected. You need to talk to Gilbert Gale again.'

'I intend to do so, madam. I have always thought it a better prospect. How Gale would love to find Waters in possession of illegal treasure!'

'It wouldn't release Arabella from the marriage,' I said. 'Not unless Waters is executed for it.'

'The queen is the head of the Church of England. She can annul marriages,' said Brockley. 'Did she not once annul one of yours, madam?'

It was true. She had annulled my marriage to Matthew de la Roche, Harry's father. She had also, for good measure, let me believe that Matthew was dead. Not until much later, after I had married Hugh, did I learn that Matthew was alive. Once after that, and very briefly, we had come together again and Harry was the outcome. I would never regret that.

Nor was any of that to the point just now. 'Go into Cutpenny,' I said, 'and talk to Gilbert.'

TWENTY-ONE
Lanterns in the Night

Arabella's Narrative

'You will remain in this room until you give birth,' said Mrs Truebody. 'When the time comes, I will attend you. I have skill in such matters.'

I could only hope that she had. Her face when she said it was cold and hard, like marble. I wondered what Mr Truebody had been like.

The room was nothing like the chamber that I had shared with Sylvester. Waters House had extensive attics, and some of them had been turned into spare bedchambers for the personal servants of people who came to visit. I had been put into one of these. Its ceiling sloped almost to the floor on one side. It had a bed with no hangings, some blankets and a thin fleece coverlet, not in use but folded inside a chest-seat, under one of the windows. There was a washstand, a small clothes press, two hooks behind the door, for cloaks and bedgowns, and a chamber pot.

It was dreary, being so confined. I was too bulky to want to go walking but the locked door preyed on my mind. I was very conscious of being a prisoner, at Sylvester's mercy.

For the moment, however, I wasn't given any more ill treatment. I was given regular meals though uninteresting ones, and I was given washing water.

I did once manage to communicate with the outer world. Now and then, I was taken to another attic while Mrs Truebody swept and dusted my prison and put clean basins on the washstand. This other attic overlooked the front courtyard. One day I heard a horse whinny so I looked out of the window and saw Mistress Stannard and the Brockleys there. Brockley looked up and saw me. But I couldn't signal to him, or open

the window and call, because Mrs Truebody came into the
room just then to fetch me and snatched me roughly back
from the window.

'You're not to have aught to do with anyone. Master's orders.
You're supposed to be away visiting! Come with me.'

I did as I was bid, though I was thinking hard. I had been
doing so ever since that odd occasion when I had overheard
the conversation between Sylvester and Captain Julien. I had
begun to work out what it meant. Theobald Roebuck was the
jeweller who had cut and set my emerald pendant, but he had
been arrested. So there was something wrong about him. There
was something wrong about my brothers' privateering. It
wasn't legal for some reason. They and Captain Julien wanted
to move to Italy, to sail in and out from a port there, presumably. Sylvester was concerned in it all and might have to get
away quickly, and wouldn't want to carry heavy baggage with
him. That could mean me but I supposed I could be left behind
if necessary. I wouldn't mind being left behind by Sylvester.

But there had been something about the profits from the
last voyage having been taken to a banker, and something left
over from the voyage before that was still here, but must be
moved from a dangerous hiding place to a better one and
retrieved later. I turned it over and over in my mind, getting
it straight. I ought to tell someone, only who? And how?

Thinking about it at least helped to pass the time. I found
it hard to sleep at night. I would lie awake for hours, sometimes all night, and then next day I would feel exhausted. Not
that it mattered. I could stay in bed all day if I felt so inclined.
But that I never did. It was better for me, I knew, to rise and
dress and wash, even though I had nothing to do but think,
and gaze out of the window.

I kept telling myself that things could have been worse. My
room was at a corner of the house, and had windows on two
sides. One looked east and the other looked south. The eastern
prospect was just above the topiary garden but since my attic
was high up, I could look beyond the garden, see the tops of
the trees in the orchard, and catch a remote glimpse of fields
and the low hills far away. It gave me a sense of distance. The
southern outlook, by contrast, gave on to the thick bushes that

grew on that side of the house, and beyond them to a wood. Neither prospect offered very much of interest, but on clear nights, I found interest of a sort in the moon and stars.

I had been well enough educated to recognize the Milky Way, and when I was awake in the small hours, from the powdering of stars, I could pick out the constellation of Orion, and the misty net of the Pleiades. I also watched, fascinated, the cycles of the moon.

The eastward window was the one with the chest-seat below it. During the nights when the moon was full, or near it, I took to wrapping the fleece round me, and perching there to watch the ground mist appear, like silver gauze in the pale light, and drift across the fields, and see the moon climb the sky and journey across it.

Gazing at these things passed many a wakeful hour for me and kept me from remembering how very afraid I was of the future. Whenever I thought about that, I quailed. And then my anger would burn again. If my mother hadn't forced this marriage on me, if I could have married Gilbert, I would have been safe. Yes, he and I had sinned, but it was for love, and we had wanted to set it right, had wanted to marry. But I had been denied any right to choose and this was what had come of it.

I was gazing out one night just as the moon had reached the full, when I noticed that beyond the topiary, in the formal garden, there were lights. Lanterns! Two of them. They seemed to be moving purposefully. They disappeared into a dark mass that I thought was a shed, and then emerged again and began, as it seemed, to go to and fro as though whoever carried them was quartering the ground, searching for something.

They came nearer. They entered the topiary garden and seemed to be moving back and forth. When their search actually brought them right under my window, I pushed it open and I heard them speak to each other. It was a brief exchange and I couldn't make out any words but I recognized the voices.

Brockley and Gilbert! Gilbert, my Gilbert! He was down there, out of reach but nevertheless within a few feet of me! I opened the window wider, leant right out of it and said their names, softly but clearly. Both of the shadowy figures below froze and then looked up.

'I'm a prisoner in my room,' I said. 'It's me, Arabella.'

'Bella! Oh, Bella! Are you all right?' Gilbert's upturned face was just below me, white in the moonlight. 'No one has seen you for weeks! Everyone has been wondering about you!'

I blurted out the truth. 'I'm having a baby but . . . but he thinks it isn't his. So do I. If so, then it's yours. That's why I'm locked up here. He is so angry. I don't know what he intends for it, or for me. I'm very afraid.'

'It's *my* child?'

'Yes, my darling. I think it must be.'

Gilbert came as close to the wall as he could and Brockley stepped back, as if to give us some kind of privacy.

'Dear God! I have worried so about you. I heard you were with child – I have wondered whether it was mine. There was that one time when it might have happened; I have always worried about that. Are you safe so far?'

'Yes. For the time being. I hoped I could make them all think it was his and was premature, but whether or not he would have guessed, Mrs Truebody can't be fooled. She knows too much.'

'I don't want my child brought up as his!' Gilbert positively hissed the last two words. 'Listen, my love, if we can find a ladder, we can get you out of there, now, tonight. I'll take you away. We'll leave this district, go away to some distant part of the country, set ourselves up as a married couple . . .'

I could see Brockley shaking his head and I heard him murmur something which sounded like a protest.

'Waters is my husband,' I said miserably. 'He owns me. He would pursue us and bring me back. The law is on his side. But if you know I am here, that is some comfort. I know you're not far away. The future is just a . . . a darkness.'

'Well, if he throws you out, then come to me. He won't pursue you then. Come to me anyway if he makes your life unbearable. I'll be ready. We'll get away, far away. To Wales, or Scotland. I'm a skilled man. I can earn a living anywhere.'

'It's a dream, Gilbert. I would love it so but I can't make it seem real. We would have a tiny baby to look after while we were on the road. *Listen!*' I had suddenly realized that here was my chance to tell someone what I had overheard Captain Julien saying. 'This is important. It's about . . .'

Too late. A door had banged, someone was shouting and there were lights – lanterns and flambeaux – rushing towards us. There was Hammond, his dressing robe flapping round his ankles, a flaring torch in his hand, and there was Sylvester, half-dressed, in breeches and shirt, brandishing another, and others were following, grooms and footmen. I broke off and then shouted to Gilbert and Brockley to run and they had the sense to do my bidding. They fled into the darkness and though they were pursued, the receding shouts didn't suggest that the pursuers had caught their quarry. *Oh, Gilbert, be safe!* I prayed. And cursed myself because I hadn't thought quickly enough and I had missed my chance.

Sylvester had not followed the chase but had stopped below my window. He was looking up at me. 'So you were having an assignation with your lover, were you, madam?'

I was too terrified to answer and after a silent moment, he turned and went away. I sat down on the bed, wondering anxiously whether Gilbert and Brockley had escaped. Then I heard feet on the attic stairs and suddenly, the door was flung open and there was Sylvester.

I saw Mrs Truebody behind him. She had evidently just been aroused from bed, for she was in her night-rail. She was carrying a lantern. She stood in the doorway while Sylvester strode in. He seized hold of me, shook me furiously so that my head jerked wildly back and forth and I feared that my neck would snap. Then he thrust me away, so hard that I went over backwards and found myself lying flat on the floor. He instantly dragged me up again and did it all again. I was no more than a stuffed doll in his hands. I don't know how long it would have gone on, except that Mrs Truebody intervened.

She stepped up to us and said, quite calmly: 'Surely that's enough, Master Waters. Let's get the mistress back to bed. So unwise, dear Mistress Waters, to have a secret meeting with Gale. You are married, after all. It was very foolish.'

There were voices below and Sylvester, leaning out of the window and demanding news, was now being told that the miscreants had had horses waiting for them and had escaped. Relief on their behalf poured through me but carefully, I neither stirred nor spoke.

Sylvester turned angrily away from the window and barked to Mrs Truebody that but for my condition, he would throw me into a cellar. 'You would probably let her out! Women! All right, see to her, put her to bed. And tell Hammond to get that window secured so that she can't open it and hold any more stolen chats with other men.'

Mrs Truebody came to me and pushed the bedcovers back. She caught hold of my ankles. 'Let's get you in.' I wished she would let me be. I felt strange, unwell, and I wanted to be alone to cry out my fear and my longing for Gilbert.

Mrs Truebody said: 'It's three of the clock, in the morning. All folk should be in bed at this hour. You just get between those blankets.'

'I can't!' I gasped. Something very weird indeed was happening to me. Water seemed to be running out of me. 'I'm . . . I'm having an accident. I'll make the blankets all wet. I don't understand it but . . .'

'What?' And then Mrs Truebody was fumbling about with me, in a personal and horrid way. Then she straightened up and said: 'Ah, well, all the excitement was too much for you, it seems. I think, my dear, that you're about to have your baby.'

'What? I'm having it now?'

'More or less. Doubt if anything much'll happen for a good while yet but I'll call Madge to bring a towel so you can clean yourself, and she'll fetch some candles. We'll stop with you.' She looked over her shoulder. 'Better you leave this to us women, sir. It's going to be a long night.'

Sylvester uttered a sound like a furious snort. 'I don't wish you a happy outcome, madam wife. On the contrary, I hope you die in your unlawful childbed.'

He marched out of the room. Mrs Truebody followed him, leaving me to sit there, terrified anew, wondering what would happen next. However, she was back in a few moments and shortly after that, Madge, looking excited and half asleep both at once, hurried in with a basin in one hand, a branched candlestick in the other and a long towel over one arm. She gave everything to Mrs Truebody and went away again, to return after a while with a jug of steaming water.

Meanwhile, I tried to mop myself up and then Mrs Truebody pushed me down into the bed. Quite kindly, she said: 'Don't be frightened. I have had children. I know all about it. Madge and I will look after you. Get some sleep while you can.'

But at that moment, the pains began, and there was no more sleep for me that night.

I would not have believed that anything could hurt so much and yet not kill me. The night passed. Dawn came in through the unshuttered window. I tried to take some rest, tried to swallow the broth that Madge brought me, but always another hideous pain would grip me and then it was impossible to rest, eat or even think.

The misery went on all day. Madge brought me more broth and I did manage to swallow some of it, and I was aware of Hammond coming in and doing something to the windows of my room. Darkness fell once more. There was only candle-light. I knew that other people were in the room; Mrs Truebody and Madge, taking turns. l was exhausted, longing for sleep.

And then, in the dawn, came a last ghastly moment when Mrs Truebody was standing over me, commanding me to push and my body was doing it anyway, and the pain was beyond belief. I heard myself scream. And then it was over. I heard the baby cry, though it was a feeble sound. Mrs Truebody and Madge were both there, attending to me, though I couldn't make out what they were doing. There were more contractions, but not such bad ones, and then they stopped. I tried to sit up against my pillow, and asked to see my baby.

'I am sorry, madam,' Mrs Truebody said. 'It died. It was premature, a good few weeks from the look of it and it didn't have the strength to live. It gave one little cry and then . . . better not see it. We'll take it away and bring you some more broth. Then you can have a good long sleep and wake up feeling better. Take heart! It won't be long before we'll be helping you bring forth the first of the master's children.'

'Was it a boy or a girl?' I demanded.

'A girl, God rest her soul. Now, settle back. We're looking after you. We're cleaning you up and then you should have something to sustain you. Bread and milk, with honey, I think, and some wine. Madge, see about it.'

I let them clean me, I ate what they brought me and drank a little wine. My body was quiet now but my mind was in anguish. I wanted my baby. They should have let me hold her, even if just for one moment, even if she was already dead. They should have let me!

For all my fears, the anger that had been smouldering inside me for so long grew a little more.

It was two days before Sylvester came. I had been thankful for the respite, since my husband was the very last person I desired to see. However, in the end he was bound to come. I greeted him with a still face and waited to hear what he had to say.

'I understand that you are recovering. Good. I want you on your feet as soon as possible. Those two rapscallions have got away. I doubt if they only came to talk to you, my love. There are signs that they have disturbed a garden shed and actually dug up a raised flowerbed. I have a suspicion concerning their real purpose. Can you guess at it, my love?'

I shook my head, bewildered.

Sylvester sat down on the end of my bed, in a positively companionable manner. 'There are things you had better know because as my wife you are likely to discover them anyway. I am capable of making sure that you don't betray me – should you wish to do so. Are you aware, Bella, that your brothers Hector and Stephen are privateers?'

'Yes, of course. They rob Spanish treasure ships. Like Sir Francis Drake. My mother and I always worry, because it's so dangerous.'

'The treasure they bring home,' said Sylvester, 'isn't right-fully theirs.'

'I don't understand.'

'Well, there's no need for you to understand everything. Take it from me; that is the case. I fancy that that woman Ursula Stannard, who has a reputation for poking her nose into things that don't concern her, is now nosing into their business. Our business, since they and I work together. Roger

Brockley's presence in my garden the other night certainly suggests that. I *think* that Brockley and Gale may have been searching for a cache of gold and jewels. I can't think what other purpose they could have had.'

I said nothing. I must not appear to know more than he had told me himself. He was staring at me, hard. 'I wanted to marry you because you are so beautiful that you invade my dreams, damn you.' His compliments were angry, not affectionate. 'But I also felt that it would act as a bond between me and your family. Those two things together were what made me decide that I must force your mother to give you to me.'

'What? You forced my . . .! How did you force her?' I sat up straight and pulled the thin pillow upright behind my shoulders.

'Well, husbands and wives shouldn't have secrets from each other,' Sylvester said, smiling. 'I've told you, haven't I, that your mother gave poison to Father Eliot, whose death was so unexpected? I simply threatened to accuse her publicly.'

I gaped at him. At last, I said: 'Yes, you did say something like that before but I didn't believe you. I thought you just said it to hurt me. Now you're saying it as though it's true, but it's my mother you're talking about! She would never do such a thing, and whatever for, anyway?'

'As to that, Eliot could of course have taken an overdose of one of Mother Lee's dubious potions. He was a remarkably foolish man. But your mother didn't like him and she did once warn me that she thought he had somehow learned of the activities of your brothers. Perhaps he threatened to inform on them. He would have said it was his duty as a man of God. Your mother *could* have acted on that, to protect her sons. Anyway, as I said to her, if I once set a rumour going that she had had a hand in his death . . .'

I was outraged, and worse. I felt as though my whole world were being violently shaken about, as though to dissolve my links with everyone I had ever loved, my mother, my brothers. My anger now was so great that I forgot to be afraid.

'How dare you say such a hateful lie about my mother! And how could you spread such a rumour without saying *why* my mother should do such a thing? You could hardly shout to the world that it was because her sons – and you – had broken the law yourselves!'

'Oh, I would have attributed Eliot's death at your mother's hands to something else . . . He was very hot against witches, you know. My rumour would say that she poisoned him because he threatened to have her tried for witchcraft. I could start a whisper that she had used magic to kill someone.'

'You couldn't be so cruel!'

'To tell the truth, I think she did poison Eliot, you know.' He said it quite calmly. He might as well have been saying, *She has a bad cold every autumn* or *I think she knitted a scarf for Father Eliot as a Christmas gift.* Once more, my brain reeled. 'But it's over now,' he assured me and he actually smiled. 'Your mother is safe enough, and Father Eliot can be forgotten, and I have you safe, as well. Beautiful as ever and free at last of the burden of someone else's baby. You are all mine now, and you may be assured that none of your family will come to harm through me.'

I just stared at him in bewilderment. He said: 'But with Mistress Stannard poking about I think it best to move away from here. Away from England, indeed. English winters are so cold and dark. Captain Julien, whom you briefly met, who is your brothers' partner, also recommends that we should move our business elsewhere. We therefore intend to transfer ourselves to Italy. We shall sometimes have dealings with Amsterdam, too – that's where your brothers are now though Italy will be our principal home.

'Your brothers are a trial sometimes,' he said thoughtfully. 'Captain Julien and I packed them off to Amsterdam with the profit from our latest voyage, because they really must learn how to deal with financiers; how to argue about valuations and so forth. This is the first time we've let them deal with bankers on their own. But Julien has followed them to find out how they've managed – he'll repair any mistakes they've made. At sea, my Bella, Hector and Stephen are splendid young men, as handy with sails as with swords, fearless and competent. Ashore, faced with men of finance, they are like timid children. But they are learning. However, what matters to us is that as soon as possible, we will remove to Italy.

'We will have to pretend to be Catholic, of course, but what are a few observances? We can use a desire to live in a Catholic country as a reason for wanting to establish ourselves in Italy. A few Hail Marys are a modest price to pay for a life in the sunshine. And in Italy it will be easier to dispose of treasure. Business will prosper. You will be happy. You'll bloom. And my sons will be born.'

'Please tell me,' I said, 'where is *my daughter* buried?'

'Oh yes, your bastard baby. It is a good thing that matters have turned out as they have. You will be able to travel, unencumbered. She is buried in the grounds. We've raised a cairn of stones over her. There were plenty of loose stones to be had – remember how that storm earlier this year wrecked a gardener's cottage on your mother's land? Hammond and I got the stones from that.'

'So she's not in consecrated soil?'

'She was base-born. Consecrated soil was too good for her.'

My poor little daughter. Gilbert's daughter too. In her brief life she had never, even for a few minutes, known the comfort of my arms. Her mother's arms. As for me, I had never even seen her. That was when my heart broke. I had heard people say that, and hitherto I had thought of it as – just a saying. Now I knew better. I felt my heart break. I felt it shatter. And then I felt as if the broken pieces had fallen into my smouldering anger and made it flare into such a blaze that I had to clutch the edge of my bedcoverings hard, to keep my rage silent. I said: 'I would like to be alone now.'

Somewhat to my surprise, he stood up at once. 'I will leave you. You have much to think about. No doubt, being just a woman, you will for a while have soft feelings for the little cuckoo you nearly brought into my nest. But when you have a lawful baby, you will forget this one. When you are better, you will be freed from this room, but you must never leave the house unless someone is with you. You might get into mischief if you have too much liberty. Farewell.'

He went out and didn't lock the door but I had no wish to leave the room. I turned over, pressing my face into the pillow.

We were to go to Italy. I was to produce a lawful baby. I would have to sleep with Sylvester again. The thought was appalling. I hated him with a strength that was far beyond words.

I pounded the pillow with my fists and cursed, until, in my exhaustion, I fell into a fevered sleep.

TWENTY-TWO
Sheer Obstinacy

Ursula's Narrative

T he morning after the moonlight treasure hunt, Brockley came to me before I had breakfasted, and told me, firstly, that it had been disastrous, and secondly that he and Gilbert had nevertheless been able to exchange a few words with Arabella, who was locked up while waiting to give birth to Gilbert's baby. She was well, Brockley said, but understandably frightened. And thirdly, that because of this, Gilbert had tried to urge Arabella into such dangerous and impossible schemes that Brockley said he could hardly believe his ears. I could hardly believe my ears, either. Brockley was seriously disturbed.

'I could believe, madam, that he meant every word and if he can get in touch with Arabella again, he may try to persuade her.'

'Let me think about this,' I said. 'Please ask Dale to bring me some breakfast in my chamber.' I certainly needed to think. Having broken my fast, I asked Dale to dress me in the one formal gown I had brought with me, a silvery blue and pale rose damask. I enhanced it with my biggest farthingale, a stiff ruff and a blue velvet hood with moonstones in it. Then I sent for Brockley. 'We are all going into Cutpenny to see Master Gale,' I said.

'In such a fine gown, ma'am?' Dale asked, puzzled.

'You will see why,' I told her.

Gilbert Gale's thwarted romance wasn't my business, and Heaven knows, I said to myself, I have defended the wrong thing once already. But I had a sense of responsibility towards Arabella. From what Brockley had told me, she seemed to have a fair amount of good sense herself, which was a blessing. But she was imprisoned and in disgrace and therefore frightened of the future and frightened people can do foolish things out of panic. Also, I had certainly been responsible for sending Gilbert and Brockley out in the night to search Waters' land for the treasure cache. Any outcome of that *was* my business.

The morning was cold, so we needed cloaks. I hid my finery under my warmest one. Then I took us all into Cutpenny, on foot.

We found Gilbert's shop open, with a heavily built cob tethered outside it, while Gilbert conferred with a large man in dramatically puffed breeches, a quilted doublet and a mighty ruff. We arrived in time to hear him saying how pleased he had been with a sideboard that Gilbert had once made for him. Now, his son was to be wed and he wished to give the young pair a bridal gift of furniture.

We tactfully retreated and walked up and down the street, waiting until the bridegroom's father had finished his business. It seemed like a long time but eventually he came out, with surprising nimbleness got into the saddle of his weight-carrying cob and rode away. 'Now,' I said.

Gilbert was waiting for us. 'I saw you hovering outside but that gentleman – he lives in Oxted – is an old customer of mine and it's a pleasure to work for him. Come in. My back room is warm. If anyone wants me, they'll shout.'

He led the way through a door at the back, which opened into a sparsely furnished parlour, though it did have a fire in the hearth. He looked tired but I was in no mood to care. I signalled to the Brockleys to stand by, slipped my cloak off and handed it to Dale, and sat down in the only chair in the room that had arms. Thus enthroned and – I hoped – looking like a king's daughter, I rested my forearms along the wide wooden chair arms, looked sternly at Gilbert and said: 'You are quite mad. Do you realize it?'

Gilbert, on the verge of sitting down as well, stopped short and looked, if not intimidated (Gilbert Gale would take a good deal of intimidating, I thought), but at least impressed. 'Master Brockley has told you about last night? You are saying that I am mad to want to rescue Mistress Arabella? She is in need of help! She is afraid.'

'That I can believe. But she can't escape from her husband's house. She is the wife of Sylvester Waters and she is to all intents and purposes his property. You *know* that.'

'*She is frightened*,' repeated Gilbert, now standing very straight and speaking with determination. 'I am ready to take her to safety.'

'It makes no difference! I sent you to search Master Waters' land for a cache of treasure, and if you were caught at it, you were to say that you were doing a little poaching and didn't realize you were on his land. I told you, for the love of Heaven, don't get yourselves caught inside his garden because then the excuse of poaching wouldn't do. And then you *do* go and get yourselves caught in the garden! As for Mistress Arabella – would you really abandon your home and your business and set out for Scotland, or anywhere else, accompanied by a heavily pregnant Arabella or perhaps with a very small baby, and possibly pursued by an outraged Sylvester Waters? Really? Now, let us be practical. How much of the Waters property did you manage to search?'

'Just the garden,' said Brockley. 'We can go again tonight and look over the farmland. We have finished with the grounds of the house.'

'No,' I said. 'Now, both of you, listen. Firstly, there is to be no more talk of running off with Arabella. She wouldn't be able to run very fast, as I trust you now realize, Master Gale. And as for the search, I am calling it off.'

'And leaving it unfinished, madam?' said Brockley, in the most obstinate voice that I had ever heard him use.

'Yes, Brockley, exactly that. This whole treasure hunt is too dangerous. Also, the more I think about it, the more I realize how absurd it is. There, you were right. We are making fools of ourselves. Even Cecil didn't quite visualize how impossible it would be. And if you are caught, God knows what will happen to you. We don't know if the cache even exists and if it does, it could be anywhere! We have hardly any chance of finding it and are running serious risks if we try.'

'I still think we should try. Cecil has asked it,' said Brockley, undeterred. 'We can take care. We *might* be lucky.'

'Mistress Stannard!' said Gilbert. 'I accept now that it would as yet be dangerous to Arabella to steal her out of that house, though I shall always be ready to try, if it seems that there is more danger in leaving her there. However, turning to the search, we are sure that no treasure is hidden in the topiary garden or in the kitchen and flower gardens beyond it. But we haven't examined the fields or the barns. It would be folly to neglect those, after we have come so far. I shall pursue the search alone if I must, even if Master Brockley feels he cannot disobey you.'

'There are times, madam, when I have had to disobey you,' said Brockley. 'With regret, and only because it seemed right. As you know.'

I looked at the pair of them with exasperation and they looked back at me. I knew Brockley in this mood. He was ranged with Gilbert and their masculine minds were made up. Whatever I said, they meant to finish the search. They no doubt considered themselves to be two determined men. I considered them to be two very obstinate ones. I had been fairly sure that to dress as a royal daughter and speak in the voice of one would impress them. But Brockley knew me too well and Gilbert perhaps didn't know me well enough.

'As before,' said Gilbert, infuriatingly, 'Master Brockley and I can meet on the track to Waters House. Perhaps not tonight; you may be right there. On Monday night, perhaps, to let a few days pass between our attempts.'

I protested but in vain. On Monday evening, Dale added her pleas to mine, but after dark, Brockley slipped quietly out of Evergreens. Dale and I went to bed and tried to sleep.

Tried but none too successfully. In fact, I lay awake nearly all night, except for an uneasy doze towards dawn. I was aroused by Dale. It was almost light and she was fully dressed, and distracted. 'Ma'am, ma'am, it's daybreak now and Roger isn't back!'

I was wide awake and out of bed on the instant. In the night, I had had time to think and to make desperate plans that I hoped would not be needed. Now it seemed that they were. 'Washing water, Dale. And a respectable gown – not the damask though – and a moderate farthingale. Breakfast first because we don't know what the day will bring but after that, we shall pay a visit to Waters House. Hurry!'

Breakfast was difficult, because Joan was present. She asked where Brockley was. Dale looked agonized. I said calmly: 'I believe he went out early. He is concerned about his horse – Firefly showed signs yesterday of throwing a splint.'

Dale, gallantly, asked: 'When are your sons expected home, Mistress Mercer? You must be missing them.'

'I always miss them,' said Joan. 'And worry about them. I don't know why they're not home now. I had a message about the ships needing repairs after being damaged in a storm on the way home and having to go abroad for special materials to do the repairs. I don't like the sound of that. When they put to sea again, I shall worry every day and every night. My husband always said that a ship that had to have serious repairs done, was never the same again. Well, they travel in company, the *Peregrine*, the *Osprey* and the *Silver Mermaid*. They can look after each other, I suppose. I hope!'

Her face was full of anxiety. But I was anxious too. Just what had happened to Gilbert Gale and Brockley last night? Where was Brockley now?

Dale had made one brave effort but she was now subsiding into a dither, glancing continually at the window and fidgeting. I thought it best to hurry with the cold ham and the bread and honey and the small ale, and get us both out of the house. We would go to Waters' House and hope for the best. If Brockley and Gilbert had been caught, Sylvester Waters wasn't likely to believe that we were merely calling to ask after Arabella's welfare, but we would still claim that we were, and trust to luck and our own eyes and ears and hope to learn something. I looked warningly at Dale and somehow kept her silent until we were out of doors and out of earshot of Joan. Then, of course, the dam broke.

'Ma'am, where *is* he? He ought to have been back long ago. That man's got him, the way he nearly did before. But what will he do with him – them?'

'I don't know, but we're going to find out. We will behave like two ladies visiting a neighbour and see what transpires. One thing is hopeful – I don't think he will dare to harm us. He knows quite well who I am.'

We left in the ordinary and expected manner by way of the gatehouse, calling good morning to Jankin, who was tending his vegetable patch with the help of one of his sons. We turned right, on to the track that would take us to Waters House.

We were perhaps a furlong and a half along it when we heard someone calling: 'Mistress Stannard, *Mistress Stannard!*' The call came from behind us and was pitched oddly low, as though whoever it was didn't want the sound to carry too far. We turned round and there was Gilbert Gale, emerging from a patch of bushes, looking dishevelled but beckoning to us urgently. We turned back and hastened to meet him.

'Where's Roger?' Dale said, before anyone else could speak. 'Where *is* he – what happened to you? Tell me he's safe, please tell me he's safe!'

'Yes, he's safe, though bruised – they knocked us about when they caught us last night and he got the worst of it. But' – Gilbert was grinning – 'we were shut up in an attic but – well, Mistress Arabella will tell you the tale and what a tale it is!'

At close quarters, I could see that Gilbert had a cut on his face and that his treasure-hunting garments, his woollen shirt, well-used leather jerkin and mended breeches, were all much the worse for wear, grubby and with fresh tears in the breeches.

'We're being hunted, of course,' said Gilbert. 'For the moment we've taken refuge in my house, though I crept out at dawn to watch for you. Mistress Arabella's there too.'

'Arabella! But I told you, she can't run away from her home . . . Waters will be after her like a bloodhound!' I said. 'I pity her sincerely but I know the law. Did you find anything, by the way?'

'We didn't find any gold ingots,' said Gilbert grimly. 'But just wait until we tell you – as we had to tell Arabella – what we did find. Please follow me now. Not on this open track. I know another way. It's a trifle long but it will bring us to my back door.'

It was more than a trifle long. It was an hour before we at last reached a narrow lane between the smallholdings on the north side of the village street, and the backs of the cottages. Gilbert pushed a gate open and we hastened in through a rear garden, mostly planted with vegetables. A moment later, we were in through the back door of his home.

We found Brockley and Arabella in Gilbert's back room. Brockley had a bruise on his left cheekbone and his clothes, like Gilbert's, were grimed and torn. Arabella was in a plain brown gown with neither ruff nor farthingale. As I came in, she looked me in the eyes and said: 'I will not go back to him. And if we can make the truth come out, I shouldn't have to.'

'What happened?' I said.

'A great deal,' said Brockley. 'Not just what we have found, but what Mistress Arabella had to tell us. We need to move quickly, before that man Waters leaves the country.'

TWENTY-THREE
The Anger Grows

Arabella's Narrative

It was plain enough that Sylvester meant to keep me as a wife, whatever my sins and shortcomings. He wanted me, it seemed, because of my beauty and because I represented a bond between himself and my brothers. Though he and they seemed to be firmly entangled already. Perhaps it really was just my beauty that he desired, as though I were a jewelled brooch he could wear in his hat.

My damned beauty. I hated it now, as much as I hated him. I couldn't imagine that I looked very beautiful after that hideous premature childbed, but Madge brushed my tangled hair and washed me, and after only two days I had stopped wanting to cry all the time and even the bleeding had grown less. Madge encouraged me to look into the small silver mirror that I had brought with me from Evergreens and I saw that I looked almost like myself again. Except that my eyes were subtly changed. They had become the eyes of a woman with a certain kind of knowledge. Too much of it and not happy knowledge, either.

The child had been born in the early hours of Friday morning. At supper time on Sunday evening, Madge brought me a loose, informal gown from the press in our marital chamber, and Mrs Truebody urged me to rise, to put it on and go downstairs to have supper with Sylvester. I was no longer locked in but now that I was free to leave my room, I would rather have stayed in it. I didn't want to have supper with Sylvester; I wished with all my heart that I need never set eyes on Sylvester again. He had taken my baby from me. He had told me horrible things about my mother, too. But of course, sooner or later, I must see him again; there was no avoiding it. So it might as well be now.

Sylvester greeted me graciously. I responded stiffly. Much as I hated him, I also feared him. I didn't trust his smile and his plans for our future appalled me. Go to Italy? Live there, far from all familiar things and totally in his power? God help me, no!

He bade me be seated, so I did. He said he hoped that I would soon be quite well again. All was ready for our journey to Italy. Hammond would be coming with us and so would Madge. Mrs Truebody would remain to take care of the house. In due course, Hammond would return and arrange to let it. In Italy, Sylvester said, he trusted that I would soon be able to take my place once again as his wife. I would have to learn Italian, of course, but that would be an interest for me as I settled down in my new home. The more gracious he sounded, the more afraid of him I became.

And then, just as Sylvester was describing the features of Rome to me, I blurted it out. 'My baby. Did you at least say a prayer for her?'

The interruption had startled him. He looked taken aback. But he answered. 'No, of course not. Why should I? Oh, I suppose you would want to. I am an indulgent husband. Before we leave for Italy, Hammond will show you the cairn and you can say a prayer, if you wish.'

'Thank you.' I forced it out. My poor child. No loving arms, even for one minute. No name, no consecrated resting place. Not even a prayer. I would have liked to kill him.

On Monday, I rested all day but again, I was commanded to take supper with Sylvester. I made myself appear submissive. He smiled approval. He thought he had me subdued, penitent and cowed.

He was wrong. During the twenty-four hours since supper on Sunday, I had made up my mind, or my mind had made itself up, without reference to me. I would not ever again be a wife to this man. I would never lie with him again. I would not, *not* go to Italy with him. I quaked, trying to imagine how I could refuse these things. But refuse I would. Somehow. *Somehow.* The right moment would come and I would seize it. I must!

The moment came much sooner than I expected.

During that second supper, we conversed about trivialities. Afterwards, I once more retired. It was far too soon anyway for me to return to the marital bedchamber, so I was still in my attic cell. I fell asleep quickly, only to be awakened in the depths of the night by a racket outside. I got out of bed and went to the window. Hammond had fastened it shut but I could still see out of it. The moon was just past the full but only just. The garden was bathed in silver light.

It was also dotted with lanterns, all moving about quickly. I couldn't hear anything but I saw the lights converging and I caught the flash of a sword and then I did hear something, faintly, but I knew that voice. Brockley was swearing. And then, I was sure, I heard Gilbert shouting, *Let me go, let me go!*

Then I saw a group of men – they had half a dozen lanterns between them – coming towards the house, marching, or dragging, two shadowy captives. They passed close beneath my window and I caught Sylvester's voice, saying – I was sure he was saying – *Put them in the attic!*

The shadow figures and the lanterns moved towards the side door and disappeared. I left the window and went to my door, opening it a crack. I could hear nothing and if the prisoners had been brought to any of the attics in this wing, I surely would have done. As it was, the silence was total. No boots or voices, either bullying or protesting. No slamming of doors.

But Waters House had two wings, extending eastwards from the two ends of the main building. My attic was at the end of the southernmost wing. In the main house, there were guest rooms on the top floor. However, there were attics in the northern wing. If the prisoners hadn't been brought to this wing, then they were surely in the northern one.

I sat down on the bed to think. I was coming to a decision. It was a decision that frightened me so much that for a few moments, I thought I was going to be sick. And yet the decision held. I waited for what seemed a long time, because I must leave time for the captives to be bestowed and for their captors to retire. But at length, trembling, I stood up and made ready.

I had a candle and it was a thick, long-lasting one. I was

able to find my shoes and dress myself in the old brown gown that I had worn during most of my imprisonment. I had no cloak and I would have to do without. Taking my stout candle, which had burnt down a fair way but still had a good deal of life in it, I crept out of the room, and stood listening. There was still no sound.

Cautiously, I started down the stairs. There were windows here and there was moonlight enough to let me see my way. One storey down – there were spare bedchambers here – then down again and round a bend in the stairs and here were the doors to one of the three parlours in Waters House, and to Sylvester's study. There was still no sound.

I went silently into the study and to its window, which looked towards the other wing. Surely, there was a glint of light there, high up, yes. That must be an attic window. I had guessed right. That was where the captives had been taken.

If only I could reach them! If I couldn't release them I might at least talk to them, through a door. I could talk to Gilbert again! The very thought of talking to him ran through me like a warm stream. And I would be able to pass on what I now knew. They might eventually be able to pass it on further; I could hope so, anyway. And I might be able to help them. I might!

The utter silence began to oppress me. To be alone in the dark with only the flickering flame of one candle by which to see my way was frightening. The candle shadows swayed, stretched out into fantastic shapes. But a candle was all I had.

I wouldn't have dared to go on, except for my festering anger, my hatred of Sylvester, my fears for Gilbert. In the eyes of many, Sylvester had a right to be angry with me but he should have granted an innocent new-born the decency of a proper grave. *I would no longer be his wife. I was not going to Italy.*

Trembling badly but persevering, I crept to the ground floor, where a long gallery stretched the length of the main house, from the south wing to the north. I tiptoed through it and found myself on the ground floor of the north wing. I became muddled in the darkness and all but fell down the stairs that led down to the kitchens and the servants' quarters. The same staircase also went up, through all the floors of the north wing to its attics.

I had never been into the north wing before except to visit the kitchens. Aware that the servants were sleeping below me, I climbed with great caution, now shivering with the cold as much as with my fear. At the top I found a door leading straight into an attic. In the doorway, I recoiled from a vista of strange candlelit shapes and menacing dark corners. Then, venturing in, I saw that the place was strewn with abandoned pieces of furniture, battered chests and a heap of moth-eaten old curtains. A low door in the middle of the wall at the far end led into another attic, littered in the same fashion. A clothes press with a door half off momentarily blocked my way and I banged my nose as it swung. I nearly dropped my candle. Trembling, I edged round the door and on to the other end of that attic, seeking a further way out.

At first, I couldn't find one. Nervously clutching the candle, I crept along the wall, first one way, then the other. Then to my relief I found that there *was* another door, at the extreme left-hand end of the wall. I tiptoed through it and found myself in a narrow passageway. It had small windows though they didn't provide much light, for they looked to the north. There were doors to my right. I opened the first two, holding up my candle, and made out that they were small bedchambers, like the ones above the central building.

They were quite ordinary, with simple door handles and no locks on the outside though they had small bolts inside, I suppose in case the occupants needed privacy. The third, however, had two stout bolts on the outside, both drawn shut. I held the candle close to see. Then I put my ear to the door and listened.

At first there was only silence but then . . . that was a snore. Surely, surely, that was a snore. And this couldn't be the bedchamber of some manservant or groom whose loyalty was only to Sylvester, not with those closed bolts. I tapped on the door, and then tapped again, louder, and then more loudly still and once more pressed my ear to the door. Inside, there were grunting noises and then voices. I couldn't make out any words but I knew those voices. I banged on the door with a clenched fist and then dragged the bolts open. I opened the door and stood there with my candle positioned to illuminate my face.

A moment later, I was in Gilbert's arms. For a little while, all we could do was cling and kiss, until Brockley, who was still sitting on the straw pallet where they had evidently fallen asleep, cleared his throat in a noticeable kind of way and we broke apart.

I spoke first. 'What in the world is this room? It has bolts on the outside. Does Sylvester make a habit of imprisoning people here?'

'I fancy,' said Gilbert, 'that in the past, maybe a generation or two ago, there was a wayward lass like you, my love, who didn't want to marry the man her parents had chosen for her. So she was bolted in on bread and water until she said she would obey.'

'I could have borne the bread and water,' I said. 'But not the other. I'm sorry, Gilbert. The other was too hard for me.'

'No one blames you for that,' Brockley said soberly. 'I heard it happening.'

The memory sickened me and I didn't want to talk about it. I said: 'Why have you been in the grounds at night? Were you searching? What were you looking for? When I saw your lanterns the first time, it seemed as though you were seeking for something. You were going back and forth so carefully. What was it? Did you find it?'

'We were searching, yes. We didn't find what we were looking for, but . . . wait.' Brockley and Gilbert looked at each other. In the light of one candle, I couldn't make out their expressions. Then Brockley said: 'It doesn't matter what we were searching for, only what we found. It was something . . . it's serious. We must report it to Mistress Stannard. But we're not sure whether we ought to tell you, my dear. It's so shocking. Look, we shouldn't waste time. We should be getting out of here.'

'Wait!' I said. 'I have something important to tell you.' And then I got it out in a gabble. 'There's-something-wrong-about-my-brothers'-voyages-they-sail-with-a-friend-called-Captain-Julien-and-my-brothers-have-taken-the-profits-of-the-last-voyage-to-some-bankers-but-there-are-leftovers-from-the-voyage-before-

and-these-are-being-left-till-it's-safe-to-collect-them-only-they're-
not-safe-where-they-are-so-they're-being-moved-and-I-expect-they-
have-been-by-now-and-Sylvester-and-my-brothers-and-Julien-are-
moving-to-Italy-and-me-with-them-because-a-London-jeweller-
called-Theobald-Roebuck-is-in the-Tower.'

'Say that again, slower!' said Brockley.

I did so, though nervously, for I too was afraid every moment
that we would hear ominous footsteps approaching. At the
end, I said: 'But what is it that you've found, that you don't
want to tell me about? I ought to know – whatever it is.'

Brockley began to shake his head, but then stopped. He
looked at Gilbert. 'It will come out eventually. We have to see
that it does. Gale, I think it's up to you.'

'Must I?' Poor Gilbert sounded appalled.

'I think so. Mistress Arabella, sit down.'

I sank down onto the pallet. The room wasn't bare. Despite
those massive bolts on the wrong side of the door, this too
seemed to be a disused servants' bedchamber. The straw pallet
had no coverings but in itself it was a good enough mattress.
There was also a clothes press, two stools, and a bucket. I
looked up at Gilbert, dear Gilbert. The moonlight, glinting in
through the open door, showed me that his face was bruised.
It also showed me his eyes, his kind eyes, looking at me but
with such sorrow that I was frightened. 'Gilbert, what *is* it?'

He said: 'The child . . . our child . . . I have just held you
close and it seems to me – you have had the baby, haven't
you?'

'Yes. A daughter. She was born too soon. At dawn on Friday.
She died at birth,' I said shortly.

'Yes. We realized that something of the sort must have
happened. I know. Dear God . . . and here you are on your
feet, creeping through attic rooms to rescue us! You ought to
be still in bed being cosseted!'

'There's no cosseting to be had in Waters House,' I told
him.

'But it's shameful . . .!' Gilbert's voice failed.

Brockley said: 'We were searching for a cache of unlawful
treasure. I expect you have been told that your brothers are
privateers but they are not, they are simply pirates. There's no

time now to explain any further. Listen. We found a cairn and wondered if that marked the hiding place . . .'

'A cairn?' The word came out in a gasp.

'Yes. Does that mean something to you?'

'Sylvester told me he'd buried my baby in the grounds and raised a cairn over her. He wouldn't have her buried in conse-crated soil. She should be lying in the Cutpenny churchyard, and Father Dunberry should have said the burial service over her!'

Just saying those words brought all my outrage to the surface. 'I'll never forgive him. It wasn't her fault that she wasn't his. She was innocent! What had she done? Did you find . . . her? Did she have a coffin? I didn't want to ask Sylvester.'

Brockley and Gilbert looked at each other again. '*What is it?*' I said. Shouted, if one can shout in a near-whisper. '*Tell me!*' I could have slain them. My mind was already creating horrors; visions of ghastly malformations swam before my eyes.

'We moved the stones,' said Gilbert, and I could hear that he was controlling his voice with difficulty, 'looking for treasure, and we found her instead. She hadn't been given a coffin. She was wrapped in something, that was all. I drew the covering down. I realized that this must be your – our – baby. I wanted to see the face of my child. I didn't know until you told me just now that we had a daughter. I just wanted to see my baby's face.'

'Yes? And?'

'Our daughter didn't die at birth,' said Gilbert, his voice cold and clipped as he said the unbearable. 'She was strangled. Not by hands but by a twisted silk cord. It was still round her neck. It was the sort of thing a man might use to tie a dressing robe round him. Even in death, the baby's eyes were . . . were . . . prominent and bloodshot. Our daughter was murdered, Arabella.'

I felt as though I had always known it. The decision I had taken in my room acquired a final step.

'We must get out of this house,' I said. 'I'm coming too. I will not stay here. I have already decided that I will not be his wife again and this is my moment to escape. Better go out to the rear. The lodge keeper has mastiffs.'

'No, you can't!' said Brockley. 'He will only hunt you down.'

'I can! Sylvester Waters has murdered our daughter, Gilbert's and mine. I am not bound to stay with a murderer! I *will* not stay with a murderer. What did he intend to do with you, I wonder?'

'He didn't see us at the cairn,' said Brockley. 'We put the stones back and we were well away from it when we were caught. I think he means, at the last minute, before he runs off abroad, to hand us over to the Caterham constables, calling us intruders, suspected of trying to rob the house. Perhaps, for the moment, you should stay here and pretend . . .'

'I've just told you! Sylvester means to take me to Italy with him and in any case, I *can't* pretend! Could *you*? I am so angry!'

It occurred to me suddenly that of all my family, the only one who had ever shown any glimmer of understanding about me was Stephen. What was it that he had said to me, that day when we met at Mother Lee's cottage? *You'll tame him . . . you'll deal with him, given time . . . you're not the little mouse you sometimes pretend to be, that Mother makes you be.*

Fiercely, I said: 'My mother tried to teach me that ladies should never be angry, that we should always be meek and complaisant, but I am none of those things. I am not meek. I am angry and it's a just anger and I have a right to it. *I am coming with you!*'

TWENTY-FOUR
Heavy On The Wing

Ursula's Narrative

The next few days were confused. The Brockleys and I took Arabella home, for she could scarcely remain with Gilbert, no matter how much they both wished it. Her natural refuge was with her mother. We were greeted by an outraged Joan, who demanded, arms akimbo, to know the meaning of this and whether she was being asked to shelter her disgrace of a daughter and if so, why.

'Master Waters has been here, my girl. I know how you tried to pass off your bastard brat as his! He came here, searching for you. And now you want me to protect you from his justified wrath!'

'I didn't even know I was pregnant until Mrs Truebody explained things to me!' Arabella shouted at her. 'You told me what Sylvester would do to me on our wedding night but you never ever said a word about how babies begin!'

'Such things are not for women to talk about. I remembered how it was for me when I married, not knowing beforehand what marriage meant, so on your marriage eve I told you that much. But as for starting babies – are you a wantwit? Do you have to be told the obvious? What did you think might happen when you and Gilbert Gale . . . when you and Gilbert Gale . . .!'

Here Joan stumbled over the right words and Arabella said: 'I *didn't know*. It was all so natural.'

'*Natural!* You unspeakable . . .! I pity Master Waters with all my heart! But he came wanting you back and back you will go. If you refuse, well, I made you marry him, didn't I? I can make you return to him in the same way.'

'If you try, I will fight you tooth and nail. He is about to flee to Italy because he fears that he is under suspicion and he wants to take me with him but *I will not go!*'

This time Arabella did not shout. Her voice was as cold as a blade of ice. Her eyes were full of anger. For a moment, I saw her mother in her.

Brockley interrupted, with equal coldness. 'Mistress Mercer, your daughter's baby, your granddaughter, was murdered. We found the body. The baby was strangled with a cord of twisted silk. It was still there. Master Waters has committed the crime of infanticide. And there is more. Arabella has heard Waters and one Captain Julien saying some interesting things.'

'What? What are you talking about?' Joan turned on him.

'Let me explain. Firstly, Sylvester Waters, for whom you are so sorry, took a living girl baby from her mother's arms and strangled her with the cord of a dressing robe and buried her in an unconsecrated grave. He had the decency to protect her from foxes and the like by raising a cairn of stones. That is all that can be said for him. At least one of his servants must have helped him. Hammond, probably. We found the cairn when we were on his land. We investigated it. Then we rebuilt it. It took two of us to move those heavy stones. And also . . .'

Brockley, silencing Joan with an upraised palm, repeated the gist of the conversation that Arabella had overheard between her husband and Captain Julien.

'What? What are you saying?' Joan became bemused, unable to take any of it in.

'What does all this matter?' Arabella shouted. She seemed to have lost interest in treasure or dubious privateering. She was obsessed with her baby. 'What matters is that my child should have a proper funeral. She should be laid to rest in the Cutpenny churchyard. She should have a name. Gilbert and I have chosen one. Her name is Gilbertine and Father Dunberry should baptize her.'

'He won't,' said Joan shortly. 'She has been dead too long.'

Whereupon, Arabella burst into furious tears. I drew her into my arms. She buried her tears and her cries of rage in my shoulder. Brockley, patiently, said: 'The cairn must stay as it is. Because it, and what lies beneath it, are evidence of the crime that Sylvester Waters has committed. Things must lie undisturbed at least until one of the Caterham constables has seen them. And they must hear about these plans for hiding treasure and running away to Italy.'

'And how will you explain what you were doing, prowling round Sylvester's garden in the middle of the night, with lanterns?' demanded Joan.

'We'll tell the truth,' I said, over Arabella's tousled head. 'Your sons, Joan, are suspected, under the cloak of trading, of piracy. No question of privateering; they have been evading payments to the Treasury. Furthermore, they are suspected of piracy not just against Spanish shipping, which would be legal as long as they were licensed by the Crown and the Treasury received a share, but against our own English ships. But evidence is needed. I have been charged with the task of trying to find out where they conceal their treasure when they first bring it ashore. I was to search near their home. Others are searching at the coast.'

'What?' Scarlet in the face, Joan bridled furiously and began to shout that her sons were being falsely accused. When the storm abated for a moment, Brockley informed her coldly that for the moment, since her sons were not at home, very little could be done about them directly. But as for Master Waters, they had left the cairn as it was until a representative of the law could examine it and what lay under it. Then, no doubt, Waters would be arrested and might have some interesting tales to tell, quite apart from facing the charge of infanticide.

Joan's shocking response to that was to say that her wicked daughter had probably murdered the baby herself to spare her husband the embarrassment of having another man's child under his roof. Whereupon Arabella had to be held back from trying to claw her mother's face. I doubt if, at that moment, Arabella was entirely sane. She at last desisted, weeping, and begging, over and over, that Gilbertine should have a proper burial.

Page was sent off to fetch a constable from Caterham and came back with the two we had met at the time of Mother Lee's death. One, Master John Rawlings, was a large, middle-aged gentleman with a spectacular moustache, who was normally the owner of three flourishing businesses – a hiring stables, a clothing warehouse and a book-binders – in Caterham.

The other, Master Thomas Dunn, was a skinny fellow barely past his youth, who worked in his father's brewery. Both were at first inclined to disbelief when they heard our story, but they did finally let Brockley and Gilbert take them to Waters House to see for themselves, and also to confront Sylvester, though not until they were reinforced by extra men. On Brockley's recommendation, they sent back to Caterham for the men who acted as their volunteer aides in case of any violent affray. In the late afternoon, they went up to Waters House in a body.

They found that both Sylvester and Hammond were gone, and that there was indeed a murdered baby underneath the cairn.

Many of the Waters House servants were under orders of dismissal and had been bidden to leave within a week. A few still remained in their posts, however. Mrs Truebody and Madge were still there and what they had to say matched Arabella's account. Joan's nasty suggestion that Arabella had killed her own baby was thoroughly refuted.

'Mrs Truebody and the maidservant Madge both say the same,' John Rawlings told us. 'The baby was taken from her mother, weak but still living, and put in a cradle in the room next door. Mrs Truebody herself carried it there and confirms that it was alive then. After that, she had you to attend to, Mistress Waters. You were in your bed and could not leave it. A little later, Master Waters went to see the child and came back saying that it had died. Mrs Truebody had been with you all the time. Master Waters said he and Hammond would attend to the matter and then he called Hammond and they went off, presumably to where the dead child was. No one asked questions. Mrs Truebody and Madge both said that no one ever argued with Master Waters. About half an hour later, Madge says she saw Master Waters and Hammond go out of the house, Master Waters carrying a wrapped bundle.'

No one had said anything about the father of the child. Joan tried to but caught such a savage look from Arabella that she stopped.

There were laws against fathering illegitimate children. But I had been born out of wedlock myself and so had my son Harry. Harry's father was long dead and had been a Frenchman anyway and I could laugh, trying to imagine anyone arresting King Henry the Eighth on a charge of fathering children outside wedlock. For years, his illegitimate but acknowledged son Henry Fitzroy had been reared as a possible heir, if his marriage couldn't produce a lawful one. I didn't know how much danger Gilbert would be in if anyone mentioned him, but if no one else mentioned him, I certainly wouldn't.

'And now the bird has flown,' said Dunn regretfully, his mind still on Waters.

Arabella snorted as though stifling a giggle and said: 'Sylvester is a heavy bird to be taking wing! He was preparing to go to Italy so now, I suppose, he has gone. He will probably meet my brothers there. I doubt if they mean to come home.'

'We'll pursue Waters,' said the older constable. 'Or you'll remain wedded to him, ma'am. But if we get him – I think you'll be rid of him soon. Meanwhile, you can arrange your poor child's funeral.'

The pursuit set out. It would be a complex business, since they would have to declare themselves to the constables in the parishes through which they would have to travel, but they assured us that they wouldn't let that delay them much.

Meanwhile, little Gilbertine was at last brought from her makeshift grave and Gilbert said to me that he would make a coffin for his daughter. Father Dunberry had been approached. He said severely that surely we all knew that it was against Church law to baptize a dead child. However, he agreed that she could have a grave in Cutpenny's churchyard. When did we wish to hold the funeral?

I urged Joan to attend the funeral along with the rest of us. If we showed a united front to the village, there would be less gossip, I told her. Heaven knew that there would be enough anyway, with Master Waters suddenly leaving the country and being pursued by the law, while his wife was left behind with

her mother. Sullenly, Joan consented and joined in with
Arabella and Dale and me as we prepared suitable clothing
for the ceremony.

Dale and I both had black gowns with us, but they were
too smart for this grim occasion. Trimmings must be removed
and fullness taken out. Joan said that the neckline of her one
black gown had never seemed a perfect fit; now, perhaps, was
the time to put it right. Her maid Jane was unwell with a heavy
cold ('I won't let her near any of us,' said Joan), so Joan was
doing her own alterations. Arabella too had repairs to make.
Her clothes were mostly still at Waters House but one old
black gown had been left behind when she married. It was
suitable enough but it needed some repairs. The four of us
sewed together in silence until Joan tutted and shook her gown
out.

'The cuff's torn. When did that happen? Just look at this! A
whole strip has been torn off. Why did Jane have to fall sick
just now? I hope I've got some black material that will do.'

Grumbling, she reached into her workbasket where she had
a compartment for odd pieces of material, for use in patching,
and began to rummage in it. As she did so, I suddenly realized
that Dale was trying to catch my eye.

I opened my mouth but she shook her head, put a finger to
her lips and then mouthed: *Upstairs.*

A few minutes later, leaving Arabella and her mother to
continue sewing, I set my work aside, beckoned to Dale and
went with her out of the room and upstairs to my chamber.
'What is it?' I asked, as I closed the door.

'Ma'am, do you remember when we found poor Mother
Lee, you took a piece of black wool material out of her hand?'

'Yes. I did.'

'It was a strip, and when Mistress Mercer held her torn cuff
up to look at it better, what was missing was a strip, too. I
was sitting beside her and I could see the shape of the piece
that was missing. Have you kept the stuff we took from Mother
Lee?'

'I think so. It's still in the hidden pouch in the gown I was
wearing when we found her. The brown one. It's in the press
behind you.'

Dale groped in the press, found the gown, searched in the hidden pouch and finally produced the torn piece of cloth. We sat staring at each other.

'We can't be sure,' I said.

'We can make sure, ma'am. Wait until Mistress Joan is out of the way – she is going to Caterham this afternoon to buy some linen. We can look in her clothes press and see if this piece matches the repair in the cuff.'

'But why in the world should Joan want to harm Mother Lee? She used her headache remedies!'

But there were times when Dale's intelligence worked more swiftly and accurately than mine or Brockley's. 'Ma'am, what if Mother Lee knew what the Mercer boys were up to? She might have become a threat to them somehow – perhaps she had an attack of conscience and threatened to report them. That might frighten Mistress Mercer and make her very angry, too.'

I thought about it and then said: 'Call Brockley. We'll wait until Mistress Joan goes off to Caterham. Then we'll examine the repair to her cuff. And after that . . . I wonder. I think we should go up the hill to Mother Lee's. This very afternoon.'

'Go up to the cottage?'

'Yes. It's because of what Arabella overheard, about moving some treasure left over from an earlier voyage. I have had an idea. We thought of it earlier but for one reason or another, set it aside. But now – all of a sudden, I think it's obvious!'

.

TWENTY-FIVE
Rope and Nails

'No doubt about it,' I said, holding the mended cuff of Joan's black gown to the light. She had repaired it, stitching a strip of matching black material neatly into place, but the stitchwork gave the shape of the original tear. A strip about four inches long had been ripped from the cuff, ending where it met a seam. Both the shape and the texture of the material matched the piece that had lain so long in the pouch in my old brown gown. The Brockleys, one on either side of me, were nodding their heads in unison.

'We leave all this for the moment,' I said. 'Now, let's go up to Mother Lee's cottage.'

'Madam,' said Brockley, 'do you really think that the treasure may be there?'

'I don't suppose it was taken there until after Mother Lee was dead. But then, where better to hide it?'

We went equipped for a serious search. We had two spades, a chisel and a hammer, a box of nails of various sizes and a coil of rope, all filched from a shed in the Evergreens garden, our own lanterns and a tinderbox. Brockley doubted that we would need either the rope or the nails, but I said we should bring anything at all that *might* be useful.

I was riding astride, in an old gown that could easily be bundled round me, and Brockley and I carried a spade each, placed blade uppermost, handles resting on our left feet and held fast in our left hands. We rode slowly. However carefully we balanced them, the spades were difficult to carry. The rope coil was slung round Brockley's shoulder. Dale had everything else in saddlebags. It was windy weather and autumn leaves whirled round us as we went up the hill, but at least it was dry.

The clearing at the top was hushed. Yes, the surrounding woods rustled and creaked in the wind, but no donkey galloped to the gate of the little field; no goats bleated, no chickens cackled. No smoke rose from the chimney. The cottage stood empty.

'Do we just walk straight in?' asked Dale nervously.

'There won't be much point in knocking,' said Brockley reasonably. 'I doubt if anyone's home.'

We dismounted. Brockley eased girths, ran up stirrups and secured our mounts to the gate of the empty field. We went to the cottage door. It was shut but as it had no outside lock, it opened easily when I pushed it.

Inside, it was full of shadows and it smelt. There was rotting straw underfoot. I led the way across the main room, into the kitchen. It seemed bare; most of the pots and utensils had gone to the auction. I turned away and threw open the door into the little bedroom. Mice skittered across the floor. Dale squeaked and jumped, clutching her skirts tightly round her. The blankets on the bed were still there. They looked grubby. Presumably, no one had thought them worth offering for sale.

'So,' said Brockley. 'Where do we begin?'

'If you wanted to hide a chest or two of treasure here, where would you put it?'

'Under the floor,' said Brockley. 'We never thought to bring a broom! We need to sweep this mucky straw out.'

In the lean-to we found a worn broom that, like the blankets, had probably been dismissed as worthless when the rest of Mother Lee's goods were taken. However, if its bristles were battered there were enough still there to let Dale make short work of the straw in the main room. Then we studied the floor.

Most such cottages had floors of hard-packed earth, but this one was covered with wooden planks. They didn't look old and I somehow couldn't imagine Mother Lee having such flooring put in. It would have been costly, ordering it, taking the measurements, getting the planks cut to size and laid. But if the earth floor had been disturbed, then the Mercer boys might have found it worthwhile to lay the planks as concealment.

Brockley knelt down and tried to poke fingers into the cracks between the planks. 'I want to see if any of these boards seem looser than others.' He shuffled backwards and then stopped, peering closely. 'It's so shadowy here. Madam, please light a lantern.'

Dale was already at work with the tinderbox. The lantern was lit and set down beside Brockley. He moved here and there with it, peering closely at the floor. He looked up.

'Most of the planks are nailed down; there must be battens underneath them. But there are some planks here that don't have any nails in them.' He edged sideways. 'Yes, look! These planks don't stretch the length of the room! This part of the floor is made up from shortish lengths of planking, just laid end to end, and there are no nail heads. Let's have it up!'

This was easy to say but not so easy to do. In the end, Brockley managed it with the chisel, inserting the edge between two planks and finally heaving a loose board out of its place. Once one board was up, the rest came up easily. When all the unsecured planks had been shifted, a pit was revealed. We all went down on our knees to peer in.

It was fairly deep and well made, with more timber planks to line it and hold its earthen sides in place. And within it . . .

'There's a box, or a chest, down there,' Brockley said. 'And other things too but that's the biggest.' He stretched an arm down. 'There are ropes coiled on top of it.' He stretched further and then said: 'Fran, hold my feet. I've almost got to stand on my head.'

We held a foot each and Brockley slithered headfirst into the pit. 'The ropes are wrapped round the box and then the ends are left on top,' he said, his voice sounding strange and hollow. 'They're for getting this big box up. Haul me out. I'll bring the ropes with me.'

Panting, we dragged him back onto the floor. His hands were full of ropes and when we examined them, we saw that there were two long ends, both ending in loops. 'To give a grip, I suppose,' said Brockley. 'We'd better haul away and see what comes up.'

Nothing came up. Whatever was in the boxes was heavy.

'What have we got horses for?' asked Dale. 'And haven't we brought rope? If we used it to lengthen these, then . . .'

'If I bring my Firefly into what he'll think is a strange and unnatural stable and then ask him to pull things like a mere workhorse,' Brockley said, 'he'll kick the place to pieces. And Blue Gentle might find anything so heavy hard to shift. But, madam, your Jaunty . . .'

'Jaunty is both strong and good-natured,' I said. 'I'll bring him in.'

I did so, and we used the rope we had brought, combined with the ropes from the cavity, to create a chest harness. We padded it with Brockley's cloak, positioned Jaunty carefully and then I took his bridle and coaxed him forward. He rolled his eyes and laid his ears back but I stroked his nose and talked to him and at last, trustingly, he came with me. Brockley and Dale lent their weight to the ropes as well. The box came up, swinging, bumping against the timbers of the pit. Then with a lurch and thud, it thumped onto the floor. It was well secured with several turns of rope.

I released Jaunty, petted him, promised him rewards of apples and led him back into the open air. I tethered him and came back to find Brockley on his knees, using his belt knife to saw through the ropes round the box. This took some time, but at last, the box lay before us, untrammelled. I recognized the timber it was made from. Mahogany. It was a chest rather than a box, with a hinged lid and brass fittings. It had no lock, just a catch.

'Your privilege, madam,' said Brockley.

I knelt beside him and fumbled with the catch until I found the trick of it. I pulled the lid back. The hinges squeaked. Then we saw.

'God's teeth!' said Brockley.

No wonder it had been heavy.

'Gold!' said Dale, awestruck. 'Gold bricks! There are ten – a hundred – fortunes here! And what are those other things, still down in the pit?'

Brockley made another perilous dive and without equine assistance, came up with a heavy leather bag gripped in his two hands. He made a second dive and this time fetched up a polished box, much smaller than the chest, but heavy for its size. It was square, roughly two feet by two feet, and nearly as much deep. He set everything on the table and we gathered round. I loosened the drawstring that held the bag closed and let some of the contents slide out on to my palm. Dusty, greenish stones, but I recognized them.

'Emeralds,' I said. 'Not yet cut, but they're emeralds all right.'

'There are two more bags down there,' said Brockley. 'Probably more gemstones. What about this shiny box?'

It had a lock and there was no sign of a key but Brockley broke it with the hammer. Inside, there were objects wrapped in soft woollen material, presumably to protect them from each other. I counted them. There were twelve. When I unwrapped one, it turned out to be a small golden goblet, with a pattern of rubies and pearls round the bowl and the foot. If we had ever had any doubts about whose treasure cache this was, they were now dispelled.

The Brockleys looked at me, asking for instructions. I said: 'Put everything back except for one of those gold bricks and a few emeralds.' I tried to lift one of the bricks and almost dropped it. 'I never knew gold was so heavy.'

'I'll wrap it in something and carry it down,' said Brockley. 'The emeralds can go in your hidden pouch, madam.'

'Yes. Otherwise, just leave everything as it is,' I said. 'Can we secure the cottage door?'

Brockley thought he could. 'I'll take one of those planks and nail it across the door. There are some good long nails in the box we brought from the shed. You were right, madam! We needed both ropes and nails.'

I stood up. 'I think we have to confront Joan. It won't be pleasant.'

TWENTY-SIX
Loosing the Knot

Once back at Evergreens, we handed our horses to Eddie, and Brockley, ignoring Eddie's inquisitive expression, carried the wrapped brick indoors. We had cut off a piece of blanket to muffle it in. Inside the vestibule, we stopped and looked at each other.

'We have to do it,' I said. 'We must arrange things in the parlour. Then I'll bring Joan. I must find Arabella, too.'

Arranging things in the parlour came first, and was interrupted by Page, who walked in uninvited and wanted to know what was going on. Brockley closed the door, and then he and I, taking turns, explained. Page was usually expressionless but now he looked appalled. 'Master Brockley – Mistress Stannard – I am employed by Mistress Mercer. I owe her a duty. I owe her my loyalty.'

'Even in these circumstances?' I asked him.

Brockley, addressing me, said: 'Madam, I have worked for you and with you for many years and I not only owe loyalty to you, I also give it with affection. But if I found that you had done what Mistress Mercer seems to have done, I would have to lay both loyalty and affection aside. You know that, I think?'

'It would be the same the other way round,' I said, and found that just saying those words was painful, as though they were rooted in my stomach and being dragged out on a fish-hook. In fact, Brockley and I, when we looked at each other, read potential betrayal in the eyes of the other, and hated ourselves for it, and were thankful for our own clear consciences.

But Page was nodding. 'Very well. I won't hinder you.'

'We would like you to be present,' said Brockley. 'Then you would understand completely. Do you agree, madam?'

'Yes, I think I do. Page, do you know where Mistress Arabella and her mother are?'

'Mistress Arabella is in her chamber, I believe, madam. Mistress Mercer is in the kitchen.'

'Please fetch Arabella. She needs to be here. She will have to know all about it, anyway, and it's best that she knows from the beginning. It will mean a hateful scene. You had better warn her of that. I will bring Mistress Mercer. And keep the maids away.'

Page nodded, and went. Brockley and Dale went on making the arrangements. I went in search of Joan.

I found her quarrelling with her cook. In fact, she was pouring a tirade over the muscular and wizened James Mitchell, who was standing with his feet apart and arguing back. One of the kitchen maids – Phil Drew, I thought – the spit boy Silas Hazel and his impudent brother Samuel were listening with immense interest, no doubt relieved that they were not the targets for Joan's wrath.

The argument apparently concerned a mound of roundish, brownish objects on a dish on the well-scrubbed table.

'I keep telling you! Will you stop arguing! Yes, these things are roots – like carrots or onions – and you may never have seen them before but believe me, they are fit to eat; I have eaten them at Master Waters' table. Why are you never prepared to try new things? Peel them, cut them all to that size' – she pointed to one of the smaller objects – 'and boil them in salted water till they're tender, then make a syrup, adding rosewater and Grecian amber, for their sauce and believe me, they'll make a dish fit for the queen.'

'But, madam, what are these things *called*?'

'Potatoes, you fool. You a chief cook and you've never heard of them? They come from the New World . . . Yes?'

She swung round to face me. She didn't know it but it was the last time she was ever Mistress Joan Mercer, lady of Evergreens, in control of her kitchen and her table. I pitied her in that moment. But I said: 'Mistress Mercer, please come to the parlour. Something has arisen that can't wait.'

Something in my voice must have warned her. I saw her lose colour. She turned away from the cook, saying over her shoulder, 'Cook them, damn you!' and came with me.

I brought her into the parlour. We had placed a table in

the middle of the room, and on the far side of it, Dale and Brockley had seated themselves. Arabella and Page were both there, at one side, sharing a settle. They rose courteously as we entered and then Page set a chair for Joan, facing the table, and stationed himself in front of the door. He gave me a small nod as he passed me, a signal that he was now wholly on our side.

I joined the Brockleys behind the table. On it was a gold brick, lying on its piece of blanket to protect the table top. Beside this, displayed on a piece of white linen, were half a dozen uncut emeralds, one gold goblet and a piece of torn black fabric.

Joan stared at them and then glared at me. 'What is this? Is it some kind of jest? Am I to play a guessing game?'

I said: 'We found a whole cache of those gold bricks under the floor of Mother Lee's old cottage. We also found what looks like a big collection of gemstones including one whole bag of emeralds like this one. And we found a set of goblets like the one we have here. They are clearly *not* family heirlooms, or why would they be stored among what are obviously the proceeds of piracy? But if they are the proceeds of lawful actions against Spanish treasure ships, why have they not been disposed of openly?'

Joan opened her mouth as if to speak and then closed it again.

'Well, we can answer that ourselves,' I said, 'for we know that your sons have been attacking English shipping as well as Spanish and I certainly doubt they have a royal commission. But we have more to say, concerning that piece of black fabric. If you look closely, I think you will find that it matches the tear you found in the cuff of your black gown. You found it when we were making ready for tomorrow's funeral. The funeral, in fact, of your granddaughter.'

'My base-born granddaughter,' snapped Joan. She turned to glower at Arabella, who stared inimically back. 'I have seen the body. That was a child not far from term. But my shameless daughter had only been six months wed. I took her in because you all expected it, not because I wanted her here. Left to me, she would have been turned out to fend for herself.

If you had been a modest, obedient girl, Arabella, none of this would have happened.'

Arabella looked at her mother with hatred. A hatred so visible and intense that it made me shiver. Then she found words.

'So I am to blame, am I? *I* didn't murder Mother Lee. *I* haven't robbed her majesty's vessels! I have been sold to a man I detest, as though I were a sackful of onions! If you had let me marry Gilbert Gale, none of this would have happened and my child would have come into the world safely. And you still say the fault is all mine!'

I raised my voice and said loudly: 'Let us not waste time on irrelevances! The torn piece of your cuff, Joan, was found gripped in Mother Lee's dead hand. She tore it – she can only have torn it – from the clothing of whoever strangled her. What had she done to you, Mistress Mercer, that you had to murder her, poor old woman that she was?'

'Poor old woman! She was . . . she was . . .!'

Her eyes veered from side to side, as though seeking a way of escape. I had never seen eyes look so hunted, or so fierce. But there was no way of escape and the few words she had spoken had already damned her.

She tried, however, holding her head up and continuing to glare. 'What nonsense is this? So Mother Lee grabbed at something her assailant was wearing! Well, it wasn't me!'

'Was it not?' I said. 'But just now, you cried out, *She was . . . she was . . .!* She was what? It didn't sound like a compliment.'

'I won't stay here and be accused like this!'

She spun round to flee the room, but Page was blocking her way. She shouted at him to move. Quite deferentially, he said: 'I'm sorry, madam,' and stood fast. She swung back, to face me. I said: 'What had she done to offend you?'

'Offend me!' She seemed speechless.

Brockley said: 'You may as well tell us what happened between you and Mother Lee. We would like to understand. The law will make you speak anyway when we hand you over. As we intend to do.'

The dissolution of a personality is never a pleasing spectacle, not to me, anyway. I suspected that Walsingham enjoyed it but I did not. I had seen it before, and loathed it.

It happened to Joan Mercer now.

She tried to escape. She tried to push Page out of the way and when he wouldn't move, she hammered at him with her fists. Firmly though not roughly, he caught her wrists, walked her over to her chair and sat her down in it. She kicked his shins but he withstood her, holding her fast until she stopped struggling. Then she screamed and dissolved into a wild crying. Dale produced a handkerchief and went to her to mop her face. After a while, the wails stopped and Joan sat there, pale as skimmed milk, trembling and looking wildly round her.

I said: 'Joan, we know that you murdered Mother Lee. Please tell us why.'

'It was such a silly thing to do,' Brockley observed. 'With her gone, how would you have got hold of your headache medicines?'

'Yes, indeed,' I said. I was her landlord; she was also my hostess. She had invited me to her daughter's wedding. And how was I repaying that invitation, her hospitality? I loathed her and I loathed myself. I repeated my question. 'Why did you do it, Joan? *Why?*'

She stared at me out of eyes bleary with tears and fear and then answered me. 'Because Hector boasted in her hearing! She found out what he and Stephen were doing and she wanted to be cut in, to have shares the same as us and the proceeds already had to be shared too many ways. The ships' crews have shares, and what's left over had to be spread five ways, between me and my sons and a man called Captain Julien and Sylvester Waters. She said to me, give me a share or I'll tell. So I gave her those goblets. She could use them or sell them. She liked them at first, thought they were pretty. But after a while, she started wanting more. I had to get rid of her. Mother Lee was a greedy old hag! She said her silence was worth more than a pair of goblets, even gold ones. What need did she have for a fortune, an old unlettered woman like her? *She* never boarded any ships herself to fight for the treasure!'

'You mean she threatened to tell the authorities?'

'Oh, no. Not that.' Joan's voice became sly. 'The treasure

would have been seized and she couldn't have a share in it then. Oh, no, she had another way of getting her withered old hands on it. She had another hold over me. None of your business! So I went up there one day and saw to her. As for the medicines, I had a good supply already and I helped myself to some more before I left her. And before I killed her, I made her tell me the recipe. I know all about her secret ingredient now. I think it's the truth though I'd try it on one of the mastiffs before I used it, just in case. Ah, how she begged for her life, the old besom. How I frightened her! She was no witch, able to cast a spell to save her from me. She gibbered and cried. The tears ran down in her wrinkles and fell on her gown. She struggled but I was stronger. She clutched at me with her horrible hands; the nails were long and yellow – *ugh!* That's how my cuff was torn. But I thrust her skinny old arms away and she was sobbing and pleading as I put my fingers round her throat.'

There was a paralysed silence as we all absorbed this dreadful description. I felt the bile rise in my throat.

But not in Brockley's. When he spoke next, it was in a voice so hard that it shocked me. I knew him as a loyal servant, as partner and at times accomplice; once I had imagined him as my lover. Now, and it seemed to be for the first time, I realized what a terrifying enemy he could be.

'So you confess,' he said. 'A very comprehensive confession too. When was it that you and the boys took to hiding the treasure up there? You may as well speak out. Tell us all. If you wish to mitigate the manner of your death, that is your only chance. What you have done is monstrous. You could burn.'

Joan had been glaring at him. Now her mouth sagged open and she began to shake. She too had recognized that tone; she too had seen in her mind the picture that Brockley had drawn for her. She had quailed. Her voice trembled as she spoke. 'We used to keep the things the boys brought back in Sylvester's cellars until we could get rid of them through a man called Roebuck, but when *you* people came to the wedding, Sylvester Waters and Captain Julien – him that the boys sail with – began to get nervous. Sister of the queen, known to be an agent, Master Waters said to me, and you bring *her* here!'

Her bleary eyes transfixed me. 'He got more and more worried when you were here but it wasn't till after Mother Lee was dead, when we heard that Theobald Roebuck had been arrested, that Captain Julien thought of moving it up to the cottage. The cottage was empty, he said: no one would interfere. Sylvester and his man Hammond bought timber to make floorboards, and took everything up there and dug a pit for it. Well, that's what they said.'

'That's right. It's what they did,' I told her. 'What was the other hold she had over you?'

At that, Joan closed her mouth again and sat shivering but silent, until Arabella said: 'I know the answer to that.'

We all turned to her, and I recoiled, horrified. I had never seen a face so full of triumph. And malice. I could barely recognize her.

'I wouldn't have told,' she said, 'until she tried to pretend that all this was my fault. But now – I am angry. I have been angry for a long time. And now I will hold it in no longer. It is something that Sylvester told me. I can remember his very words. *Did you know that your mother poisoned Father Eliot? He had found out too much about things your brothers were doing, and she did it to protect them but it wasn't a nice thing to do, all the same.*'

'My own daughter!' moaned Joan. 'How can you say such things about me? It's all lies!'

'I am sorry to say,' said Page sadly, 'that it is not.'

Every head now turned towards him. He said: 'I have known for a long time that Master Hector and Master Stephen were pirates, taking Spanish vessels and maybe not paying tax on their spoils, but it wasn't my place to worry about that. Only today have I learned that they've been robbing English vessels too.

'I didn't know about it when I helped Waters and Hammond dig the pit under Mother Lee's floor. They paid me fair and I asked no more. But that was then. What I've heard just now in this room has changed things.'

He paused, but we were all silent, waiting for him to go

on. Even Joan, though her face was smeared with her tears and she was taut, like an animal ready to spring.

Page said: 'One morning back in Father Eliot's days, I was in the church, supervising the cleaning as I often do, and I saw some bits of rubble on the floor. I looked up and saw a place where light was coming through the roof. The rubble was coming from there. A repair was needed, so I went to the vicarage to tell Father Eliot. His housekeeper, Mrs Brewer, didn't want me to come in, said Father Eliot was ill. Mrs Brewer's a good woman but she's not too bright, not reliable with taking messages. I said I would leave a note for him and she let me go into his study and use his desk. His bedroom is next to his study and I heard Mistress Mercer in there, saying that she'd brought his foxglove remedy from Mother Lee for him, and here it was, though it was a new medicine, and the dose for this one was two spoonfuls three times a day. Yes, madam, you did say that. I heard you.'

Joan stared at him, with a kind of amazement, as though he were a piece of furniture which had suddenly found a tongue and spoken. Arabella looked grimly satisfied.

'I didn't think aught about it,' said Page. 'Two or three weeks later, he died, but I still didn't think aught about it, till a fellow we had here on the farm fell down at his work, clutching his heart and saying Mother Lee knew what medicine he needed. Mistress Mercer there never expects me to run errands like going up to Mother Lee . . .'

'It's beneath your station. You're not an errand boy,' said Joan in a strangled voice.

'No, but I do go up there on my own account, now and then,' said Page. 'This time it was urgent, so I just threw a saddle on my horse and went. Mother Lee gave me a foxglove medicine and said he was only to take one small spoonful twice a day; it was strong stuff and it could do more harm than good, even kill if you took doses too big and went on taking them.

'And then,' said Page, still in that sad voice, 'I opened my big mouth and told her what I'd heard you say, madam, when you were telling Father Eliot what dose to take, of foxglove medicine. She just looked at me and said: "Indeed. That is

very interesting," and she smiled in a way that I didn't like
though I was halfway home before I began to understand. I
worked it out in the end. You had told Father Eliot to take a
dangerous dose, and less than three weeks later he died. He'd
probably been taking overdoses all that time. And I had just
told Mother Lee about it. I had given her power over you,
madam, if she wanted it.'

'Is that right?' I said to Joan.

The hatred in her eyes was blistering. Her fear had melted
into fury, like metal liquefying in a furnace. She looked
murderous. 'Hector opened his big mouth in the Crown tavern
and that old fool Eliot realized what my boys were doing. Or
part of it. He knew they weren't sharing their spoils with the
Treasury but even Hector wouldn't be daft enough to talk
about English shipping! But he said too much, even so. Eliot
sent for me and said I must put a stop to it. Just gave me
orders, would you believe it?'

She sounded as though she expected us to sympathize. I
didn't like to look at her face. Her eyes were glaring and her
mouth was twisted. Her words had come out in husky jerks.
She was hardly recognizable.

'I said it was all nonsense,' said Joan. 'I said it was just
Hector's romancing, but he said no, he thought it might well
be true and if I didn't make it stop, he would go to one of the
Caterham constables and report it. My sons were at sea then;
he said I must deal with them when they returned. A few days
later, he got ill, something to do with his heart – it had happened
before – and he told his housekeeper to go up to Mother Lee
and get some medicine for him. He said she knew what medicine. Mrs Brewer met me just at the foot of Mother Lee's hill.
I was going to see Mother Lee and I was going myself because
even back then the maids didn't care for going up to the witch
on the hill, as they called her. Even Jane didn't. Or Mrs Brewer.
She asked if I'd fetch Father Eliot's potion for her. She
said she could tell me what to ask for, and so I went instead
of her.'

Suddenly, Joan threw back her head and emitted a harsh
laugh. 'So now you all know! And this is the end for me. All
right! I fetched his medicine for him, because Mrs Brewer

was frightened of Mother Lee. Mother Lee told me the dose and warned me that to take too much could kill. That was my chance to protect my boys. Yes, I told the old busybody the wrong dose! He was going to ruin us all! I was mighty glad when the villagers tried to swim Mother Lee, when they were saying *she'd* murdered him. Only you had to interfere and rescue her!'

'But why didn't you speak up, man?' Brockley demanded, of Page. 'You knew what Mistress Mercer had done. Why did you keep silent?'

'Because, as I said before, a servant owes loyalty to his employers, Master Brockley. My father was butler to Mistress Mercer's father and he taught me from early youth that a butler, or a steward or any man employed in a position of trust, must be loyal, always, even if he doesn't approve of his employer. He may leave his employer, but never betray him. Besides, I wasn't sure. I thought I might have misheard, or not be remembering aright or maybe Father Eliot didn't die from the foxglove potion but from something else. What I thought I remembered was so dreadful, so unlike anything I had ever encountered before in my life! I wasn't quite certain even just now, until Mistress Mercer admitted it. Only now have I understood that yes, what I only suspected, or feared, before, is the truth.'

I gazed at my erstwhile hostess in gathering horror. 'You first disposed of Father Eliot – because he threatened your sons. And then disposed of Mother Lee because she knew what you'd done. What hold does *Waters* have over you? He made you give Arabella to him, didn't he? And he's a villainous piece if ever there was one.'

'Oh, he's part of it all,' said Page unexpectedly. 'He's a man of business. Hector and Stephen need someone like him. They're pirates and that's all. They don't know how to make financial arrangements. Waters came in because he knows about these things. Though Captain Julien knows more. It was Waters, I think, who brought him in. I believed they are distantly related.'

'I suppose the boys told you all that,' said Joan bitterly.

'Hector does talk,' said Page. 'That's true enough. I learned it all from him, in the days when I thought he and Master Stephen were simply robbing Spanish vessels. I was happy enough about that.'

'He made me force Arabella to marry him, by threatening to report that I had killed Father Eliot,' said Joan savagely. 'And a bitter joke it is, for he didn't know, he can't have known, that it was true! He thought he was just making up a threat that might hold. He said he would tell people that I did it because Father Eliot believed I was a witch. He was in love with Arabella, you see. In love with her! What does he know of love?' Once again, she threw back her head and laughed, and this time the laughter went out of control and turned to hysteria.

'Excuse me a moment,' said Page, and walked out of the room. Dale went over to Joan and slapped her. The wild laughter stopped. As much as anything for the purpose of keeping things calm, I asked an idle question. 'What *is* this Captain Julien's second name? Or doesn't he have one?'

'Of course he has one,' said Joan, snuffling. 'It's de la Roche. That's his full name. Julien de la Roche. What's it matter to you? He's young. Mighty self-assured, like a man twice his age, but young.'

De la Roche. Young. 'What does he look like?' I enquired.

'Nosy, aren't you? Looks a lot like your Harry, if you want to know.'

You remind me of someone I know. You've got a reckless look like his. Hector had said that.

Thank God, I thought, that I hadn't brought Harry on this second visit to Evergreens. Thank God he wasn't here to learn that his French half-brother, as wild and careless of his safety as his father Matthew, was a rogue privateer. Though it was odd that he had been ready to attack a French ship. English ships, working for the queen whom Matthew had considered an enemy of his religion; those would be fair game. But French ships? And then I remembered. Capitaine le Boeuf was a Huguenot. Oh yes, that fitted.

Dear Harry, who will one day be the Master of Hawkswood: stay at Hawkswood. Give your heart to it. I pray that you will never meet your pirate half-brother. The same wild blood that runs in his veins, runs in yours. Don't let it betray you.

Joan was quiet now, though her eyes were full of rage and terror, mingled. I suddenly remembered how when I went to her room, on that first morning that I spent at Evergreens, Gladys' voice had spoken in my mind. *That woman is poison.* I had sensed her nature without realizing it. Her eyes now were those of a caged and savage animal.

Page suddenly reappeared. 'I thought so. I saw them from the window. There are riders on the track to Caterham. I think Sylvester Waters has been captured.'

TWENTY-SEVEN
A Proper Use For Freedom

' It's all over,' said Father Dunberry, as Jane Hayes led him into the parlour. Jane had been questioned but it was clear enough that she had had no part in the crimes committed by her mistress. She was deeply shocked by them. She had also wept for her mistress. Jane Hayes was a good soul and I wished her well in whatever future she finally found for herself. For the moment, she was acting as Arabella's maid. For the time being, Arabella, who had quietly, if not quite legally, possessed herself of her mother's money chest, was the mistress of the house, and paying their wages, or most of them.

'It was over two hours ago,' Father Dunberry said. 'I said prayers for them until the last, warning them to repent while they still could and afterwards, I saw them taken away for burial. You are a widow now, Mistress Waters.'

So that was that. The executions in Caterham had taken place. None of us had wished to be present. I had interceded for Joan to the point that she had not burned. She had been hanged alongside Sylvester Waters. It was over now and they were no longer in the world. Hector and Stephen Mercer were still free, but they were not likely to reappear at Evergreens. Under questioning, Joan had admitted that they were in Italy. Her talk of damaged ships and going abroad to fetch repair materials was just a story to account for their absence, should anyone enquire. Later, she would have joined them in Italy.

We were gathered in the Evergreens parlour: me, the Brockleys, Arabella Waters and Gilbert Gale. Joan did not own Evergreens and therefore it couldn't be seized, though Waters House had been. Waters had dismissed many of his servants but after his arrest, most of them had stayed where they were, not knowing what was to happen next. What happened was

that the house was closed and they were told to go, but they
hadn't gone penniless. Arabella had paid them off. I had
accepted her as my tenant, for the time being, until such
time as she and Gilbert married. She and Gilbert Gale were
side by side, not holding hands, but together.

Arabella asked: 'Was it very dreadful? I hope . . . I hope
. . . my mother . . . was it quick?'

'Not very,' said Father Dunberry, with tactless satisfaction.
'They died hard, as they deserved. Their deaths were probably the longest ten minutes of their lives.'

'Ohhh! And I helped to bring them to it!' Arabella sprang
to her feet and fled from the room, her hands clutched to her
mouth.

'You were talking about her mother,' I said to Father
Dunberry.

'And her husband too. Not much of a husband, I gather and
not much of a mother, either,' said Dunberry. 'Though marriage
is a strange thing. It has its own power. She may mourn him,
and surprise herself. Now, Mistress Stannard, I take it that you
will soon be going home? But what of Mistress Waters? Does
she remain here?'

'As long as she needs to,' I said, coldly. I was never going
to like Father Dunberry.

He had now turned to the subject of marriage. 'I suppose
I shall soon have to conduct another wedding,' he said, turning
to Arabella. 'Usually I wouldn't approve of re-marriage so
soon, but on this occasion, I will do so with a good heart.
Mistress Mercer and Master Waters were an evil pair. A pity
they didn't marry each other!'

'We have all thought that,' said Brockley.

The following week was one of the strangest I can remember.
Arabella had retrieved her belongings from Waters House, and
she spent a great deal of time going through her gowns
and linen with the help of Jane Hayes, doing repairs where
needed. She was curiously quiet. I tried to distract her by
reminding her that the banns would be heard for the first time
next Sunday, and that she would soon be Gilbert's wife, and
she smiled and thanked me, but still in that oddly quiet way.

She was grieving for her mother, I supposed, and perhaps for her own part in bringing Joan to her death. Where there had been anger, now there might be guilt.

On most days, very correctly taking Jane as a chaperone, she went into Cutpenny for an hour or two, and visited Gilbert. He would soon turn her thoughts into happier channels, I told myself.

The executions took place on a Friday. It was on the following Friday that to my surprise a boy from Cutpenny came to Evergreens with a note from Gilbert Gale, asking me to call on him, without Arabella and as soon as I could. Would I send a reply, saying when I would come, or if possible, would I come at once, with the messenger.

It was mysterious and it felt urgent. Arabella was in the garden, out of hearing. I fetched a cloak and told the boy that I was coming with him.

'I am glad to see you,' said Gilbert, when we arrived. He set his work aside and pressed a coin into the messenger's hand. The boy went off, looking joyful.

'He's a good lad,' Gilbert said. 'His name's Henry Hobson. He's the grandson of our apothecary but he doesn't take after that old grump. He's interested in carpentry; I've taught him a little and he's very handy. I am thinking to take him on as an apprentice. Please come through to my parlour.'

In the parlour, he asked me to take a seat and then took one opposite to me. I said: 'What's the matter? You asked me to come at once if I could. It sounded urgent. What is it?'

'It's Arabella.'

'I guessed that it must be to do with her. She has been moping, I think, probably because of her mother. I've been hoping that you could help her. Are the banns to begin on Sunday as I understood you were planning?'

'No. I can't arrange them because of Arabella. She says she can't marry me.'

'Why ever not?' I said, much taken aback.

'Because of her mother,' said Gilbert. 'Joan Mercer poisoned Father Eliot and strangled Mother Lee. She was a killer. Arabella says having such a mother has tainted her. She says that we would never be happy; that I would always remember the stock she came from and that sometimes, perhaps after some small argument, I would find myself looking at her oddly, wondering . . .'

'Oh, poor Arabella!' I had never thought of this. 'If only she'd told me! I might have talked her out of it. Why should she carry her mother's sins on her back for ever? I'll do my best, Gilbert, though of course you can't start the banns until she's ready. Christmas is near. I'll stay on for that and try to make it a merry season. A little mirth and jollity may do her good. By the time the new year comes, she may be thinking quite differently.'

'It isn't just that,' said Gilbert. He sounded odd, diffident. I looked at him enquiringly.

'What is it, then?'

'Arabella is right. I *would* find it hard to forget what her mother did. I might – if ever we were quarrelling – find myself looking at her, wondering. Even now . . . she told me yesterday that she couldn't marry me. I tried to argue with her and she was annoyed – and for a flash, one brief moment, I saw her mother in her.'

I kept my face still but I could remember the moment when I had seen the same thing. He had paused but I said nothing and after a moment, he resumed.

'Her eyes . . . Joan Mercer was there in her daughter's eyes. Arabella has the right of it. I still love her – by God, I do. But the idea of marrying her has become . . . disturbing.'

'So what does she intend to do? Remain alone at Evergreens as my tenant? She can't do that unless I agree and I don't think I would. She would be too near to you, for one thing. It would be awkward for you both. But I don't want to take her into my household as another ward. I have had wards enough and besides . . .'

I looked at him and said lamely: 'I suppose that at heart, I feel as you do. I didn't know it until now.'

'She doesn't want to stay at Evergreens.' Gilbert looked miserably down at his feet. 'And I don't think the idea of becoming your ward has as much as crossed her mind. She speaks good French. She intends going to France, where they still have convents, and become a nun.'

'What? She can't do that! She isn't a Catholic and . . .'

'She intends to become one. What does it matter? she says.' He raised his head and his young, handsome face was full of a dreadful sadness. 'It's like a bereavement. It's as though she were dead. She is dead to me, now. And if I could call her back to life, I wouldn't. She is doing the best thing and it hurts more than I can say. I just wanted to tell you, to explain. I don't want you to dissuade her. Just to help her, perhaps with travelling, when she leaves England.'

'I will go with her myself. If it's what she truly wants,' I said.

'We had better not tell Father Dunberry,' said Gilbert, with a gleam of wintry humour. 'He would be furious!'

'No. Better let him think that she has simply joined my household. I won't stay on here for Christmas after all. I had better take her back to Hawkswood for Christmas and in the new year, when the weather allows – and given that Walsingham allows, and given that she doesn't change her mind – we'll travel to France. I can't leave England without Walsingham's consent and he may not consent to this. His loathing of what he calls Papistry is near to madness.

'But,' I added, thinking aloud, 'Arabella is the daughter of one cold-hearted killer and the widow of another and her brothers are traitors. Privateers who turn pirate, who cheat the Treasury and attack our own shipping are regarded as such. He may feel that a French convent is welcome to her, though he may not let me go with her. I will find someone else to take her, in that case.'

It did occur to me that if he refused to let her go, either, I probably would have to take her as my ward.

I also knew that when she said she and Gilbert couldn't marry, she wouldn't change her mind. Gilbert knew it, too.

'There'll be someone else for me, one day,' Gilbert said. 'Though not quite yet. It's not fair, that she would have to pay for her mother's transgressions. But . . .'

'Don't torment yourself,' I said. 'I'll go back now and talk to her. If she comes back to Hawkswood with me for a while, well, as it happens, one of my servants at Hawkswood – Ben Flood, my assistant cook – is a Catholic. I know that he slips

off now and then, either to Guildford or to Woking – I don't
enquire – and hears an illegal mass. It is presumably conducted
by an illegal priest, but if Arabella is to become a Catholic,
she will need instruction. And if necessary the priest, or Flood
himself, may be able to find someone who can escort her to
France, if I am not allowed to go.'

There was a silence for a moment. I was thinking about the
strange new life to which Arabella meant to commit herself,
the long unchanging years during which – surely – she would
sometimes pine for the life she had denied herself, the life of
man and home and children. I wondered if her Mother Superior
would let her sometimes keep vigils to pray for her mother –
or perhaps for the soul of Waters too. I knew what Father
Dunberry meant by saying that marriage had its own strange
power.

To Gilbert, I said: 'Will you want to see her again to say
farewell, before we start for Hawkswood? I think we can leave
in a couple of days' time. Page can be left in charge at
Evergreens until I find another tenant. I'll try to find one who
would like to employ the rest of the existing staff. Including
Jane Hayes if possible. She's a good seamstress.'

'I think I'd rather not see Arabella again,' said Gilbert
unhappily. 'I don't think saying a painful farewell would be
good for either of us.'

'No,' I said gently. 'I think you're right.'

The journey home to Hawkswood was strange. It was very
unlike our first arrival, in the spring, when we sang as we
rode through woods where there were young green leaves on
the trees. There was no singing this time, and we were travelling through a winter landscape, of leafless trees and a silver
sun that had no warmth in it.

Our number had increased, for now Arabella was with us,
on her white ambler, and beside her, on a pony, was her maid
Madge, from Waters House. She had appeared suddenly at
Evergreens and asked if she could resume her work as
Arabella's maid. Arabella had agreed, for the time being.
Madge, when informed that her mistress intended to leave the
country and enter a house of nuns, merely said that she could

be any kind of maidservant, if there was a niche for her at my home. She was a pleasant lass, I thought, and said she could join us.

The only groom now left at Evergreens was the freckled Hal Jankin. Arabella had sold most of the Evergreens horses, leaving only a pair of heavy horses for the farm. Evergreens was almost empty now of human life, until new tenants should arrive. I would let Brockley do most of the negotiating. I personally hoped it would be years before I set eyes on Evergreens again, if ever.

We didn't hurry, letting our pace be set by the mule cart where the baggage was, but we were not talkative, either. We had too much to remember, and little inclination to reminisce about it. But when the chimneys of Hawkswood House came in sight, I felt my spirits rise. Home! And this time I could stay there, seeing to the happy duties of my own place, preparing for Christmas. I wondered if Christmas festivities would do anything to change Arabella's mind though what I was to do with her if it did, I could not imagine.

We rode into the courtyard and as usual, much of the household was there to greet us. Old Gladys was much to the fore, lame but determined. And for once, her expression had nothing in it of *I told you so.* It struck me suddenly that when, in Joan's sick room, I thought Gladys' voice had warned me that she was poison, the voice I had actually heard was probably my own. I had been told once before that I had the ability to sense evil. I had done so then, in all probability.

But here was Harry, pushing in front, obviously excited. He helped me out of my saddle before Brockley could reach me. 'Mother! Are you well? Oh, I have so much to tell you!'

'Let poor Mistress Stannard catch her breath!' said Ben, who was just behind him, smiling broadly.

'What is it?' I asked. 'It looks like happy news, and that will make a change!'

Peter Dickson, however, was there as well, grabbing Harry by the shoulder. 'Let your mother get indoors and out of her cloak and into the hall with a wineglass in her hand, boy! Help with her baggage if you want to be useful!'

But very soon, when I was indeed seated in my own hall,

where the fire was crackling cheerfully and I did have a glass
of wine in my hand, I heard it all.

'It's Cobbold Hall, Mother!'

'Cobbold Hall? Does it have new tenants now?' I asked,
recalling that at Wilder's funeral, I had wanted to ask
Christina Ferris about it but hadn't felt it was the right
moment to do so.

'Oh *yes*!' said Harry, all aglow. 'People called Blake, and
they have a family. Two sons and three daughters and oh,
Mother, the eldest daughter, Eleanor, she is just a year younger
than I am and she is the most beautiful creature I ever beheld!
Her laugh is like music. She has hair like rich brown silk and
eyes like stars!' At that moment, his own eyes resembled stars.
'Mother, I really think . . .'

'My son,' I said, 'I do believe that you are in love, for the
very first time.'